Endangered Species

The Great North American Sasquatch Novel

Other books by Ken Coffman

Fiction

Steel Waters
Alligator Alley, by Ken Coffman and Mark Bothum
Twisted Shadow, by Ken Coffman with Mark Bothum
Glen Wilson's Bad Medicine
Toxic Shock Syndrome
Hartz String Theory
Endangered Species
Fairhaven

Nonfiction

Real World FPGA Design with Verilog

STAIRWAY PRESS

Books can be ordered from:
Stairway Press
www.stairwaypress.com
1500A East College Way #554
Mount Vernon, WA 98273

This book is a work of fiction. Names, characters, places and incidents are the products of the author's fevered imagination or are used fictitiously. Any resemblance to actual events, locales or persons (living or dead) is entirely coincidental.

ISBN 0-975-43149-8
ISBN-13 978-0975431398

Dedication

For Pat Shaw

Pat and I are good friends. In fact, we're such good friends, we can disagree, scold each other, squabble and argue—and our relationship survives. Even thrives. We've shared Starbucks coffee, friends, enemies, rumors and innuendo, pink flamingos, Cabo Wabo tequila, Maurizio Russo Limoncello and a pop song about pirates.

"After all, I am, in so many ways, your creation," Pat said.

This one's for you, my friend.

For literary inspiration, I thank William Gibson. He writes books that are not disposable. That's the greatest compliment I can think of for a writer.

I thank my first-readers for criticism, encouragement, guidance, proofreading and miscellaneous instances of merciless harassment and browbeating.

Judy Coffman, Stacey Benson, Mark Bothum, Ken Lomax, Adina Pelle, Colleen Powell, Maureen Blando, Gary Croft, Dale Edwards, Tommy Lee Bolser, Pat Bertram, Beth Hill, Wanda Hughes, Disco Dave, and Helen Verrall.

Author notes on Endangered Species

I hope you enjoy my odd tale—which includes various and sundry flights of fancy. During the long review process, I got comments suggesting I dump the alternate story lines and flesh out Graham and Clayton's backwoods adventure—crafting them into a more linear...and dare I say it...a more *normal* novel. Obviously, if by some miracle this book is converted to a screenplay, that's exactly what will happen.

One of the advantages of creating an 'indy' publishing venture is that I can craft the story the way I want. To me, the heart and soul of this novel is the love story between Maria and Willie. I thought about stripping that story thread out, but I just couldn't bear to do it. Perhaps I'm doomed to obscurity because of artistic decisions like that. So be it.

Sometimes I wonder if I challenge the reader too much at first. Does it take a chapter or three before the ideas coalesce? What if I don't pull my stories together and instead create a meandering, unfocused blob of self-indulgent tripe? I hope the reader will show a little patience and have confidence that I respect your precious time. As always, I promise to pull things together and do my best to deliver a crafted, engineered...and satisfactory reading experience. Eventually.

KLC – October 2010

Email me at ken@stairwaypress.com if you have questions or comments. As always, online reviews are greatly appreciated.

Like the book? Tell your friends. Thank you.

Sasquatch: from the Pacific Northwest—derived from the Salish Indian word *Sesquac*—a mythical force of nature with a spirit that should be left alone.

CHAPTER ONE

Graham Wallace

GRAHAM AND HIS technician, Anderssen, stared intently at a pair of computer screens where numbers scrolled past—nearly too quick to follow. Internet Protocol addresses. The Strategic Services, LLC server farm was under constant attack by hackers, viruses and worms from around the world, but mainly from Romania, Hong Kong and Malaysia. They examined the Java source code of a persistent port scanner routine that emerged from the Philippines a few hours earlier.

Graham was a solidly-built young man, tending toward fat, with rubbery arms and a large belly that strained against the fabric of his polo shirt. He'd started Strategic Services in his parent's basement with an angel loan from his father ($5,000) and a truckload of surplus IBM servers he'd bought off eBay for a few dollars a pound. The shipping ended up being three times the purchase price—this was one of Graham's first hard lessons about doing business on eBay.

"It's a variant of Rabid-C, so we can block the scan code with a hookworm," Graham said, while unconsciously cleaning his teeth with a fragment of a yellow sticky note.

"You got it, boss," Anderssen said.

Lili Holte, Graham's personal assistant and handler, stood in the doorway.

"Graham? What are you doing? You were supposed to be at the Big and Tall shop a half an hour ago."

"Oh, yeah. I forgot. Maybe I can go tomorrow."

"We've been over this, Graham. The tailors won't be able to finish if you don't get in there today. You said you'd do it."

"We're under attack."

"We're always under attack. Anderssen can handle this, right?"

Anderssen nodded.

"Go ahead, boss, I got it."

Reluctantly, Graham got up. He patted Anderssen on the shoulder. "Hookworm variant G," he said.

Anderssen nodded. "Goes without saying."

"I'll walk with you and make sure you don't get lost," said Lili.

"I can find my way," Graham said. "I got this company to thirty-five million in sales without wearing a monkey suit."

"Our intelligence backgrounder says Powell puts a big value on style and professionalism," Lili said. "You need to show him you can play the CEO game. We've been through this a thousand and thirty-three times."

"I said I'd do it," Graham said. "You don't have to mother me."

"Yes I do."

The Men's store was a few blocks away from the Strategic Services office complex. The sky was dark and, though it wasn't raining, the brisk wind carried misty and damp air that threatened to carry off Graham's hat, a plaid-wool Tam o'Shanter. They walked as fast as Graham's stubby legs could manage. He stopped to look at the computer book titles in the window of a Borders bookstore, but Lili tugged at his arm to hurry him along. Once in the men's shop, the clerk immediately recognized a difficult customer and made a few hasty measurements of Graham's inseam, arms and shoulders and led them toward a rack of suits.

Noting the Tam o'Shanter, the clerk said, "We have some very nice Scottish tweeds that you might enjoy."

"My hero, William Wallace, would not stand for a single instant of this nonsense," Graham said. "Give me a broadsword and a horse, and then I'll be well-dressed."

"Wee Willie Wallace never tried to land a fifty-million dollar computer services contract, so just shut up," Lili said. "If you keep complaining, it will just take longer. Bear it or hire a stuffed-suit MBA to play president—you refuse to do that, so here we are."

"Kill me now and get it over with."

The clerk held up a dark blue jacket and dress pants.

"Obviously, vertical stripes will be his friend," the clerk commented to Lili.

"Take these and put them on," she said.

As Graham walked toward the dressing room, Lili whispered to the clerk.

"I'm sorry to put you through all this."

The clerk shrugged. "With Microsoft so close, we get lots of skeezy geeks here. We're used to it."

Willie and Maria

Maria came home. In Willie's study, a waterfall of Chopin's cascading piano notes spilled from a barely-audible Bose CD player. Over a delicate section of A flat Polonaise, Willie heard her throwing the locks and latching the security chain.

Her heavy cloth purse landed with a thump on their end table and her car keys jangled as she hung them on the key hook screwed into the hallway wall. Willie was frozen with concentration while trying to hold his hand perfectly still to make a clean straight line with a sable brush.

Watercolors are devilish in their complexity—the colors are transparent, and therefore, mistakes cannot be covered up. Colors must be allowed to dry before new paint is added; otherwise everything dissolves into an ugly smear. His reference photographs were scattered on his workspace, but he was not trying to copy the pictures...he was nearly hypnotized by the task of capturing the natural harmony of their cabin, towering trees, and mist-shrouded background hills with a few sweeping brushstrokes. He tamped Holger Danske Black and Bourbon tobacco in his Sasieni Walnut pipe, struck a wooden kitchen match, and applied flame.

"Damn you, William Jefferson Washington Walters, I've told you a thousand times. If you insist on smoking that disgusting pipe, crack open the window so the poison can be thinned out a little." She used his full name, so he knew she was genuinely perturbed. "I don't know why you insist on smoking that nasty neurotoxin anyway," she said as she jerked the window open.

Willie rotated on his stool.

"Tobacco is a mild stimulant and appetite suppressant with calming psychological effect on serotonin uptake levels in the brain. Plus, I enjoy the mechanical routine of giving my hands something to do. I did a spreadsheet with all factors weighted and applied to a polynomial formula and the result was positive for continuing this—when performed in moderation—nearly harmless habit."

"Do you have to be analytical about everything?" she said. "That tobacco makes my cashmere sweater smell like a whorehouse ashtray. I wish you'd stop smoking it."

With his pipe jutting from his jaw, Willie looked at her calmly. Her long name was Maria Allegra Catalina Fidelia Paz Ofelia Francisca Gitana Alvarez and she was a little thin for Willie's taste. Tall, about five-foot-nine, she seemed even taller when wearing high heels. With her black hair pulled back, it curled around her shoulders in ebony waves. She'd been born in Mexico City and her English was generally impeccable, but when angry, the fluid Mexican cadence of her accent slipped through.

"Aren't you supposed to be working on a column for USA Today?" she continued.

"I'm working on it. Turning ideas over in my mind while I'm painting."

"You are, on occasion, a most aggravating person," she said, while turning on her heel to leave.

"Don't leave me that way," he said.

Standing with her hand on the doorknob, she took a deep breath. She looked back at him over her shoulder.

"You're right." She walked back and gave him a kiss on the cheek.

"I'll come out in a few minutes, pour you a glass of wine, and we'll talk about what went wrong in your day," he said.

"It's a date," she said.

Knowing better than to wait for Willie, Maria pulled a wine glass off their kitchen rack and poured herself a healthy volume of Tisdale Merlot. Tired, she stood, leaning against the kitchen counter, and sipped. She thought back to the first time she'd heard Willie (in the classroom, he insisted on being called Professor Walters) speak.

She had prior opportunities to take one of his elective classes as part of her University of Washington Medical School class load, but was scared off by the student's informal data exchange which classified professors as easy or difficult, rational or non-linear, undemanding or difficult.

If pressed, she might confess a vague prejudice.

Was this teacher a long-winded African-American affirmative-action social-promotion nonsense-spewer?

In sociology, it is difficult to discern between insightful genius and moronic self-referential socio-babble. With topics like *Discursive and Social Practices in the Construction of Exclusion: a Comparative Study*[1], how could a person discriminate between pure genius and complete horseshit?

By reputation, Professor Walters was distant, pedantic, often humorless, harsh, intolerant and highly impatient with lax thinking. On the other hand, engineering and math students universally loved him. There was cult-like, proctological Internet blogging and chat-room analysis of his studies, printed columns and electronic journal publications.

How long was it since day one of Master's class SOC590A, The Emergent Clusters of Post-Pragmatic Socio-Economic Holism?

Could it really be eight years already?

Yes, eight years ago, uncommitted to the class, she'd sat in the back of the lecture hall and scanned optional offerings in a course catalog. If this one didn't work out, she'd transfer to SOC 587, *Deviance and Social Control* or SOC 467C, *Social Differentiation in*

---

[1] Augusto De Venanzi, as published in The Electronic Journal of Sociology, 2004, ISSN: 1198 3655, see http://www.sociology.org/content/2004/tier1/venanzi.html

Immigration and Ethnicity. Either would be an easy A for a bright, female, immigrant med student. She needed easy elective courses in order to be able to devote sufficient time to really tough core classes like GMS AN 700, *Morphological and Functional Histology of Cells, Tissues and Organs*.

At first, she felt sorry for Professor Walters as he stood behind his lectern and stared at a remote corner of the room—motionless and wearing a vacant expression. Standing there so long, while students whispered and fidgeted, she wondered if he had stage fright or if this was some sort of Asperger fugue. Clearly, he was borderline autistic—obsessive-compulsive in the way he shifted his weight from foot to foot and repetitively stroked his lecture notes.

Could she recite the first words she'd heard him speak? His booming voice was a deep rumble and still carried a Fishtown, Philadelphia lilt.

"I am obsessed with efficiency. Production efficiency and mechanization create luxury—luxury that allows an adolescent to spend time in Internet chat rooms and playing video games instead of working in corn fields. It creates the luxury of time for an activist to obsess over endangered rodents. I'm talking about efficiency in manufacturing, where products are produced abrasivelessly in the remotest parts of the world. I'm talking about efficiency in fulfillment channels that fluidly cross geographies and borders. I'm talking about the advances of biotechnology—technology that programs a batch of salmon to grow in the sea, and then swim upstream to my holding pond—even directly into my net—without requiring oceanic trawlers. I'm talking about the efficiency of neotechnology, where data flits around the world in low-friction optical packets."

There was almost a minute of silence while he seemed to collapse inward—frozen and entranced. "I'm sorry, I digress," he said. "I'm talking about *one* global economy and *one* global marketplace. That brings us to the main topic of our class, cleverly titled The Emergent Clusters of Post-Pragmatic Socio-Economic Holism. Let's start with the friction of optically-transmitted data. Does anyone know what I'm talking about?"

Several hands raised and Maria was surprised to see hers was one of them. Professor Walters pointed at her.

"I don't know you. What can you offer?"

"Well, P-professor Walters," she said. "Are you drawing a parallel between the physics of work wasted as heat in a machine and the value of a data-transaction loaded down with the cost of packet transport, regulation and taxation?"

"Yes," he said. "Do you have anything to add to that correlation?"

"No, sir, but I believe the subsidiary implications are interesting."

"I agree," he said.

As he said this, Maria realized she was smitten.

Who is this man?

He was smart and his wife was sick. Otherwise, she knew nothing about him.

Shaking her head to dispel the memories, she realized her wine was warm—she'd been leaning against the counter for a long while.

Was Willie's autism contagious?

That was silly, of course. She was simply tired—losing her mind all on her own. Poking her head in the doorway, she caught a peripheral out-of-focus glimpse of his painting. His work was often like a stereogram, an image hidden in semi-random watercolor dots you can stare at forever without making sense of them.

She realized he'd painted a picture of their cabin in the Canadian wilderness. Her heart seemed to stop and her breath caught in her throat. It was crystal clear; all at once she could see the slats and knotholes of the siding, the overhanging evergreen trees and even the chairs arrayed on the porch.

When her eyes refocused on the painting, it dissolved into colored dots and try as she might, even with the memory of the image to overlay on what her eyes saw, she could not recover it. It was maddening, just like her obtuse man.

She pulled the door closed quietly and prepared for bed. After a half-hour of reading the same page of her Stephen King novel without it making any sense, she reached for the light switch. At that instant, Willie came in and used the bathroom.

She could see his shadow as he stood in front of the toilet bowl; he never seemed to care how public or private his toilet activities were. Thick at the waist and thighs, he came out and threw his dirty clothes into a pile by the door. He towered over her—she looked up at him. His graying hair stuck out in wooly, asymmetric, nappy lumps, and somehow, absurdly, a white pin feather from her pillow stuck out of the hair on his forehead. He held out his arms and flexed his flabby muscles.

"Are you prepared to worship my magnificence?" he said.

She held out the blankets so he could slip in, and then peeled off her t-shirt.

"Any time, any place and forever," she said, before turning off the lamp.

Clayton Powell

"You might remember this from the film Close Encounters," the pilot said over the intercom while executing a wide loop around the Devil's Tower rock formation. Clayton lifted the Cessna Citation's window shade a few inches and peered out.

"It looked bigger in the movie," Clayton mumbled as he slammed the shade back down.

The Cessna Citation business jet landed smoothly at the Gillette-Campbell County Airport. A hired driver, wearing a brand new cowboy hat and ostrich-skin boots, drove a shiny Hummer H2 and deposited Clayton at the train station where a uniformed train crew unloaded and reloaded his luggage. The train was an old-fashioned steam engine with three Pullman cars and a boxcar followed by a caboose.

Clayton was unimpressed with the period details—like the conductor dressed in a blue suit wearing a tall hat with a pocket watch in his vest pocket connected with a long silver chain. Clayton glanced at the complicated shafts and linkages that transported locomotive power from the steam engine to the wheels. The whole thing was nearly deafening with its hissing, rumbling and vibrating. Trickles of sooty black smoke puffed into the air.

"She's a beaut, ain't she?" the conductor commented. "United Pacific 838, fully restored. One of the last fully functional steam locomotives in the United States. Turner kicked in four-hundred grand and the Wyoming Steam Engine Society put in hundreds of hours of volunteer labor. A genuine relic of the old frontier."

"I'm here to shoot buffalo, not for a history lesson," Clayton said. "Do you have any antique cold beer on board? I'd love to wet my whistle."

"Of course, sir," the conductor said coolly.

From Clayton's point of view, it took far too long to get the train rumbling on the track and once it was up to speed, it was barely able trundle along any faster than about twenty-five miles per hour.

At this rate, it will take all day to get anywhere.

Outside his window, while he sipped beer from a long-necked bottle, the rolling landscape hardly seemed to change.

Finally the conductor announced, "We're nearly there."

"About damned time," Clayton complained.

He followed through to the box car. They'd set up a chair for him to sit on and a spotter, wearing a buckskin leather suit, scanned the horizon with a pair of field glasses. A rack held several black powder rifles. Clayton settled in his seat, and then picked up a rifle.

"It's a period reproduction of a Sharps Model 1863 .54 caliber sporting rifle. They kick like a bull moose, so we set up a brace. Otherwise you'll fire once and we'll send you home with a busted-up shoulder."

"Just shut the hell up and find me some buffalo. I'm not here for a community college course in wild west minutia. Are five rifles going to be enough? Can you reload these blunderbusses fast enough to keep up with me?"

"We'll keep up, sir," the spotter said dryly. "Get ready, here comes one."

Clayton wiggled his ass to settle it deeply into the chair and slipped the walnut stock of the rifle into a wooden brace that fit snugly against his shoulder. He slipped on shooting glasses and massaged foam plugs into his ears. The sway of the boxcar was rhythmic and he saw a large black buffalo sweep slowly in front of the sights. He timed carefully and gently squeezed the trigger. The rifle erupted with a rolling thunder and the buffalo shuddered briefly before its legs collapsed and its body thumped to the ground. Clayton held out the spent rifle and was handed another. He took careful aim and fired.

Scattered cowboys on horses herded the buffalo near the track.

"Watch for the drivers," the buckskin man said sharply.

"I know which end the fire comes out of," Clayton said, irritated, while holding out the rifle and gesturing impatiently for a replacement. After five shots and five mortally wounded buffalo, Clayton said, "This is bullshit. Hand me my gun case."

"Sir, your contract only allows you to use the black powder rifles of the period."

"What is your boss going to say when he finds out you could have made a million dollars in one day? I said, get me my goddamned case."

With a sour look, the buckskin-suited man kicked the aluminum transit case toward Clayton.

"I'm not having anything to do with this," he said before turning on his heel and walking toward the caboose.

Clayton unfastened the latches and pulled out his fully automatic AR-15. It was a Leitner-Wise .499 caliber with modified gas piston recoil control and a 14.5-inch barrel. He slammed in a huge clip and ratcheted back the bolt. A group of about twenty buffalo grazed a hundred yards from the railway.

Clayton selected fully-automatic and aimed carefully. The air split with a deafening roar for a few seconds, and then Clayton smoothly detached the clip and reloaded. A single buffalo, standing on top of a hillock, raised his head at the clamor and Clayton nailed him with a short burst. The buffalo's massive head exploded in a satisfying spray of blood. Sweeping the horizon, Clayton located and dispatched other small groups of the stolid beasts. Finally, the last clip was expended and Clayton was exhausted and bored. He poked his head out of the boxcar and scanned the killing field.

At least twenty-five dead heaps.

Not bad.

The buckskin man, with a beet-red, angry face, came back into the boxcar.

"Asshole. Over the radio, they said you killed one of our horses and one of our men has a broken leg. This is not part of our contract."

Clayton turned toward the man. He reached into his jacket pocket and pulled out a single .499 round. He held it against the light for inspection, then opened the rifle chamber and inserted it. Then, he turned and aimed carefully at a man on a horse cantering after the train. He fired and the horse collapsed. The rider jumped clear and waved his arms and shouted at the train.

"I don't give a flying fuck," Clayton said calmly. "Shut your shout-hole and add the expenses to my bill."

Quimby Markham Chatsworth III and Robert Kinsley

Doctor Chatsworth was a smaller man than Robbie expected. He was slender and dressed in a business suit with crisply-creased slacks and tiny little shiny black shoes. Wearing a snow-white handlebar mustache and a welcoming smile, he waved—gesturing for Robbie to enter his office.

"Doctor Chatsworth, what an honor," Robert Kinsley said as he reached forward to shake the hand of the Environmental Protection Agency's Western Regional Division Senior Principal Scientist. "I can't believe I'm in Washington State and that I might actually work for you. I am totally committed to the goals of the EPA. This work, saving the planet, is the single most important thing I could do in my entire life. And there are so many fields and areas and opportunities to work on. I mean, there's global warming and protecting endangered species and salmon recovery and stopping clear cutting and wetlands preservation and banning pesticides and improving water quality and subsidizing energy efficiency and—"

"Please sit, Mr. Kinsley," Dr. Chatsworth said.

"Oh, I'm sorry, I know I talk too much but I'm just so excited and there's so much to—"

"Please," Doctor Chatsworth repeated, gesturing at the guest chair with his free hand. Still firmly in the grip of his handshake, Robbie felt strong pressure that twisted his hand and forced him into the seat. Dr. Chatsworth's face was impassive, but Robbie noticed an imperious, cold look in his eyes.

Robbie's confidence evaporated. His mouth was dry. Vertigo disoriented him and he averted his eyes from the Doctor's withering gaze.

That look.

It chilled him and threatened to suck his life away. It dampened his enthusiasm. The Doctor settled in his chair and leafed through Robbie's cover letter, CV, letters of reference and resume.

"Generally, people go with a resume *or* CV. I don't think I've been presented with both before," Doctor Chatsworth said.

Should I apologize? Explain how I couldn't decide between the two, so I went with both?

It was Robbie's summer break after his junior year at Harvard and all he wanted was to escape from his parents and grab a resume-enhancing internship…one that would sparkle on an otherwise lackluster college record. Academics were not his strong suit.

With the right recommendations and Dad's promise of a generous endowment, could I be reinstated?

As much as it pained him, he might have to see if Dad would talk to Uncle Edwin—

"Mr. Kinsley? Are you with me?"

Robbie shifted his eyes and focused in the general direction of the voice penetrating his foggy fugue.

Oh shit. I can't think of the right thing to say.

"Ah, yes, yes, sir. I am."

"How agreeable for you. Tell me, Mister Kinsley, how does a young man get expelled from Harvard?"

Oh, no, he knows. How does he get his information? Does he know the answer already? Is he testing me?

"Um, well, there was a student demonstration and I got carried away. It seems that I sprayed indelible red ink on Victoria Summers' ermine coat."

"The wife of the former president of Harvard. Nice. You ruined her coat. Yes, I suppose that would do it. I imagine that cost your father a few dollars."

"Fur is cruel. Endangered species get caught in those traps."

"Yes, of course." Leaning forward and switching gears, Doctor Chatsworth said, "If you can assemble a coherent thought or two, what is the essential nature of government?"

Robbie's thoughts raced.

What the hell is Doctor Chatsworth talking about?

I have to say something—quick—or this guy's going to think I'm a complete idiot.

"Service," Robbie said hesitantly, "service to the public? Serving the public interest?"

That sounded pretty good.

"What would you have us do, Mister Kinsley, if what's in the public interest is uninteresting to the public? What if they don't have the aptitude to understand trade-offs and necessary compromises? What if they don't have the time or inclination to explore critical issues fully—to reach properly-reasoned conclusions on these issues you are so intensely passionate about? How would you *make* these issues important to them? Or, expanding on my theme, how do you secure public support for, and commitment to, a given course of action when the public benefit is subtle or convoluted?" Doctor Chatsworth spoke with a measured intensity—a carefully-crafted formality that hid more than it revealed. "We're at war, Mister Kinsley. We're the defenders at the gate—the only protection Mother Nature has from the miners, loggers and road-building marauders. Whether we like it or not, there are people who like parking lots more than they like forests. People who prefer corn fields and tree farms over pristine wildlife habitat. People who mock us when we protect the earth's gentle, defenseless creatures. What do you do when the facts lead to an obvious and reasonable conclusion, but the public willfully ignores our expertise and suggestions? Would you wave a sign at a demonstration? Would you falsify test data[2]? Would you damage construction equipment? How far would you go?"

Robbie squirmed. With his teachers and his parents, he could answer or evade at his whim. If he knew the answer, he could answer. If not, he could make a joke. Usually, he would toss out buzzword slang and affect an air of bemused detachment.

That will not work here.

"No, sir, the end does not justify the means."

Doctor Chatsworth exploded.

"I hate lazy thinking. For everything we do, there is a necessary calculation. The *end* of making a salary to feed your family justifies the *means* of getting up in the morning and going to work. Everything we do comes from weighing the reward compared to the required effort. Don't hide behind lame platitudes."

"To compel the public to act rationally, we must educate them, of course," Robbie found himself answering. "I would educate the public. I would use carefully thought-out public school programs, after-school TV specials, public service announcements and the like. Once they understand, they'll do, well, like you say."

"Like *I* say, Mister Kinsley? What exactly are you getting at?"

Oh shit, oh fuck, oh crap. What the hell is with this guy? Usually when someone calls somebody 'Mister' they mean it as a sign of respect. When he says it, it sounds like an insult.

Robbie sought refuge in silence.

Dr. Chatsworth leaned forward. Slowly and crisply he articulated and lingered over each syllable.

"Can you think?"

---

[2] This is a reference to the 'Lynxgate' controversy where U.S. Forest Service Rocky Mountain Research Station field technicians submitted false lynx fur samples to "test the accuracy of the DNA testing". According to the AP story *Controversy Surrounds Canadian Lynx*, November 16, 1998. "We're talking about listing an animal [Canadian Lynx] that has not been seen [in Oregon] in over thirty years," said Senator Gordon Smith, R-Ore. "If we're going to do that, we might as well list Sasquatch."

Robbie winced; he didn't know what made him feel more doomed—each fatal phoneme emitted with exaggerated emphasis or the suspension of sound between syllables with enough stillness that he could hear the Doctor's office clock tick twice in each and every silent chasm.

His thoughts no longer raced; they fled. Doctor Chatsworth's eyes drilled him through dilated-in-fear pupils, burning through his retinas and bone into the lonely space of his cranial cavity.

Nature abhorred the vacuum of Robbie's brain.

Doctor Chatsworth leaned back in his chair and smiled.

"I'm sorry, that's just part of my interview style; I don't mean anything personal by it." Idly, he stirred Robbie's papers around on his desk. "If I understand your family background properly, Senator Edwin Kinsley is your uncle on your father's side?"

Ed Kinsley was the junior senator from New Hampshire and a newly-appointed member of the United States Senate Committee on Energy and Natural Resources.

"Yes, sir."

"Welcome to our project, Mister Kinsley. I'm sure you'll find your time here rewarding and worthy. Talk to Sherry, she'll show you your desk and make sure your computer gets hooked up and configured."

CHAPTER TWO

Graham Wallace

GRAHAM STOOD IN front of the restroom mirror and eyed his image with horror. The suit fit well—Lili had selected a colorful, splashy silk tie to complete the outfit. The only problems, beyond a day's growth of scraggly red whiskers, were his open-toed sandals and white socks.

"I feel like I'm selling my soul to the man," he said.

"Take off the sandals and put on the wingtips I set out for you," Lili said.

"I'm more comfortable in my sandals," Graham insisted.

"That's too damned bad. Just do it."

"All right, but I'm not tying them."

Once he changed his shoes, Lili adjusted his necktie.

"You're so pretty," she said. "You almost look like a man I'd agree to have sex with."

It was unconfirmed—but widely believed at Strategic Services—that Lili was a lesbian. Graham assumed she was being ironic and ignored her sexually-suggestive comments.

Staring at his image in the mirror, Graham shook his head.

"This is not right. I'm—"

"Graham, you have people depending on you to win this contract."

"not—"

"People's jobs are at stake."

"doing—"

"You already said you would..."

"this!" He unraveled the necktie. "Fancy clothes have nothing to do with slinging code and providing secure services. If he can't understand that concept, then we don't need his frickin' business anyway."

"I knew this was coming," Lili said, throwing up her hands. "You're impossible. Have it your way. Flush this contract down the toilet and see if I care."

"I'm wearing my Birks, Bermuda shorts and a Pink Floyd t-shirt."

"At least wear a polo shirt and a pair of slacks, or I quit. You don't have to be such a drama-queen."

"You're the one threatening to leave your stock options behind and quit, so who's the d-queen? A polo shirt? Okay, I agree. I'll make that sad sacrifice to the unholy Gods of commerce."

"Fine, jerk," Lili said over her shoulder as she left the bathroom.

In the hallway, she made eye-contact with a few loitering coworkers.

"I tried," she said, "but what can I do? He's the boss."

Willie and Maria

The contents of the hall closet were heaped in a pile; it was an esoteric aggregate of tennis rackets, cross-country ski equipment, assorted pieces of scuba wetsuits, golf shoes, cardboard boxes of baseball cards and inexplicably, an over-full sewing basket she'd been searching for.

Willie, with a long-dead pipe protruding from his mouth, walked in and watched her sort through the junk.

"What, my sweet, is it you're looking for?"

"We almost left without our camping utensils. I'd like to see you eat your instant oatmeal with your fingers."

Willie froze and stared at a corner. Maria sighed and continued her search. There was no telling how long he'd be lost in thought...and what those thoughts might be. He might be musing about his next magazine column, forgotten topics from last week's lecture series, climate change in Greenland or where the camping utensils might be stuffed away.

They were supposed to be on the road already—halfway to Harrison Lake in British Columbia, but she was still trying to round up errant items they'd need on their trip.

"The utensils are in a plastic box on the top shelf in the garage—behind the inflatable raft."

"What are they doing there?" Maria asked before she could stop herself.

"We were trying to avoid throwing everything in the closet because we can never find anything in there," Willie said mildly.

Harrison Lake is a deep, forty-mile slash of blue water just north of the U.S./Canada border. For the last five summers, they'd parked their SUV at Harrison Hot Springs and spent three weeks at a shoreline cabin, accessible only via water. They spent their days fishing, making love, reading trashy novels, writing, relaxing and hiking in the area. No cell phones, no Internet access and nearly complete isolation.

"Would you go get them please, and then throw them in the truck?"

Willie looked genuinely confused. "Go get what?" he said.

"The camping utensils," Maria said patiently.

"Oh, sure, of course," Willie said, eager to please.

Maria thought back to the first time she'd been alone with Professor Walters. She had an appointment to talk to him about a mid-term paper she was writing.

She could even remember the final title, *The Cycle of Ignorance—Statistical Generalizations in the Measured Competence of Public School Teachers*. Doctor Walters' office walls were decorated with a motley assortment of *No Smoking* signs and framed diplomas hanging crookedly. One hung upside-down, but she was too intimidated to ask if it was a wry criticism of the issuing institution or simply an unconscious error. He had four books splayed open on his desk and a small library of old books on floor-to-ceiling shelving protected by glass doors.

"Please leave the door open," the Professor said. "I have a personal policy of never being alone—behind closed doors—with a female student. There is enough foot traffic in the hallway—witnesses—to head off wild accusations or dishonest allegations. A virile, attractive man, as I am often described by female students, must use extreme caution. See?"

Maria nodded.

"Let me ask you, dear," he continued. "A petition is circulating to ban smoking in our offices. What do you think?"

Maria was scared of Professor Walters and her mind considered many possible replies.

Obviously, he smoked, so he'd naturally be opposed to smoking restrictions?

"I think smoking is a disgusting habit—an offense against nature and a health hazard forced on the innocent by selfish polluters."

Professor Walters sighed. He looked at his pipe while turning it over in his hands.

"I have a theory that smokers will be demonized and discriminated against. The nanny state will do everything possible to stamp us flat. It will take a decade or two, but we'll be despised and persecuted."

"Well, just quit. It will do your lungs good."

"You may be right—the evidence against heavy smoking is clear and there are no credible questions about those health hazards. However, the evidence for smoking in moderation—a cigar or two a day, a bowl or two of pipe tobacco, or a pack of cigarettes—is not as clear. To vex the anti-smoking zealots, the span of correlation includes a health benefit, probably caused by lower body weight and alleviated stress. Also, I'm worried about a society where the state has the means and power to enforce anti-smoking regulations. Will a police state like that be a place to pursue happiness? And, let's expand our thinking. Aren't there other human behaviors that might not measure up? Overeating, watching television, jumping out of a perfectly good airplane with a parachute, riding a motorcycle without a helmet and driving by yourself to work instead of carpooling? What if the state decides these things don't benefit the general public? Their ability to create mischief would be unbounded." Professor Walters rubbed his forehead and dropped his pipe in a large onyx ashtray. "But, you didn't come here to debate public policy." He scanned his notes. "You are looking for guidance on your midterm paper. Ten single-spaced and typed pages, due a week from Friday. How is it coming along?"

"I'm not sure you'll approve my topic."

Suddenly, Professor Walters leaned forward, interested.

"Isn't it my job to evaluate the strength of your argument and debate your facts and philosophical basis, not to approve or disapprove your topic? The university should be a venue for open discussion of anything. Do you have a working title for your paper?"

"I'm calling it something like *The Dumb leading the Dumb, how our Public Sector Teachers are Filtered, Groomed and Molded*."

Professor Walters went into one of his trances. This was the first time she'd observed this behavior up close and it was alarming. He didn't seem to breathe. Uncomfortable, she had nearly decided to slip out when he regained consciousness.

"Is this some weird insult directed at me? After all, I am a public school employee."

"No, sir, not at all."

Professor Walters chuckled.

"Don't mind me…I'm messing with you. There is a white paper based on research by the California Teachers Association that measures the competence of public school teachers. However, if you look at the underlying data, it actually demonstrates the opposite. It's called something like *A Case for Higher Teacher Compensation* published in Golden State Educator. You can find it online. And, come up with a better title. Get back with me in a week and we'll see how you're doing."

She gathered up her papers and prepared to leave.

"Miss Alvarez?"

"Yes."

"Just so you know…I'm a married man with a personal policy—I don't have sex with my students. I'm irresistible to some. You should know my rules before your fantasies get out of hand."

Maria was flustered.

"You are a presumptuous old man," she said. "I don't see how such a thought could enter your head."

"Some women are attracted to powerful men—men they assume will nurture and protect them. Some women are attracted to evil or self-destructive men they think they can save. Some women are attracted to men with exemplary intellects and I sense you might be one of those. I don't mean any offense; I just want to make sure the ground rules are clear between us."

"You are an aggravating and deluded man. I'm here for guidance on my midterm paper."

"Of course, young lady, that's excellent. We're on the same page and all is well."

Clutching her books and papers to her chest, she was angry as she left the room and entered the stream of foot traffic in the hallway.

What an arrogant, egomaniacal old man.

She realized—under her sweater, her nipples were erect and swollen. This made her angrier.

Robert Kinsley

For some reason, instead of the ballpoint pens, lined legal notepads and yellow sticky notes he'd asked for, the General Services Administration had sent him yellow highlighting pens, six boxes of large paperclips and a carton of white correction fluid.

This was in spite of Departmental Quality Assurance Guidelines which specifically forbade any use of this correction fluid. He double-checked the online requisition form to make sure he'd entered the item numbers correctly, and he had. After a half hour of walking around and trying to exchange correction fluid for legal notepads, he gave up and returned, beaten, to his desk.

It wasn't really a desk; it was more like a drafting tabletop teetering on a pair of file cabinets—one permanently locked with both a combination lock and ancient padlock. The age of the drafting tabletop was unknown, but someone had carved *LBJ for the USA* into the surface—which provided a crude carbon dating.

He removed a large Smokey Bear poster from the wall behind his desk and hung up a framed picture of his parents. It was depressing. The paint on the wall was faded behind the poster and his photograph was too small to provide adequate cover, so he removed the photograph and pinned back up the poster.

It showed a sad Smokey bandaging a bear cub's burned paw with the large question—WHY?—in the background.

Robert reread Washington Administrative Code 232-12-619 Section 2B. It is unlawful to take bullfrogs except by angling, hand dip netting, spearing (gigging) or with bow and arrow. A hunting license is required to take bullfrogs. He was busy highlighting this section in bright yellow when Quimby Chatsworth stopped by to check on him.

"Bullfrogs?" Quimby said.

Robert jumped. "Sorry, sir, you startled me. I didn't know a permit was required to hunt for bullfrogs. Why are we regulating bullfrogs? Are they endangered?"

Quimby tested the surface of Robert's desk. Finding it safe, he perched on a corner.

"A very good question. First of all, if we allowed unlimited bullfrog harvesting, then certainly, they *would* be endangered. They'd be hunted and killed until none were left. Therefore, reasonable preventive measures are appropriate to protect the public commons. However, there is a more important underlying concept in play. Who owns the wildlife of our wonderful state?"

"I never thought about it. I suppose it either belongs to no one or to itself or maybe it belongs to the person who catches it."

"I find myself appalled at your ignorance. I hope you're not a typical Harvard student. It's not the simple reality of the frog that is important, it's the principle. The bullfrog belongs to the people and we are the people, get it?"

"So, we own the bullfrogs?" Robert asked tentatively.

"No, you fool, aren't you paying attention? The people of Washington State own the bullfrogs. We simply administer for the frog's welfare on behalf of the owners. We tax and issue permits to harvest on the people's behalf. We're like their conscience—their beneficent father figure thinking things through for them so they won't be troubled by miniscule details. Without us, there would be anarchy and chaos and all of our beautiful wildlife would be wiped out. However, it's a delicate balance. We would never be directly granted our power to do our good work. We need to be soft and subtle because the people will never be mature enough to give up their freedom to allow us to serve their thoughtful needs. That's the mystery and the challenge of our age. How do we achieve and hold the power to serve the public interest when the issues are so complex and counter-intuitive? That is why I pressed you about the means to do our work. We need funding to protect wildlife, so we tax, collect fees, and issue permits, but the public resists paying. We need power to intervene on behalf of the frogs and fish and birds and foxes and the rest of nature's splendor. Enforcement is necessary, but often, it is unpopular. That's why I'm glad you decided to keep the Smokey Bear poster."

Robert glanced behind. "I'm sorry sir, Smokey the Bear? I'm not following you, sir."

"First of all, it's Smokey Bear, not Smokey *the* Bear. Second, look at that poster. Notice how Smokey is anthromorphed with human features. It's creepy if you think about it—a bizarre, pagan crossbreed of humankind and bear. Anyway, the message is simple. It's a cartoon and that's how we interact with the public. Collectively, they will not study the issues and formulate intelligent conclusions, so we predigest facts for them and lead them gently to the right point of view. I like that poster because it is such a beautiful example of our work."

"Excuse me, sir, but what exactly does it mean? Only *you* can prevent forest fires? I don't get it. Most forest fires are started by lightning."

"Who's talking about forest fires? Are you really so dense? The real message is that trees and animals are as important as people. That we have to spend public money and infringe on public liberty to protect the beautiful, noble and cute animals of the forest. I hope I didn't make a big mistake hiring you. You are trying my limited patience."

Quimby muttered and grumbled as he walked away.

"Whew," Robert said.

He looked up as a cold can of Mountain Dew was placed on his desk. A butch-looking woman dressed in forest service green from head to toe, smiled at him.

"I'm Betsy," she said.

"Thanks," Robert said, while popping the top on the soda can.

"Just leave a quarter in the kitchen the next time you're in there. It's the honor system."

"Does Doctor Chatsworth hate everyone or is it just me?"

"No, don't worry about it; he hates everyone equally."

Clayton Powell

The trophy room was thickly-carpeted and lit with high-pressure Xenon fixtures creating illusions of daylight and shadows on the dioramas. A jaguar stood in a shroud of leaves mirroring the scene where Clayton had shot him in the Brazilian jungle. The hollow-point round had blasted off the skullcap just above the eyes, but the taxidermist had done a good job of sewing up the fur; only by running a thumb over the cranium could the fracture be detected.

The prize cat of his public collection was an eight hundred and forty-three pound Siberian Tiger bagged in tall grass on the shoulder of Russia's Sikhote-Alin Mountains. He'd used a Gibbs Summit .45/70 to make the kill. Just thinking about it, he felt a twinge of muscle memory in his dislocated shoulder. And, the cruelty of the cold Siberian winter still haunted his bones.

The walnut-veneered door to his private collection was not invisible, but it was unmarked and did not draw attention to itself. An inset deadbolt lock discouraged the uninvited—the room held trophies that could put him in jail for the rest of his life. Beside the kitchen staff, no one else was in the house. Still, Clayton looked around carefully before inserting the intricate key into the complex lock.

There were so many bald eagles around that bagging one was passé, but Clayton liked them, so there were a score, with outstretched wings, hanging from the ceiling on invisible wires. Most were shot along the Skagit River in northwest Washington State. With his Australian walking stick, he nudged them so they oscillated in soothing circles like mobiles in a child's crib.

In the bear section, his favorite trophies were a pair of Kodiaks and a two-hundred-and-twenty-five pound black-masked Panda cat-bear bagged in inland China. One corner was dedicated to elephants, both Indian and African.

Behind a beaded curtain lay the real prizes of his collection. He stopped and stroked the forehead of the first man he'd killed, a swarthy Egyptian who was one of the beaters for a boar hunt in the West Rhodopi Mountains of Bulgaria. The kill was an accident; Clayton had been a little too quick on the trigger as the man popped out of a thicket of brush. For the right money, the taxidermist was willing and since Clayton shipped many large crates for business purposes anyway, he decided to see if he could include the man's embalmed carcass as cargo.

The shipping went smoothly, so here the man stood with his head poking out of the brush, just like when he'd appeared in the crosshairs of Clayton's 15X scope. The dead man's fellow trophies were an assorted lot—a homeless man taken with a knife under an overpass in Philadelphia and the only female in the collection, a fat woman he'd strangled in an alley in Amsterdam. She'd put up the most fight; for a heroin-junkie whore, she was surprisingly fast and strong and very nearly turned the tables. She kneed him in the groin and almost split Clayton's skull with a cobblestone.

Something was missing from his collection. It felt incomplete. Sometimes he thought about adding children—there were plenty in Brazil or Thailand that would not be missed, but that was probably taking things too far. However, he found the thought interesting and was amused by his nearly unlimited depravity.

What was left?

He was unexcited by sea mammals and the rarer of the small land breeds were boring…killing a platypus or an ocelot didn't seem worth the trouble.

Surely there is something in the world worthy of my attention.

He was confident that with patience, the world would provide and his collection would grow. In the meantime, he had a grizzly bear bow-hunting trip to Canada to look forward to.

What gives me the right to take the life of an eagle, a tiger, or a man? Is it an immoral and pathologically-sick symptom of a deep-seated mental illness?

On the other hand, what sort of simpleton really believes that all humans are equal, when this is so obviously untrue? An accountant toiling over a spreadsheet in Toledo is not the equal of the President of the United States. A high school football player is not the equal of the Pope.

And, a skuzzy cock-sucking prostitute, walking the backstreets of Amsterdam, is not my equal. Me, the eminent, wealthy Clayton Powell.

Isn't it self-evident by the fact that I am drinking brandy and stroking her tanned skin while her soul screams in eternal hell? She could have won our skirmish, but she didn't. I am, ergo sum. Quod erat demonstrandum. Therefore it is proven. I lived, she died.

The rhino could have taken my head off with a powerful rake of its giant horn, but, weakened by bloodloss; it collapsed and died at my feet.

Winners and losers, that's the way of the world.

In time, it will be my turn to be crushed, defeated and destroyed. But not today. Now I run my fingers through the dead slut's hair and enjoy the heat of her leathery skin under infrared lamps and I can moisten her perfectly-preserved leathery breasts with Germain-Robin XO brandy from my glass.

And dream.

I can dream of the proper resident for the corner, reserved and waiting, in my private collection room.

Perhaps a pope or a king?

The world will provide.

CHAPTER THREE

Willie and Maria

TRAFFIC INCHED ALONG at the Blaine U.S./Canada border crossing. Musing, Maria thought of a spreadsheet analysis she'd created a few years back which documented Willie's driving history. She meticulously worked through insurance records and created a trend calculation.

Most of his accidents were trivial—mangled fenders and scraped quarter panels—but the evidence was overwhelming and a logical case was easily made, convincing even her stubborn husband.

S*he* should drive.

Reclining in his seat and peering through reading glasses, Willie read from a thick book. It was maddening how he bounced around the text and never seemed to read anything sequentially. Besides, while moving, Maria couldn't read a single page without getting car sick. It was as if Willie's concentration was so complete that he was completely disconnected from his body.

Frowning, Maria was uncomfortable with the damage he did to the books; turning down corners of the pages to mark them, scribbling in the margins, and, if he got really angry, tearing out pages and discarding them. His system, however abusive and haphazard, worked for him. In arguing his point of view, he could quote long passages and back up his references quickly and efficiently.

Once it was their turn at the port of entry kiosk, Maria handed their passports to the customs inspector.

"Where are you headed?" the inspector said.

"We're US citizens from Seattle headed to Harrison Lake for a vacation, we'll be up there two weeks and we're not carrying any guns or fresh produce," Maria said, anticipating the inspector's questions.

He came out of his kiosk and beamed his flashlight through the windows into the cargo area.

"Father and daughter?" he asked.

Maria knew full well they did not look like kin; she had olive skin and long wavy hair and though easily old enough to be her father, Willie was black.

"Husband and wife," Maria said.

"She's my midlife crisis," Willie interjected.

"Midlife? Are you thinking you'll live to be one-hundred-and-twenty-four?" Maria asked mildly.

"Hold your evil tongue, woman," Willie responded with gentle humor.

"No firearms?" the inspector asked.

"No, as Canada prefers it, we're completely defenseless," Willie said, leaning over to make eye-contact with the inspector.

"Don't pay any attention to him; he's just an ornery, contentious old man," Maria said.

While waiting for the inspector to make up his mind about them, Maria felt the tug of memory.

In her senior year, she audited Professor Walters' Econ 511, *Microeconomic Theory and Application*. His wife was ill and he was often late or stayed home—turning over the class to teaching assistants.

Morbidly, he often abandoned the text and lecture notes and read from obscure papers with titles like *Correlation is not Causation, the Secret Link between Wearing a Brassiere and Contracting Breast Cancer*.

She feared for his sanity when he once spent forty minutes comparing the risk of AIDS viremia to the side-effects of Protease Inhibitor antiviral chemotherapy cocktails. What did the data suggest?

Was the treatment more of a hazard than the disease?

And, what were the relative risks between irrational things people did voluntarily, like riding bicycles and skateboards—compared to the societal risks of Creutzfeldt-Jakob Disease and E. coli? When he started talking about the madness of asbestos lawsuits, it seemed he would never shut up. The faculty and students cut him a lot of slack because his wife was painfully and slowly dying of kidney cancer. The class ended with a five minute silence while Professor Walters stared at the papers on his lectern.

She was concerned for him, so, on a whim after class, she stopped at a florist shop and bought a small bundle of pink carnations. The Professor's house was a tidy brick house just north of the University of Washington campus. Nervous, she thought about just leaving the flowers on the doorstep, but the door was swept open by a startled housekeeper who, warily, leaned outside the front door to pick up the afternoon newspaper.

"The Professor is not home yet."

Wordlessly, Maria held out the flowers. The housekeeper stood back and gestured.

"Take them upstairs yourself. She's always glad when company calls."

Inside, the house smelled like medicine and mothballs. She was scared silly—climbing the stairs on shaking legs.

What was she doing? This was stupid and insane. She was uninvited and had no business invading her professor's privacy.

Standing in the bedroom doorway, she took in the various IV tubes and pill bottles. Mrs. Walters had a colorful African scarf wrapped around her bald head. Reclining on the bed, she lay quietly with her eyes closed. She looked much older than Professor Walters—her cheeks were hollowed out by disease and her skin hugged her skull like damp satin.

"The carnations smell lovely, dear, but don't bring them in. I'll start sneezing and I won't ever stop. Of all the things I miss, burying my nose in a fresh bouquet of flowers is high on the list. I didn't realize that until this very instant. You're wearing a lovely perfume, dear, is it

Angelica number 7? My body is nearly done, but my mind, when the opiates recede, races in tight little circles."

She opened her eyes. Her irises were like brown puddles.

"You're a lovely one, my dear. One of the Professor's grad students? Don't make me beg. What is your name, honey?"

"Maria."

"Yes, the Professor mentioned you. Come and sit beside me for a spell."

Professor Walters mentioned her? It must be a mistake. Perhaps she was confused with another Maria...there were dozens at a school as large as the University of Washington.

In the hallway, a ceramic vase was filled with silk roses. Maria laid the bundle of carnations on the table next to them.

"Just read to me, sweet pea. The page is marked."

Feeling lost and panicked, Maria picked up a book splayed on a side table and began reciting.

"'But his isolated personality was impenetrable. No one knew what he thought about anything. People would ask his wife if he were really a socialist; she had to tell them she herself did not know. He was never without his armor; a polite, controlled objectivity which stripped the world of its emotional content and which kept those who would most have liked to pierce his personal shield at arm's length. "Tell me, Professor Veblen," a student once asked him, "do you take anything seriously?" "Yes," he replied in a conspiratorial whisper, "but don't tell anyone.[3]'"

"That Thorstein Veblen was such a scamp," Mrs. Walters whispered. "Please keep going."

Wondering how long she would have to read, Maria slowly became engrossed by the text. Several pages later, she read the phrase 'No one is exempt from the virus of competitive emulation...' and chuckled, and then read it again. She held Mrs. Walters' hand and they laughed until the ill woman began choking. Terrified, Maria held a plastic cup and straw to the woman's lips. Mrs. Walters sipped and gradually regained control.

---

[3] *The Worldly Philosophers. The Lives, Times and Ideas of the Great Economic Thinkers* by Robert L. Heilbronner

Maria dabbed at the woman's leaky eyes with a hand towel.

"Don't worry about me, dear. If I could choose it, I would love to die laughing."

"Please don't talk that way."

"I'm sorry, but at this point, I'm not afraid of death anymore. Please keep going."

A page farther along, Maria read, "'I am free to theorize with all the abandon that comes of immunity to the facts.'"

"Doesn't that sound like the Professor?" Mrs. Walters asked, grinning at the look of horror on Maria's face. "Regardless of his eminence and intellect, believe me, dear, he's still just a man with strengths and flaws and many foibles amid his transcendence."

The afternoon elapsed and Maria continued reading until it was time to rush off to her next class.

"Will you come and read to me tomorrow?" Whispering conspiratorially, she added, "As much as I love Victoria Elise, you pronounce more of the complex words correctly. And you have such a lovely voice."

Maria nodded.

"Yes, I will come again," she said.

Robert Kinsley

The staff meeting was interminable. The air in the room was stale—rank with the smell of body odor.

Robert thought back to his first day on the job. He'd experienced a spittle-punctuated litany of outrage from a pair of militant lesbians (who inexplicably hated each other for a transgression so grave no one dared to speak of it) complaining about his aftershave and deodorant.

"I'm allergic to pollen, dust and other miscellaneous indoor air pollutions, animal dander, second- and third-hand cigarette smoke, mold spores, aftershave and perfumes, air fresheners, dry-erase markers, cleaning products, fabric softeners, dryer sheets, scented detergents and solvents from new carpet adhesive and pesticides," one of them complained.

"Your selfish disregard of my multiple chemical sensitivities creates a hostile work environment," the other one hissed. "Tolerate my diversity if you expect to last around here."

While Robert was lost in thought, Quimby prepared to close the meeting.

"Are there any other important topics we need to cover?"

Robert gathered his courage and spoke.

"When do I get a field assignment?"

There was a shocked silence.

"The intern wants a field project," one of the lesbians whispered sarcastically.

Quimby eyed Robert coolly, as if seeing him for the first time.

"Once your Project Grant Facilitator has logged your Millennium Development Goal into the Business Planning and Reporting Tool and the Project Review Team forwards your plan to the Operations Evaluation Department and funding is approved by the Fiscal Accounting Department, then you will have a field assignment approved. If there are no other comments—"

"Excuse me, sir," Robert said, "but what does that mean?"

Quimby sighed. "Write a grant application, get it funded and scheduled—then you get a field assignment. Betsy, would you stay behind and explain the process to him? Meeting adjourned, thank you all for attending."

Robert was left looking across the table at Betsy.

"I wrote a lot of reports in school. I can write a stupid grant request."

"If only it was that easy," she said sadly. "You have to pick a topic that does not infringe on other grants and projects. For example, I'm working on a project to study a proposed endangered species, the Pacific sheath-tailed bat. Emballonura semicaudata rotensis. They are fascinating and important creatures and vital to our delicate ecological balance. Did you know—"

"I'm sorry, Betsy, but do we have to go into all that right now?"

"No," Betsy said, disappointed. "The problem is…how do you find a fresh, new species in danger? Even the relaxation of species definition to include geographically defined populations of wild fauna only helped for a while. There are lots of insects, flowering plants and snails, but these grant applications are very difficult to get funded. All the *cute* animals like owls and big cats are already taken many times over. Shelby is working on the Addax, Benjamin is working on the Olympic Pocket Gopher, Sandra is working on the Northern Sea Otter, Paul is working on the Washington Ground Squirrel and you don't dare think about the Washington Spotted Frog, because Quimby thinks he owns all the amphibians."

"Gray wolf?"

"Get real."

"Um, Columbia Basin Pigmy Rabbit?"

"Old news."

"Woodland Caribou?"

"Now you're just being stupid."

"There must be something. I'm not suited to a desk job. If I wanted to do desk work I'd sell financial derivatives like my father. I came out here to make a difference to the natural ecology."

"You came out here to get away from the trouble you stirred up in Beantown."

"Well that too, but there must be something here for me."

"Are you willing to give up your job here and work for a non-governmental organization or other activist group?"

"What job? I'm an intern. It's not even a paid position."

"Very well. I will make a few phone calls. Can you hang in for a day or two while I see what I can come up with?"

"Yes. Thank you."

Clayton Powell

Clayton's office was near the top of a black-glass obelisk of a building in upscale downtown Bellevue. He had many businesses, but they all reported to the holding company he called OneWorld, an intentionally bland, non-descript name.

The view from the window included a vast swath of Lake Washington, Seattle's skyscraper skyline and an annoying high-rise building site slowly eclipsing his siteline of Bill Gates' expansive property on the Medina shore of Lake Washington. Clayton could not complain because he was one of the primary investors in the project, along with a former Washington State governor and a U.S. Senator.

Clayton's meditation was interrupted by a gentle tone from his intercom system.

"Mr. Powell, your three o'clock appointment is here, sir."

"Thank you, Elise. Give me a minute, and then show him in."

"Yes, sir."

At shoulder height, a nose-smudge defaced the glass, so Clayton, with exasperation, applied cleaning fluid from a crystal spray bottle (a recycled French perfume bottle left behind by one of his girlfriends) and cleaned the spot with a linen cloth from his desk.

He'd just hidden away the cleaning supplies when his visitor walked in. Clayton reached over his desk and shook the man's hand firmly.

Mr. Chung Jien 'Jerry' Li was a small, child-like man, even for an Asian, and was dressed in a perfectly-tailored navy blue suit with a contrasting psychedelic Jerry Garcia necktie. His hair was cropped short and he peered through tiny (trendy and nearly useless) eyeglasses.

While sizing each other up, they performed the ritual business card exchange. The Asian man's card was divided into halves and printed on both sides in English, Mandarin, Japanese and Korean. Clayton's card countered the verbose, multilingual trend; it had only his name and a website address where contact information for his executive assistant could be found. After taking their seats, they stared at each other for a nearly a minute before Mr. Li broke his gaze and flicked at a piece of lint on his jacket sleeve.

"A billion dollars is a lot of money, Mr. Li." Clayton said. "If I was really just a gambler, I'd just put my money on the roulette table and spin the wheel. That pays thirty-five to one."

"You only bet on races you're running in."

Clayton laughed. "You're right. I think we can do business. However, I want the factory in Singapore and the support staff to be moved to Bangalore. And there is one more thing..."

"Which is?" Mr. Li said.

Clayton pressed the buttons on a remote control and a bullseye target, attached to a projection screen, dropped from the ceiling on the opposite side of the massive room—twenty-five yards away. Clayton opened a closet door and selected a Zebrawood long bow and a quiver of arrows. He placed the quiver on his desk and handed the bow to Mr. Li.

"I'll make it simple for you, Mr. Li. Hit the target and I'll sign."

With a blank expression, Mr. Li took the bow and made a few practice flexes. He pulled an arrow from the quiver and examined it for straightness and balance, and then took a stance. He unleashed the arrow and it hit the target, not dead center, but touching the red center circle. Mr. Li turned and handed the bow back to Clayton.

"Very good, Mr. Li. I'm impressed. You obviously did your home work and practiced."

"Are you an ignorant man who believes your primitive Native Americans invented the bow and arrow? My father taught me that Huangdi, two thousand years before Jesus was born, was chased into a mulberry tree by a tiger. While trapped in that tree, he fashioned a bow from a mulberry branch, used a vine as a string and carved an arrow from a bamboo shoot. He shot the tiger in the eye and escaped. The bow and arrow were invented in Asia four thousand years ago."

"This was a special kind of Chinese tiger that can't climb a tree?"

A momentary flash of irritation roiled across Mr. Li's face. He picked up the bow and smoothly notched another arrow. Swiveling, he turned and loosed the arrow which darted across the room and embedded itself between the eyes of a stuffed zebra head mounted on the far wall.

Clayton collapsed back into his leather chair and laughed. "Yes, Mr. Li, I think we will, perhaps, be able to do business, you and I," he said.

Mr. Li, smoothed the sleeves of his jacket and nodded in assent.

"Perhaps so," he replied calmly.

Graham Wallace

With exaggerated slowness—scanning him from head to toe—Lili looked over Graham with distaste.

"What?" he whined. "I'm not wearing the Pink Floyd t-shirt. What more do you want from me? Oh lord of the millennium, does this inhuman torture never end?" he asked, dramatically addressing the heavens.

"You can't meet Powell wearing a logo shirt from one of his competitors. That's simple common sense."

Graham looked down at the logo.

"Shit, you're right," he said.

He walked around the lab and pointed at Anderssen, who wore a black polo shirt with a Flower Kings logo. For some unknown reason, Anderssen only listened to obscure Swedish progressive rock bands like the Karmakanics, The Pain of Salvation, Kaipa, Anecdoten and others.

"You."

"What?"

"Trade me shirts."

Anderssen shrugged.

"Okay, boss," he said, peeling the shirt over his bulging belly.

Graham returned to his office.

"Now are you happy?" he asked.

"Better," Lili replied. "Now, I surfed the web. Powell likes big game hunting. You should ask intelligent questions about his trophies."

"I don't give a shit about any wildebeests he might have shot with his phallic peashooter."

"You'll be expected to make small talk. Pretend to be interested—how does that conflict with your precious hacker credibility?"

"He'll know I don't know anything about hunting."

"He'll appreciate your expressing an interest."

They stared at each other over Graham's desk until Graham backed down.

"Okay, what do I say?"

"Just ask him about his latest trip. He just got back from Africa a few months ago. He bagged a rhino. There are pictures posted on the Internet; just ask him what rifle he used and how the hunt went. That will be enough."

"The sacrifices I make for my company…" Graham said.

"You poor, abused baby," Lili replied.

CHAPTER FOUR

Willie and Maria

THERE WAS SOMETHING about the upper Fraser River delta that soothed Maria. It was probably just her imagination—she only lived two hundred miles away in a very similar climate and landscape—but the green wash of evergreen hillsides seemed composed of watercolor tints more pastel than she was used to in Washington State.

The light seems more softly-filtered by gauzy clouds; could there be less harsh UV in the Canadian sunshine?

It didn't seem logical, but she was not going to fight the buoyant effect on her mood. Compared to the creeping madness of the clogged streets of the city, the traffic on Trans-Canada Highway 1 was more relaxing as they drove in the shadows of the looming peaks of the Vancouver Coastal Mountains piled up around the valley like ancient black heaps of crumbling masonry.

Bridal Veil Falls shimmered in mist on the southern edge of the cliffs that crowded the highway. The rugged mountains, sculpted by ice age glaciers, seemed like a wall between the urban sprawl of the Vancouver basin and desolate surrounding wilderness. The contrast between suburban sprawl—housing developments and golf courses—and the wild, untamed backlands made her dizzy.

Maria tapped on Willie's shoulder and gestured at the raw landscape.

"The glaciers pushed these mountains around like playthings. It makes me woozy to think of it."

"Quite understandable, dear," he said.

He returned his attention to his reading. After a time, he said, "Perhaps this is something we should have talked about before we got married—when we talked about religion and children, you know? But, do you believe in the 'Sasquatch'?"

"Sasquatch? What brought this on?"

"All the businesses named Sasquatch this and Bigfoot that." He gestured. "Look at that truck. Would you allow Bigfoot Moving Company to transport your household goods? Think they use Bigfoot labor? And that one, see the van? Sasquatch Catering. What does that mean? They cater only to Sasquatches? Then they can't be too busy. Or they serve only Sasquatch food? What would a Sasquatch eat up in the hills? Dead rodents and blackberries? I wouldn't let them cater my wedding or corporate event."

"Willie?"

"Yes, dear?"

"Enough blabber about Sasquatches. Shut up and read your book."

"Okay."

As they continued on Highway 1, Maria tried to ignore a road sign advertising the Sasquatch Inn in Harrison Mills, and then another for the Sasquatch Indian Sweater Shop.

And Willie grinning at her.

As the miles rolled under the SUV, her mind drifted back in time.

Mrs. Walters lingered for almost a year. In that time, the books Maria read to her included Bob Denver's *Gilligan, Maynard, and Me* ("I've found that being a good childhood memory is very rewarding...") and Nikos Kazantzakis' *Saint Francis* ("He who sows, Brother Francis, also reaps in the very process, because in his mind he has a foretaste of the future harvest...").

Toward the end, the only sign that Mrs. Walters understood what was read were her fingers twitching in synchronization with the words and a quiet yearning for more written in her eyes.

One of the last things she said before completely losing the power to speak was, "Tell Willie I give him permission to be happy again. Not right away, but someday. In time."

The Professor, when Mrs. Walters whispered this, stood in the doorway. It was impossible to tell if he heard her or was thinking of something else entirely; he would come and go silently with only the subtle scent of old tobacco floating from his sweater to confirm his presence.

There would be seconds-long gaps in her breathing, but Maria would keep reading while imploring the supreme power to grant Mrs. Walters one more breath, one more minute, and one more day. Finally, on the 27th of March on a blustery spring morning, Mrs. Walters breathing stopped...and did not restart.

Out loud, Maria reread the passage from Saint Francis. "'You must respect life, Brother Francis,'" insisted the bishop; "'not only the life of other men and of worms, but also your own life. Life is the breath of God: you do not have the right to stifle it.'"

Touching his wife's cheek, the Professor stood by the bedside and looked into her empty face. He then looked at Maria with tears in his eyes.

"'They are not dead! They have but passed beyond the mists that blind us here into the new and larger life of that serener sphere.[4]'"

Standing quietly, his shoulders shook. Maria wanted to touch him but she did not dare.

"I'll make the phone calls. You should run along," he said.

Standing by the bed, the Professor's cool calmness was disturbing. Then his knees buckled and he went down hard, hitting his head on an end table—slashing a huge gash in his forehead. Pills and medical folderol cascaded across the hardwood floor. To avoid aggravating a potentially-serious neck injury, Maria should have left him and called 911, but instead she lifted and cradled his head on her lap. His eyes fluttered open.

---

[4] *There is No Death* by John Luckey McCreery. U.S. poet (1835–1906).

"Take me instead, Lord," he said clearly, while she punched numbers into her cell phone. Slowly, he regained his senses. "I'm sorry. I thought you were an angel, but you're just my grad student."

After she made the call, she looked into his eyes.

She was irritated.

"And you're an addled old man with a head wound," she said, unkindly.

"Did you hear the joke about the Florida preacher who died, mid-sentence, while giving a sermon about heaven?"

"No," she said.

"That's okay, it wasn't that damned funny anyway."

Thankfully, after that, he shut up until the paramedics arrived.

Willie leaned against the passenger door turning one of his pipes over in his hands.

"What are you thinking?" he asked as they negotiated the Agassiz-Harrison turnoff from the freeway and crossed the long bridge that loomed over the Fraser River.

"Huh?"

"Your spirit seems dampened and I wondered why."

Maria sighed. "I was thinking that we'll get to the hot springs in a half hour or so."

"Ah," he responded, "that explains the shadow that eclipsed your mood."

"Silence yourself and get back to your book."

"Yes, dear."

Clayton Powell and Graham Wallace

The meeting room on the 19th floor, where Clayton liked to close his deals, was finished eccentrically. A cream-colored leather couch, surrounded by matching leather recliners, was arranged to look toward the northwest over the Bellevue skyline though floor-to-ceiling glass panels with nearly imperceptible seams.

The floor and ceilings images were optical projections. The room appeared to float over a sheer, vertigo-inducing drop nearly two-hundred feet into a courtyard fountain; the ceiling revealed a cloud-studded blue sky. An occasional seagull would fly over to complete the fantasy that they were in a high-tech tree house of sorts—eerily suspended in space.

The deal on the table was for 24/7 merchant transaction services with firewalls, a virtual private network infrastructure, secure financial plumbing, data warehousing and backup in a dedicated earthquake-hardened facility. The contract was valued at $50M per year and the vendor-selection process was cut-throat and competitive—there were at least seven companies within a few square miles of Clayton's office that could offer these services and that did not include thousands of competitors from worldwide data havens like the Bahamas and India.

Clayton slouched in a chair and leafed through a Soldier of Fortune magazine. At a quiet knock on the door, he picked up a remote control and pressed a button to release the deadbolt lock. His visitor, Graham Wallace, was young.

Too young to be president of a competent Internet services company.

His complexion was spotted with acne and an untidy, oily wave of thick hair flopped across his forehead. He wore shapeless khaki pants and a logo polo shirt that had not seen a washing machine for a while.

Graham hesitated at the edge of the room and looked over the floor with apprehension.

"Hey, uh, Mr. Powell. I'm not really comfortable with heights. Can we do this somewhere else?"

"Shut up, Graham, and get your fat ass in here," Clayton replied.

Graham calculated a cost/benefit analysis. There wasn't much profit in the contract, but the marketing value was immense—other big companies would certain follow the trail OneWorld blazed.

Graham made up his mind.

Swallowing and trying not to look down, Graham stepped on the glass floor, testing it with his weight as if it was treacherous ice. His mind told him he was stepping off a cliff, but, resolute, he walked across the room, though with eyes nearly clenched shut as if to see as little as possible.

He collapsed into the embrace of the couch, breathing shallowly in little gasps.

"When I was a little kid, an older boy held me over the side of a bridge and threatened to drop me. Maybe I was four or so, I don't know. I've been back there since and it wasn't that far of a drop, maybe fifteen feet, but it scared me to near-to-death. I crapped my pants. Now I don't like ladders or, you know, those glassed-in elevators like they have at the Hilton? I always take the stairs."

"That's a sweet story, Graham, but surely you know OneWorld doesn't value in human weakness. If you were a real man, you'd face your fear and transcend it. The first time I shot a rampaging elephant, can you imagine how that was? A ton of anger-made-flesh coming toward me like a freight train at twenty-five miles per hour. I wanted to jump into the brush and hide like a baby, but instead, I looked it in the eye and blasted a hole through its brain with a Graham Gibbs .505 round. It slid to a stop barely ten feet in front of me. Did I shit my pants? No, I did not. I looked into the devil's face and stood my ground. You're never going to have the gravitas to run a fifteen-billion-dollar company unless you control your irrational phobias."

"That's all very interesting, sir, but could we talk about the data services contract?"

Clayton sighed. "We *are* talking about the contract, Graham. Aren't you paying attention?"

He reached over and picked up a single sheet of paper, then held it up for Graham's inspection.

"See, here it is, my friend. All drafted up, parsed and sanitized by the lawyers and ready for my signature. Now watch carefully." He folded up the contract and slipped it into a legal-sized envelope. Using a little sponge, he dampened the adhesive and sealed it. "See, Graham, it's ready to go—with priority postage already applied."

"You didn't sign it."

"Yes, but I'm *going* to sign it, Graham," Clayton said patiently—as if talking to a small child.

"I don't understand."

"Okay, let's start with the basics. To whom is this envelope addressed?"

"To your attention, care of the Harrison Hot Springs Resort and Spa."

"That's great, Graham. Are you starting to catch on?"

"You're going to sign it at the Harrison Resort? I don't even know where that is."

"But you will, believe me. Look Graham, you know I'm a rich and powerful man. I didn't get rich by doing business with people I can't measure. I'm suggesting we get to know each other on a little trip. That makes sense, doesn't it?"

"No, not really. You did due diligence....pulled our Dunn and Bradstreet report, studied our Moody's rating, talked to all of our corporate references and did credit checks up the butt. You know more about us than we know about ourselves. So, you suggest we travel to a resort to get more acquainted? I don't follow your train of thought on this."

"No, Graham, the resort is where I'll sign the contract. We'll get to know each other on a little cross-country trip *prior* to arriving at the resort. We're flying into Hundred Mile House in Canada, and then we'll hike through the south edge of the Cariboo Mountains. If we're lucky along the way, we'll bag a grizzly with a longbow."

"Excuse me? I can't take time off from work. Besides, I'm no woodsman—I got lost on a golf course once. This idea is the essence of insanity. I don't like camping and hiking. This has nothing to do with computers and security. I'm not doing it."

"Well, that would be a shame. You're so damned close to the contract that puts your company on top of the heap. I know you're planning an IPO—this contract will add a couple of orders of magnitude to your net worth when that happens, believe me. All I'm asking is for a few days' stroll in the woods to get to know each other."

Graham's fingers twitched as if he was convulsing. He sat with his eyes clenched shut for two minutes while Clayton watched him with detached amusement.

"All right, ya' bastard, I'll do it. What do I need to bring?"

"Great. I'll take care of all the supplies. I don't want to tell you what to do, but, in the spirit of friendship, I suggest you get outfitted with a comfortable pair of waterproof hiking boots. Otherwise, bring what you want and I'll take care of all the essential camping gear."

Graham stood up and swayed on trembling legs.

"I'll go with you, but can't you just sign the frickin' contract before we go?"

"Oh, Graham, I'd really like to, but I must insist you humor me on this," Clayton said with a voice dripping with false empathy. "Be a pal and drop it in the mailbox on your way out and it will be waiting for us when we get to Harrison. When we arrive, I'll pick up the envelope at the hotel's front desk and sign it right then and there. This will be fun, you'll see."

Graham took the envelope and walked, wobbling slightly, toward the door. Remembering his instructions, he stopped.

"Oh, by the way, how was that Africa trip? Fun?"

"Don't blow smoke up my ass. You don't really give a shit. Just be here Tuesday, eight o'clock sharp—outside the front lobby. I'll run us out to the airport. See you then, Graham," Clayton said cheerfully in a loud voice.

"Fucking manipulative jerk," Graham mumbled under his breath as he reached the doorway.

Robert Kinsley

Deep in concentration, Robert worked on the Atlantic magazine Puzzler.

Demands massages for the audience?

Four letters.

What the hell could that mean?

Betsy walked up and Robert tossed the magazine aside. She handed him a small piece of paper folded up into a tight wad.

"Call this number from a pay phone after six," she quietly said after looking around to verify no one else was within earshot. "Don't be stupid and call from home or with your cell phone."

"What? Give me a clue, will you? What are we talking about?"

"Here's your clue...make sure you have a pocket full of quarters when you call. Don't use a credit card. See ya."

Graham Wallace

Graham parked his car and walked into the lobby of his company. The environment was shockingly shabby compared to the lush high-rise offices of OneWorld.

Strategic Services occupied two floors of a former electrical utilities building constructed in the 1970's. The walls were concrete tip ups embedded with white rocks. The windows were narrow slits and when he approached, he always expected medieval archers to pop out to defend the parking lot against attacking barbarians.

For example, marauding corporate lawyers from Microsoft.

Inside, the carpet was threadbare and the reception desk, adorned with peeling wood-grain laminate and patched with duct tape, was harshly illuminated by hissing fluorescent light fixtures. All their money was spent deep in the building on air conditioning, racks of server/storage equipment and uninterruptible power systems.

His Corporate Manager of First Impressions (receptionist) read a tattered romance novel and chewed a huge, disgusting wad of pink gum. She was highly effective when collecting payments on past-due invoices, so no one paid any attention to her slovenly appearance or dodgy reading habits.

"Hello, Beverly. Any messages?" Graham asked with a beaten-down and exhausted tone.

"Sure, but nothing urgent. How did the meeting go? Are we in business?"

"There's a kink. We're not dead, but Powell is jerking us around. He wants me to go on a hike with him."

"What's wrong with that? You need a break. We can handle things around here while you hang out with Mr. Richboy. A few days cavorting in the woods? He probably has cooks and maids and rides around in a Bentley ATV. Sounds like fun," she said, while proffering a wad of crumpled while-you-were-out notes.

"Your idea of fun, maybe. I'd rather stay home, play Civilization and eat pizza."

Walking down the hallway, he leafed through his sheaf of message notes. George Wilkins, the manager of the server farm, passed by.

"Graham, are we in? I have important decisions to make."

"Not quite yet," Graham replied.

He entered his office and tilted back in his vinyl chair. Lili poked in her head.

"Busy? Can I visit?" she asked rhetorically while settling into the guest chair. "Don't be a black hole, I'm management, right? Inside the information event horizon. So, tell me all about the meeting. Beverly says we're not dead, gotta like that. So, what's the story? Powell is jerking us off?" she said, making the motion with her fist. "That's what he does."

Graham knew better than to try to answer until she ran out of steam. Eventually, she'd shut up and let him answer all her questions. Until then, it was futile to try to slip a word in.

"We're lucky to still be in play," she continued. "A camping trip, eh? You don't know anything about camping, where are you going? Hanging out on the beach somewhere? Don't stub your toes. Stay out of the sun—sunscreen doesn't work well on Scottish skin; you'll burn up like a bannock. Research says—if you get freckles, then you're highly susceptible to deadly melanoma. Nine out of ten doctors agree. Don't sit there like a speechless lump. Talk to me."

Graham hesitated for a moment to make sure she was really done. She sat, quietly expectant, tapping her fingernails on the hard plastic arm of her chair.

"Powell is being weird. He put the contract in an envelope and said he'll sign it when we get to Harrison Hot Springs."

"The Hot Springs? It's really nice up there. You'll like it; you can soak in the mineral water and relax. Sensory deprivation—you can use some of that, decompression. If we land this contract, you'll deserve a break to refresh and rejuvenate, and then come back rested and ready to rock. Powell's a genius, I can see it. He knows you've been rolling hard and fast toward burn-out. That's no good for a business partner. We'll hold the fort here, don't worry about us, you can drink Canadian beer and eat backbacon, get a spa treatment and a pedicure; you'll come back a new man. I'd love to go too, but you need me here, though they will have broadband up there, so it would be no problem, I can work via remote, maybe I could get away. I've been meaning to get you out of town and have long episodes of kinky sex with you—you're wound way too tight for your own good, no one can work twenty-four-seven for so long without imploding or exceeding critical mass, kaboom, see what I'm saying?"

While she was speaking, his eyes drifted to scattered papers on his desk...notes on an Albanian Al-Yosef hookworm variant attacking his Barracuda firewall.

Silent, Lili cocked an eyebrow and waited for him to respond.

"I don't think Powell is talking about sitting in the mineral springs and enjoying a sauna. We're flying into some backwoods place I've never heard of and hiking in. He says all I need are boots. Is he thinking of a day hike? I really don't want to sleep outside."

Lili sat up straight in her chair.

"All right, this is important," she said. "Let's start from the beginning and work through this thing. Where are you going?"

"It's a funny name. Hundred Mile something? It's in up in Canada, so why are they using miles? It should be One Hundred Sixty Kilometer House, right?"

Lili raised an index finger. "Shut up a minute," she said. Squeezing her eyes shut, her forehead wrinkled with deep concentration. "Holy mammal shit, I'm starting to get this. Hundred Mile House. That's up the Gold Rush Trail way northeast of Vancouver. The hundred miles is measured from the gold rush trailhead at Lillooet. That's something like two hundred miles cross country from Harrison Hot Springs. He really said you just need boots? That hike will take at least a week. Tell me exactly and precisely what he said."

Exasperated, Graham said, "Give me a minute to think. He suggested I get fitted for boots, otherwise, I should bring what I want and he'll take care of the essential camping gear."

"Shit, Graham, you have no idea what you're in for. It's beautiful up there, but outside of Alaska and the Yukon, there is probably a no more isolated place in North America. I think I get it. Clayton is trying to kill you."

"Jesus Ellison Christ, Lili, get out of here," Graham said, pointing at his office door. "Your brain has gone blue-screen-of-death. I don't have time for this."

"Graham, you'd better start using your head. Get on Bing and look up keywords like Powell, safari and death. I remember something."

Grumbling, Graham swiveled in his chair and tapped the entries in. An article link popped up and he clicked on it.

Irwin Schwartz, Founder of ElectroSyn, Killed in Kenya

> UBS - Irwin Schwartz, former Stanford University professor and entrepreneur, was killed late on Thursday while on safari in Kenya's Lake Jipe area. Dr. Schwartz sustained massive internal injuries after being trampled by a hippopotamus. Others in the safari party included Pedro Martinez, the president of Essential Postwave Technology and Clayton Powell, the chairman, CEO and President of the OneWorld Group.
>
> "Hippos, for short periods when agitated, are faster than you'd think they could be. I guess the late Professor didn't value that and paid the ultimate price for a lack of respect for Mother Nature." Mr. Powell said in an interview.

Graham and Lilly looked at each other.

"You need to bail out of this trip," Lili said.

"What are you talking about? I cleaned myself up and wore a polo shirt and I'm going to bail out now? This contract is important. I have to go."

"You'll last two days, max. For example, I'll bet you twenty bucks that Powell's *essentials* won't even include bug repellent for you. He'll have plenty for himself, or maybe he's protected by a biotech injection, but he'll give you nothing."

"I don't see the big deal. I can handle a few mosquitoes."

"You have no idea what you're talking about. Shut up and let me think for a moment." She pressed on her temples with the heels of her hands. "Okay," she said. She held out her hands as if to examine them for trembling. "I'll get you through this. You'd better have a lot of money because REI is going to love you. How long do I have?"

"I'm meeting Powell on Tuesday morning."

"This coming Tuesday?" When Graham nodded, Lili stood up, paced around the tiny office and took a series of deep breaths. "Okay, we can do this. We're going to have to be smart and work fast, but we can do it, I know we can. What are you waiting for? We have to get going, there is no time for lollygagging. Move it. Goddamn it, Graham, I said move your ass."

The underground parking lot was crowded. Lili had to wait for a Subaru Outback to clear a space before she could park. Near the elevators, by a small pond, a waterfall cascaded and a hiking trail weaved into a thatch of trees. Graham looked around in wonder.

"With a place as cool as this, why do we even need to go out into the woods?" he commented as he pressed the button to call the elevator.

"Let's take the stairs," Lili said.

"That's the long way," Graham grumbled, looking up.

She poked him in the back with a bony finger until he moved. At the top of the stairs, Graham leaned over with his hands planted on his knees and wheezed. In front of him, large wooden doors had climbing axes for handles.

"Cute," he said.

"Quit bullshitting and come on," Lili said.

Inside the cavernous building, Lili walked away briskly while Graham watched a pair of pert teenage girls wearing studious expressions, tight shorts and tank tops. Under staff supervision, they strapped on climbing harnesses and prepared to climb the massive indoor climbing rock. Lili, with a tiny older man in tow, appeared at Graham's side as he looked up.

"How tall is this thing? Two hundred feet?"

"Twenty meters," the wizened man said with distain. His thick white hair was swept back and provided a stark contrast to his leathery, deeply-tanned face.

Uncharacteristically nervous, Lili performed the introduction.

"Graham Wallace, I would like to introduce you to my dearest friend, Jean-Claude. J-C finished a climb of K2 in 1983 with stress fractures in both legs."

"Is that an Olympic event?"

A dark anger washed over J-C's face. He took in Graham's pot belly and stubby legs with cold appraisal.

"Impossible. This thing I will not do," he said stubbornly as he walked back into the main part of the sales floor. Lili took his arm and pulled him over to a rack of fluffy parkas where she held his face in her hands and spoke to him intensely. She kissed him on both cheeks and smoothed back his hair. When J-C finally nodded in agreement, she pulled him back toward Graham.

Stern-faced, J-C walked around Graham, inspecting. He pinched the roll of fat on Graham's waist and clucked.

"Ouch." Graham said. "Don't bruise the merchandise, jerk."

"You must work some fat off this man. You didn't tell me—how many months do I have to prepare?"

Lili took a deep breath.

"We have five days," she said.

"Five days? I am not a holy man or priest. This thing cannot be done."

"I am in your hands, J-C. I have nowhere else to turn. Please help me. I don't expect a miracle, just do what only you can do."

"Absurdity. Madness."

"There is only one beautiful man of genius in the world who would even attempt this. A tough man with a brave soul and towering world-class intellect. A wizard of the wilderness and messiah of the mountaintops."

"Lili, dear, I see what you're doing. Please don't try to bribe me with empty flattery. I take no responsibility, do you understand? No responsibility. Does the man-Scot have money?"

"Yes, he can pay."

"Very well, I will do what I can." Tapping a finger on his teeth, he studied Graham carefully. "This must be carefully thought through. This man is so unfit that we must work within an eighteen-pound budget for his pack and gear. We will start with boots, something lightweight, but rugged. Go up and talk to Garth. Tell him I want the Scot to be fit into Lowa Renegades with Thorlo CoolMax padded sock liners and Teko Eco Merino Wool Light Hiking Socks. Tell me, man-Scot, what is your waist size?"

"Thirty-six inches."

"Humphh," J-C grunted. He produced a cloth tape and quickly wrapped it around Graham's beltline. "Thirty-eight. Your waist diameter is ten inches longer than your inseam. Do you know what that means?"

"That I'm husky?"

"That you're fat." J-C said.

To defuse things, Lili tugged J-C away.

"Are you thinking of a mountaineering pack?" she asked.

"I should think not," J-C said. His forehead crinkled with concentration. "From what you've said, we should not reveal our coaching and preparation. It would suit the man-Scot to appear—as long as possible—as an unprepared bumbler, which will not be difficult."

"Hydration pack?"

"No, let's not go that direction," J-C mused. "Something black and plain, I think. A North Face Recon Three will fit the job. Come back after the boots are fitted and I will have a pack ready."

Garth, the shoe department supervisor, was a ruddy-faced man almost seven feet tall. He measured Graham's feet and examined

Graham's insole. "We're going to try High Profile Superfeet Synergizer Green Hiking Insoles."

After they were laced up to Garth's satisfaction, he told Graham to walk on the test trail. Graham made one circuit around the artificial trail and walked stiffly back. It was rough, with inclines, declines and obstacles, like a short patch of real trail from the deep woods.

Turning from his intimate conversation with Lili and spinning his index finger in circles, "Walk until I tell you to stop," Garth said firmly.

After several circuits Graham lost patience.

"Hey, I'm still walking, in case you haven't noticed."

"All right," Garth sighed. "Are your heels moving around? They should be firmly cupped. Are your toes sliding forward when you walk downward? I don't want your toes getting crunched up. We must, at all costs, avoid blisters; however, the boots shouldn't be so tight that you lose circulation. Everything feels okay?" Graham nodded. "Very well, I pronounce this a good fit. Tell J-C I said the Renegades were a good call."

Downstairs, J-C hefted a plain-looking black pack.

"Garth said the Renegades were a good call," Lili said.

"Of course, what do you think I've been doing for thirty-seven years beyond preparing for this challenge?" he growled. He motioned for Graham to raise his arms, and then positioned the backpack while adjusting the straps with meticulous care.

"This thing weighs a ton," Graham griped.

"It weighs twelve pounds, frivolous man," J-C replied. To Lili, he said, "Walk him three miles and bring him back. In the meantime, I will lay out a few things." He clapped his hands briskly. "There is no time to waste."

Lili tugged at Graham's arm. His face was red and he was about to speak.

Lili covered his mouth.

"The master said three miles, she said. "Come on, let's go."

Outside, barely moving traffic on I-5 sat in waves of exhaust and heat.

"We'll walk up to Broadway and back. That should do it," Lili said.

"That's uphill," Graham complained.

"Finally, the full extent of your genius is exposed for the world to admire," Lili said. "Yes, it's uphill."

"I don't see why this is necessary."

"I know and that's what worries me the most. This hill is not going to climb itself. Shall we move our collective asses?"

An hour later, at the summit, Graham, gasping, leaned over with his fat hands on his knees. His face was flushed and his sandy hair was plastered to his head. Rivers of sweat cascaded down his face.

A young man, with the front half of his hair shaved and a row of silver studs embedded in his lower lip, slipped around them. His voice was slurred, but he seemed to be saying "God is a fascist dictator," over and over to himself.

"Let's sit down and get an iced latte. I'm buying," Graham suggested hopefully.

"We'll stop for water, but that's all. We need to head back."

"I knew you were going to say that," Graham lamented, shaking his head. "My leg muscles are quivering. I'm all worn out."

"You're a pussy. The walk back is downhill and you're still complaining? Move it, boss."

Back in the parking lot of REI, Graham, wheezing, staggered to a bench and collapsed. His shirt was plastered to his torso and steady globs of sweat dripped from the end of his chin. J-C, wrinkling his nose, placed a jacket over Graham's back to estimate the fit.

"I once carried an eighty-kilogram pack over the Pyrenees with two sprained ankles and a dislocated shoulder. Even after eight days in the wild, I didn't look as bad as you," he sniffed.

"Hey, I just figured it out. God wants us to go to the center of the earth."

"Why do you say that?" Lili said.

"Why else would he make it easier to walk downhill?"

"Hmphh," J-C grunted. "Eat this protein bar," he said, handing over a Clif bar and a bottle of cold water.

"Thanks, you're not such a bad guy after all," Graham said.

"When you're done eating, you can do it again," J-C said, gesturing toward the east.

"Oh, no, it's almost dinner time. I can't do it. It will be dark before we get back here."

J-C took a stance and raised his fists. "You'll get your ass kicked by a seventy-year-old man if you don't start moving right now," he said.

"This is really stupid," Graham said bitterly.

"You certainly are," replied J-C.

It was fully dark when they got back to the REI parking lot. Graham staggered and seemed only semi-conscious. Lili planted a kiss on his sopping forehead.

"You did it," she said.

"This is worse than death," Graham complained. "Just shoot me and plant me. I can't take anymore of this torture."

"You've earned a beer," Lili said cheerfully.

"I'll vomit if I drink anything. See what you've done to me? You should be ashamed. This is obscene."

"I wish you were too sick to complain, but that's asking too much, I suppose. There's no time to waste taking you home. Let's check into the Weston. It's just a few blocks, you can do it."

"Oh, no, please just let me lay here and die in peace." She pulled at his arm until he got up. "Why does God hate me?" he said.

"Because he despises whiners, that's why."

The desk clerk assigned them to the 19th floor. After Lili opened the lock with the card key, Graham pushed by her and dived on the couch. She picked up the phone and made a call, then dampened a towel and dropped it on Graham's head.

"You're disgusting. Get undressed and wipe yourself down."

"Not with you watching."

Lili sighed. "You think I've never changed a diaper before? I have four younger brothers, for cripe's sake. This is no time to be shy."

With a twirling motion, Graham gestured for her to turn around.

"All right," Lili said.

At a knock at the door, Lili walked over and let a husky woman, dressed like a nurse, into the room.

"Gretchen? Thank you for coming on such short notice."

Gretchen nodded. "Is not problem," she said.

She wheeled in a table and started extending its sections.

Graham, with the damp towel wrapped around his loins, complained bitterly.

"What is this, the King Street Station? Hello, I'm not wearing any pants."

Gretchen, bearing a sour expression, pulled him to the table and waved her arms threateningly.

"Is this really necessary?" he asked, directing the question at Lili.

"This will go a lot easier if you quit bitching and start doing as you are told."

"Remind me to fire you," he said.

"Get on, time is not my friend." Gretchen said. "No time today to waste."

While Graham tried to clamber on the table without exposing his private parts, Lili and Gretchen whispered between themselves. After the transaction was completed, Gretchen opened a valise and removed an array of bottles and tubes.

"I don't like strange hands on my body."

Gretchen pushed his head into the supporting ring of the massage table.

"No more talk," she said.

She started with his shoulders and gradually increased the force of her fingers. After some initial pain, the heat of the lotions and the probing of her stubby fingers were hypnotic. It felt so good that he forgot to complain when she worked up his calves and thighs and worked her fingers into the meat of his butt. Lili placed a straw against his lips and he took a deep draught from a cold pint of Grant's Scottish Ale.

"Heaven and hell," he whispered as he fell unconscious.

Grunting, Gretchen and Lili lifted him with the massage table cover and heaved him on the couch. Lili tossed a bedspread over him and made sure his head was comfortably arranged on a pillow.

She smoothed his thin hair, pushing it away from his eyes.

"I'll see you in the morning," she said, knowing he couldn't hear her.

The view from the hotel was toward the southeast. Sunlight poured into the room when Lili yanked the drapes open.

"Jesus Christ," Graham groaned. "What time is it?"

"Time for coffee," Lili replied. "Try these on. J-C says they will fit."

"I think I'll pass. Maybe I'll just watch TV all day and rest up. I think that would be the best thing."

"Ha." Lili laughed sarcastically. "You're funny."

Graham looked over the clothing; it was all made of thin shiny material. "I can't wear this sissy stuff. I'm hungry, let's get an omelet."

Lili placed a floppy rain hat on his head and adjusted the strap around his chin.

"You have time for a raspberry scone and a piss, and then we're out of here."

For the twentieth time, Graham asked, "Where are we going?"

Ignoring him, Lili drove her little Japanese SUV and switched between talk radio stations.

"I didn't say," she replied.

Their route took them north on Highway 9 past farms and patches of suburban sprawl. They turned off the highway toward Granite Falls.

"I feel pretty good considering the inhuman abuse you put me through yesterday. Gretchen is a magician, a real healer. However, someone should tell her to wax that mustache."

"You can tell her yourself tonight."

"Oh, no, I'm not going to need her tonight, am I?"

In reply, Lili smiled enigmatically.

They pulled into a gravel parking area at the Mount Pilchuck trail head. J-C, already there, wore a running suit and hydration pack and stretched his knotty leg muscles. He pointedly looked at his watch and clicked his tongue.

"Promptness is respect," he said.

"Isn't this a great morning?" Graham said with false cheer. "And you, J-C, what an unexpected pleasure to encounter you here."

J-C grunted.

"Hmmph."

He pulled up the tongue on Graham's hiking shoes, adjusted the laces and retied the knots.

"Okay," he said, while picking up his extendible walking sticks. "See you on the trail."

With that, he walked away briskly and disappeared into the brush.

Graham pushed Lili against the side of her vehicle.

"Don't bullshit me. How how bad is this going to be?"

"It's a six mile round trip with a twenty-two hundred feet vertical rise. I'm carrying your water and you just saw a seventy-year-old man go for it before his breakfast. It's very do-able."

"Fine, let's get it over with."

Lili handed him a pair of hiking sticks.

"These things look like yuppie ski poles, I don't need them."

"They're anti-shock hiking staffs and they'll help with your balance and reduce stress on your knees, particularly when you're tired. However, if you want to break a leg and use that as an excuse to cancel Clayton's trip, that works fine for me."

She started loading the poles back in the SUV.

"Alright, if you insist on being such a pain in the ass, give me the damned things," Graham said, reaching.

"As you wish, my lord."

"That's more like it. Let's get this thing done."

The first part of the trail wound through shady woods and was nearly flat. They passed occasional groups— including dogs, women and children—returning from the summit. Near the one-mile mark, where the woods gave way to the first open rocky sections of loose granite, Graham stopped to catch his breath. The sun was bright and the sky a deep blue. Lili handed him a pair of wrap-around sunglasses and offered him a sweating bottle of water which he waved away.

"I feel pretty good so far. Are we nearly there?"

Overhearing, a teen-aged girl passing them smiled through braces. "Not yet," she commented with a cheerful smile, "but you've made a great start."

"Outstanding," Graham said with resignation as he waved away a black fly and continued up the trail.

After another hour of hiking, Graham was forced to take more and more breaks. His legs seemed to be made of dead pig iron.

"I feel like I'm dying. I can't catch my breath."

"It's not all your fault; we're probably close to five thousand feet of elevation at this point. This used to be a ski resort—did you notice the beautiful view?"

Graham lifted his head and looked around at large piles of fractured lumber and concrete rubble. The view extended to the north over a deep valley. Rugged mountains receded into the distance and there were patches of snow visible on some of the peaks.

"To me, a beautiful view is a river of ale and a steaming mountain of chili-cheese fries."

Lili grinned and patted him on his large belly.

"Evidently," she said, though not unkindly. "Look, there's J-C."

Graham turned to look. J-C walked across a stretch of the rock-strewn trail. His white hair puffed out of his bandana like cottonwood fluff. His legs were brown and hard like gnarled sticks.

"Hey, J-C, how is it up there?" Graham called out as J-C passed.

"No dawdling," J-C replied.

"You know, I'm starting to really dig that old man," Graham commented. "I guess that means break time is over."

He turned and headed upward.

The approach to the summit was steep and ended with a nearly vertical clamber over giant boulders to a stub of ladder leading to a lookout. Graham, breathing deeply and fighting against black spots before his eyes, dragged himself up the ladder, leaned over the railing and gasped for air.

His heart thumped in his chest and he could hear blood rushing in his veins. It took ten minutes, but finally he felt better and began to notice the 360 degree view. To the west, he could see the Puget Sound and the San Juan Islands. To the north, across scattered mountain tops, the snowy peaks of Mounts Baker and Shuksan were visible. To the south, through hazy clouds, majestic Mount Rainier dominated the scenery.

"Holy shit, it's beautiful," he said.

A little girl, trying to unlatch the straps that held her in her father's backpack, echoed him.

"Boo-tiful," she said.

"Watch your language around little kids," her dad said.

"Okay, sorry," Graham said. When the dad turned away, he crossed his eyes and stuck out his tongue at the girl. She made an ugly face in return.

"I'll take that water now," Graham said to Lili.

She handed him a bottle and a zipper bag of trail mix.

"You made it. I'm proud of you."

"Yeah, I guess I'm proud of myself too. Let's make a deal."

"What kind of deal?"

"I'm going to quit bitching and you're going to quit bullshitting. Talk to me straight, okay?"

He held out his hand to shake on the deal.

"Done," she said. "Take all the time you like to enjoy the view and then we'll start down."

"Okay," he said, munching on trail mix. He sprawled on the lookout bench and drank deeply from the water bottle. When he was fully rested, he found Lili outside nibbling on a granola bar and looking toward Mount Rainier.

"I'm ready," he said.

"Okay. Going down is less of a cardio workout and it will go quicker, but it can be more dangerous. Your legs will be tired and you'll have to watch your footing more carefully."

"You don't have to mother me."

"Yes, I do."

The trail seemed like it would never end, but they finally found their way to the parking area around one o'clock. Graham's legs were bone-tired and his lower back ached relentlessly. J-C, lounging under a tree, read a paperback book. He got up when he saw them emerge from the trees. He walked around Graham as if doing an inspection. He squatted and squeezed Graham's thighs and calves.

"Nothing broken?"

Lili unshouldered her pack and laid it on the ground. "Nothing broken," she confirmed.

"Very well," J-C said, "in spite of being grotesquely overweight and out of shape, his youth and hearty Scottish genetics work in his favor. Give him a half-hour to rest, then do it again."

"Oh, no," Graham complained, "that's simply not possible."

"I thought you were going to stop bitching," Lili said.

"I'm not bitching, I'm just saying I don't think I can do it."

"Well, that's what we need to find out. And, there's only one way to do that."

Two-thirds of the way up the mountain, Graham could only see the patch of trail directly in front of his feet. They still passed people, but his entire focus was on taking the next step, climbing the next incline and lifting his feet enough to avoid tripping on a rock or root.

Endorphin opiates kicked in and he felt a detached suicidal euphoria; if pressing his body forward hard enough to trigger a massive infarction was the only way to end this torture, then he would climb until it came on. He was beyond complaint and beyond self-awareness. His legs did not want to move, but they moved anyway.

He had the mad feeling that, in hazy history, the ability to climb after all reserves of strength were consumed was something he inherited from his Scottish ancestors. He placed the walking stick points, lifted his boots and forced his dead body upward. After an eternity, he found himself standing on a boulder looking up at the last vertical ascent to the white ladder that ended at the lookout deck.

Lili wiped her forehead with a bandana. She was sweaty and flushed. Large dark circles of perspiration decorated the cloth under her arms and a sopping patch flowed down her back and discolored her denim shirt. With quivering legs muscles, Graham stood and looked over the vista—evergreen forests stretching out like a verdant tapestry. He was not in his body—he floated somewhere above the scene and could feel the wind as it threatened to sweep him away permanently.

"You didn't think I could do it," he said.

"I hoped you'd give up so we could forget this madness. It cost a fortune to uncover all this, but did you know Clayton's father was a backwoods guide? Did you know Clayton's sister died on Mount Rainier and that he and his father continued up to the summit after the helicopter retrieved her body from the crevasse? He was twelve. Did you know his father died in the wild after chopping off his own foot when it was trapped by a tree? It was a freak accident; the tree was struck by lightning and came down on his father's tent. He was trapped for eight days before attempting to free himself with a hatchet. He bled to death. They found the body the following spring. I swear to God, you'd be safer hiking with Charles Manson. Or, perhaps a better analogy would be the cannibal? What was his name? Jeffrey Dahmer? You'd be safer traveling cross-country with Dahmer, a steak knife, a frying pan and a copy of *Cannibalism for Dummies*. Am I making my point? Clayton is certifiably nuts."

Graham pointed at the lookout.

"*You* didn't think I could do this," he said.

He crawled up the first rock and slowly inched up to the mountain top. At the apex, he leaned on the railing and gazed west, squinting into the late afternoon sun—looking over the valley at Everett and the San Juan Islands. Lili handed him a bottle of water and he drank deeply.

"Did you hear what I said down there?"

"Clayton has been on the cover of Time magazine several times. He's rich and powerful. His net worth went over a billion while he was still in his twenties. He's offering a contract that will take our company to the next level. We'll be international. We owe our shareholders the return on investment. I didn't get to where I am now by running away when things got tough."

"You are not a rough-and-ready outdoor type of person. It's time to write off the contract and face reality."

Graham turned to face her.

"It's time that you remembered which of us is the boss and which of us is the employee."

Lili's eyes flooded with tears. She slipped off her backpack and pulled out a couple of bottles of water.

"Fine, boss, carry your own water and I'll see you back at the car."

"Look, Lili, I appreciate what you're doing, I really do. Please don't turn this into some hormonal drama."

She handed him a sheaf of folded papers.

"Read through this stuff and draw your own conclusion. I'm out of here."

"Lili."

"Yes, boss?"

"Is there any more of that trail mix?"

She snorted and walked to the ladder. Graham turned and noticed the other hikers in the lookout were watching him. He shrugged.

"Women. What are you going to do?" he said.

He rested for an hour, reading the papers. His muscles became stiff and he could barely move. Looking over the pathway downwards, he stretched his back and tried to imagine what a hot whirlpool bath followed by a night's sleep in a featherbed would feel like.

Like the very pinnacle of heaven.

Over an hour later, he was back in the parking lot. Lili reclined in her car seat—dozing and listening to the radio. Graham settled into the leather passenger seat with a grateful groan.

"Are you speaking to me?" he asked.

"No," Lili said as she started the engine.

He slept during the ride back to town. At the hotel Gretchen waited with her massage table. Too tired for shyness, Graham stripped down to his underwear and flopped on the table.

"This is a man that gets comfortable quickly," Gretchen commented to Lili.

"This is a man who is a hopeless asshole," Lili said.

"Oh, my. Is he of the breaking of your heart?"

"*Give him an extra deep massage*," Lili whispered. Then, loud enough for Graham to hear, she said, "Be in the lobby at six A.M. sharp, jerk."

"Before you go, order up teriyaki or something, will you?"

"It's after five, asshole. I'm off the clock," she said as she dragged the door closed.

With a stern look, Gretchen flexed her fingers, popped her finger joints and prepared to give Graham his deep muscle massage.

The next morning, after a hot shower that slightly eased the pain in his aching muscles, Graham limped down to the lobby. Lili's SUV was parked out front. Graham, stiffly, climbed in.

"Good morning, my lovely Lili," he said, greeting her with artificial cheer.

"Don't bother trying to chat me up; I'm still not speaking to you."

"Fine," Graham replied, "be that way."

They listened to talk-radio chatter as they drove back to the REI store where J-C waited.

"I believe the pack is in its final configuration. Seventeen and a half pounds including a Platypus container of water. I'm very pleased. This is a grand, prize-worthy achievement. I had to juggle priorities carefully."

"Geez, it's a backpack, for cripe's sake, not Michelangelo's painting of the Sistine Chapel."

"You, sir, do not deserve the exquisite fruit of my genius," J-C said.

Distracted by garments hanging on a display rack, Graham said, "Hey, what are these?"

"No," Lili said.

"Utilikilt survival kilt. These would be perfect in the woods," Graham said, holding one out to gauge the fit.

"Tell him to put it back. There's no way," Lili pleaded to J-C.

J-C's face crinkled up with concentration. "Don't react with such careless haste," J-C said, "as there is merit in the idea for the man-Scot.

They would be fine when worn over Polartec power-stretch tights. He'll want the beer-gut cut, of course. Yes, I approve. We can well use the cargo pockets and waist band straps."

"He'll look like an ass," Lili said, sighing.

"That will work in our favor, for I think we want to disguise our strategy for as long as possible," J-C said. Turning to face Lili squarely, he asked, "Are you to question my methods?"

"No, maestro. I will not," Lili said sheepishly. "I'm sorry."

"Very well, we shall hear no more about it. Today you shall climb in the Verlot forest."

"Shit, these kilt-things are really expensive," Graham said, while examining the label.

"Shut the hell up," J-C and Lili said in unison.

J-C, patiently and in detail, spread out and explained the assorted contents of the backpack. Graham spent a lot of this time playing with the Garmin Quest 2060 GPS receiver until J-C snatched it out of his hands.

"Pay attention to the many uses of this utility knife," J-C said.

"That GPS-thing is way cool," Graham said.

"You'll have plenty of time to play with it later," Lili said.

In the car and headed for the hills, Graham turned off the radio.

"I'll pay you a thousand dollars cash if we sneak out and take a day off. My legs are really sore."

"No," Lili said, while switching the radio back on.

Lili parked the car and quickly pulled on her boots and shouldered her pack. Graham, in a leisurely manner, stretched his back and walked a few paces into the bushes for a piss. When he came out, he caught a glimpse of Lili disappearing up the trail head.

"Hey, wait up," he called out.

Her only response was a middle finger displayed over her shoulder.

"Shit," he whispered as he arranged his pack on his back and grabbed his walking staffs.

The trail started gently as it wound through muddy patches and scrubby alders. He felt good for the first mile as his muscles loosened and gentle slope of the trail followed the course of a noisy stream, but then it turned steep and he had to traverse rough areas—over roots and rocks. His muscles were screaming when he caught up with Lili. She casually sat on a log eating an apple. Graham's face was red. He panted like a dog.

"Ah, there you are," she said.

"You're the devil," he replied.

"Listen."

Trying to regulate his breathing, Graham looked around. All he could hear was the wind rustling in tall Douglas Firs—and a quiet torrent of water rushing over rocks. Slowly he became conscious of a crimson Northern Cardinal jay complaining and in the distance, a woodpecker tapping out a polyrhythm.

"What? I don't hear anything," he said.

"That's because you are a damned idiot. Let's move out."

Graham opened his mouth to complain, but just shrugged.

"Of course," he said, resigned to his fate as he climbed the trail and tried to keep her in sight.

His body became a climbing machine while his mind drifted through snippets of rock music, movie dialog and software algorithms. After a couple of hours, they emerged from the trees and entered a rocky meadow.

"Are we there?" Graham asked.

"No. Are you going to look around and try to enjoy the scenery?"

Graham lifted his head and scanned the setting. The pond, blocked by deadfall and a tangle of branches, reflected broken white clouds against deep blue.

"Lovely. Where are we going?"

Lili pointed up a steep cliff emerging from rough talus.

"There," she said, after sipping from a plastic water bottle and wiping her forehead with a bandana. "Wait here if your legs are done and I'll be back in an hour or so."

"What's up there?"

"Me, obviously. I'll be up there. Other than that, you'll have to come up and see for yourself."

"I can make it," Graham whispered at her receding backside.

Gasping, Graham clambered over a pile of granite boulders. The path flattened out and led to a lake held in a bowl of rubble broken off steep rocky walls. Tendrils of smoke from a campfire drifted in the air. He cast off his pack and unlaced his boots. He expected steam to rise when he immersed his aching feet in the frigid water. Once his stomach settled, he drank deeply from his water bottle.

"Don't leave your feet in there too long."

"Why, are there leeches?"

"No, your skin will get soft and you'll have trouble with blisters on the hike out of here."

Graham shrugged. "I'm not going to hike out. I think I'll just stay up here forever."

Lili gave him a stern look, but it melted into a grin. She pointed across the lake. "I think I see a wild goat. They are not common around here."

She handed him her field glasses and he focused on a white blur standing on a rock across the lake. As if shy, the goat looked at him for a moment, and then bounded up the hill and out of sight.

"Cool," Graham commented. "It's…"

"What?"

"It's nice up here. Thanks for bringing me."

She tilted her head and examined his face carefully for any sign of mockery.

"If you're fucking with me, I'll rip your guts out and feed them to that weasel over there."

"Where?"

"On your left about seventy yards out. Halfway up the deadfall."

Graham squinted until he saw it.

"Do they even eat meat? Hey, what do we have? My belly is empty."

"You're the one carrying the food. Look and see what J-C packed for us."

Graham unzipped the main pocket of his pack and pulled out foil packets.

"MRE's. Do you want the turkey casserole or the—" he looked at the other pouch, "turkey casserole?"

"The turkey sounds good, thanks," Lili replied, laughing.

From a plastic wineskin, she poured red wine into clear plastic cups.

They ate the meals with plastic utensils included in the package. Lili did not want her cranberry puree, so Graham scooped it out and wolfed it down.

"These things are not half bad," he commented as he leaned back and patted his stomach. "Look, Lili, I want to apologize for being such a butthole. I know you're just over-reacting in trying to keep me out of trouble on the hiking adventure Clayton planned. From now on, I promise to keep my mouth shut and do what you tell me to do."

"That would be a great start."

"But, if all this preparation is wasted, then, well, I'll think up an appropriate punishment. I'll put a reprimand in your personnel file or something."

"Fine. After this is over, if that's what you want to do, then so be it. Until then, your ass is mine." She got up and checked the laces on her boots. "No time to dawdle, let's hit it."

Graham groaned. "I could use a nap."

"Remember? You said no more bitching."

"I'm trying to make a constructive suggestion. That's allowed, isn't it?"

"No," Lili said firmly. "It's not."

The hike back went quickly, though many areas required slow and careful footing to avoid twisting an ankle or flying face-first down a rocky trail. The last mile, a gentle slope through a canopy of trees with sloppy muddy sections, seemed to go on forever. Graham's legs were dead and wooden and his focus was on the next step and trying to keep Lili's ass in sight. When they emerged from the trees on the gravel roadway, he was surprised. Lili helped him remove his pack and he stretched his back. He wiped his face with his woolen Tam o'Shanter and petted a hyperactive border collie.

The collie's owner, wearing an overstuffed pink goosedown jacket, walked over.

"Nice kilt, dude," he said.

"Thanks," Graham replied.

"Doesn't seem gay at all, not to me. What are you wearing underneath?"

"Blow me," Graham said.

"Touchy, ain't he?" the hiker said to Lili.

"A veritable powderkeg," she replied.

"I think I know the routine," Graham said. "Though I'm beyond exhausted and nearly dead, you're going to tell me J-C did this hike in five minutes with a broken leg and a ninety-eight pound pack and that we're doing it again. At least, let me rest for a bit first."

"No, we're done for the day."

"Don't mess with me. I may be sucked dry like the last earthly six-pack on Super Bowl Sunday, but I can do it. I may be as drained as a honeymooner's scrotum, but I can climb this damned mountain again even if it's the death of me..."

"Please stop. Your hyper-extended similes are too painful to bear. I know you could do it again if you had to, but J-C says you're done for the day. The point is to build muscle tone and reserves of strength, not kill you. We're done."

"We're not going back up?"

"Not today."

"Oh, thank God."

Graham's knees buckled and he grabbed her legs.

Lili scanned the parking area. "Stop it, this is embarrassing."

"I can't believe we're really done for the day."

"Well, there's Gretchen and her deep-muscle massage."

Graham pushed himself back to his feet.

"Shit, that woman has no mercy. I'd rather climb the damned mountain again."

The next few days were a blur. They climbed Mount Pilchuck again and again and slowly, Graham got stronger. In the evenings, Gretchen tortured his body and Graham and Lili shared vegetarian pizzas. After a pint of beer, he fell into bed and slept the sleep of the dead while Lili slept on the pull-out couch. On the last day, they stayed in town and, hand-in-hand, strolled around the Seattle Center, then surfed the Internet and caught up on e-mail with their laptops at Starbucks. His kilt garnered a few rude comments, but he ignored them.

As evening fell, Graham pulled down the Seattle Times she was reading and looked into her eyes.

"So, I'm ready?"

Lili shrugged. "J-C thinks your chances are fifty-fifty. He says you should preserve the illusion of incompetence for as long as possible. That won't be hard."

Graham flexed his biceps. "How can I possibly hide my masculine glory?"

"How indeed?" she responded. She folded the newspaper and set it aside. "You can still back out. Call in sick."

"I think I'm ready."

"Those are famous last words. Please be careful out there. I want you back in one piece. I'll be at Harrison Hot Springs, waiting."

CHAPTER FIVE

Willie and Maria

Maria parked the SUV. They got out and stretched their cramped backs. Harrison Lake glittered with reflected sunlight—forested hills surrounded the scene like a picture frame. A pack of jet skis whined like giant mosquitoes in the gap between the mainland and Echo Island. Packets of tourists strolled the sidewalk. Maria made a funny face at a little girl devouring an ice cream cone; the girl's plump face was coated with sticky chocolate.

"I'm going to get us checked in. Just leave the bags, I will send someone out to get them," Maria said.

"I'll sit here and soak up the sun and read my book," Willie replied.

"You'll pretend to read your book while watching the girls in their skimpy outfits."

"I'm shocked you would think such a thing of a cultured man such as myself. You know I only have eyes for you, dear."

"A bigger bullshitter I have never known," Maria responded with a smile.

As she waited in the check in line, she thought back to the funeral.

Perhaps she'd never really noticed his hair before, but it seemed like Professor Walters' had turned grayer in just a few short days. The graveside service was lead by a huge black pastor. She'd overheard he was a former football player—he was so large that she could easily believe it. He had a deep, booming voice and must have been a good friend because his voice dwindled into choked silence a few times as he recited the scriptures. There were over a hundred people in attendance; Maria stood at the rear of the entourage and looked over the backs of all the mourners while the wind whipped at the hem of her thin black dress. After a moment of silence, the crowd slowly scattered. Maria walked toward her car. A little black girl ran after her, calling out her name.

"Miss Maria."

"Yes, dear," Maria replied.

She turned and stooped—and took the little girl's hands.

"You have to come by the house for supper," the girl said solemnly.

"I do?"

"The Professor insists. Let's not make him cross with us."

In spite of her dark mood, Maria laughed.

Why not?

"Yes, dear, I will stop by for a few minutes."

At the house, alternating in the receiving line, the men shook Willie's hand and the women hugged him. They exchanged quiet, private words. Uncomfortable and not knowing what else to do, Maria stood in line and hugged Willie when it was her turn.

"You were a great comfort to her," Willie whispered. "And, to me. Thank you for being a soft light during a hard time."

Maria did not think her body held more tears, but, regardless, they were invoked from deep within and streamed down her face.

"It was nothing."

"No. In that, you are completely incorrect." the Professor replied. "Now, eat something. We have enough food to feed seven starving armies."

Maria heaped potato salad and eggplant casserole onto a plastic plate and scanned the room. The crowd was motley and assorted; there were many blacks, but also groups of Asians and Caucasians. A small Mexican-looking boy, wielding a massive plastic, western-style pistol, chased a giggling Vietnamese girl wearing a colorful jumper. An old, diminutive Korean woman brought Maria a crystal glass of red wine.

"You are Maria?" the woman said.

Maria nodded.

"Mrs. Walters said you were lovely," the woman continued, "but that doesn't quite capture it, does it? You look like a virginal princess from a gothic fairy tale." Maria flushed. "Now look, I've embarrassed you. Is it possible you don't know how pretty you are? Wouldn't that be precious? What can I do? Have you seen the slideshow? Of course you haven't, you just got here. When you finish your plate, go into the den, there is a small memorial and slideshow. You might enjoy that, dear."

Maria nodded over the rim of her wine glass.

After placing her empty cup and plate on the kitchen counter, she followed a knot of mourners into the den. The air was sweet with the aroma of flowers and scented candles.

A folding table held an array of framed pictures; images of the young and smiling couple.

On a ferry crossing the Puget Sound.

Grinning before the tableau of Mount Rushmore.

Posing in front of a shiny new Jaguar sedan.

The Professor in overalls removing the *For Sale* sign in front of their house.

The slide show, with a new picture every few seconds, was projected onto a screen. The images were randomized in time; a photograph of a young black girl, wearing a flower-embroidered pinafore was followed by a middle-aged woman hunched over in a motorized wheelchair, though the toothy smile was the same.

This was followed by a photo of Maria, sitting by Mrs. Walters' bedside, with a book splayed on her lap.

This was too much for Maria to bear. With eyes streaming, she hurried from the room and the house. She sat in her car and sobbed. Slowly, she regained her composure. She started the engine. The little

Vietnamese girl, with ribbons in her tousled hair, stood on the grass a few feet away and waved goodbye to her solemnly.

Maria found a smile and waved back.

"Can I help you, ma-am?"

Startled, Maria wiped her cheeks with the back of her hand.

"Reservation for Mr. and Mrs. Walters?" she said.

"Yes, ma-am. Just fill in the lines on the form where I've marked and we'll get you checked in. Just the one night then?"

"Yes, that's correct," she said.

Clayton Powell and Graham Wallace

Nervously, while Lili leaned against the building and chewed on her fingernails, Graham paced up and down the sidewalk in front of OneWorld headquarters.

He was baking and itching in his new clothes. Under his Utilikilt, he wore Gore-Tex longjohns, light-weight waterproof hiking boots and a woolen jacket covered with a Windstopper parka. He had insisted on wearing his woolen Tam o'Shanter and pairing his father's walking stick with one of the high-tech walking staffs, but Lili had stuffed a practical stocking cap into his backpack along with a lightweight hat with a veil of mosquito netting.

They had done everything possible to minimize Graham's exposed skin with gloves and a neckerchief, and then had liberally sprayed everything with Cutter Backwoods Unscented mosquito repellent.

Clayton, revving up his Humvee's diesel engine, screeched to a stop. He jumped out of the SUV and looked Graham over from head to toe.

"You must be kidding. What is that ugly thing you're wearing?"

"Utilikilt. Very practical."

"Umph," Clayton grunted. "You can leave your stuff here. I told you I'd take care of the camping supplies," he said as Graham tossed his pack in the back.

Lili's lecturing filled his head until he felt it would explode with backwoods lore and survival skills. One thing she said reverberated in his mind.

If he suggests you leave your bag behind, then you'll know the truth of it. He's trying to make a fool of you or worse—he means to do you harm.

Graham made eye-contact with Lili who seemed to be trying to send him a telepathic message of some sort. He shook his head.

"Just a few odds and ends I threw in an old bag," he said to Clayton. "It's okay, don't worry about it."

Clayton shrugged.

"As you wish," he said, slamming the big truck into gear. They roared across Lake Washington and parked at Lake Union. A Kenmore Air floatplane idled at the dock. Clayton was dressed unceremoniously in light-weight hiking shoes, khaki pants and an unbuttoned wool shirt over a t-shirt.

The only thing he carried was a small leather overnight bag that appeared to be empty. Graham suspected this casualness was all a show to keep him relaxed and off guard, but these thoughts could have been stirred up by Lili's contagious paranoia. During the flight, Clayton listened to his iPod and read e-mail on a PDA. Initially nervous, Graham eventually relaxed and admired the views of the San Juan Islands and the mountains.

From the maps Lili had made him study, he recognized the Fraser and Thompson Rivers, Harrison Lake, Hellsgate Canyon, and the Chasm as they traversed the British Columbia gold rush trail. He studied the terrain and was surprised at its variety. There were barren and stony mountains and vast expanses of arid desolation followed by deep forests and thousands of lakes as they got closer to their destination. Even from ten-thousand feet, it was obvious that the landscape was brutal and wild.

Hundred Mile House was nestled into a small valley; Highway 97 threaded through it and stretched all the way up to Prince George and beyond to Alaska.

Clayton tapped the pilot on the shoulder. "Why don't we set down in the little lake when we come here?"

"It's a water fowl reserve. Hundred Mile Marsh," the pilot replied flatly.

"Fucking ducks," Clayton grumbled as he stuffed his head phones and electronics in his bag.

The pilot landed the plane smoothly on the runway and cruised toward the hangars. A black minivan idled on the pavement—the driver popped out and opened the sliding door. Clayton threw in his black travel bag and pulled out a largish backpack. He held out his arms and rotated as the driver sprayed him head-to-toe with an aerosol can. Then, not running, but walking briskly, he walked across the tarmac toward a roadway that headed south between the small lake and a large Quonset hut. Graham stood by the van.

"Spray me too," he demanded. The driver shrugged, smiled a small smile, and complied. Clayton was fifty yards away by the time Graham shouldered his backpack, grabbed his walking sticks and made ready to follow.

"Good luck, sir," the driver called after him.

Graham waved over his shoulder.

Catching up with Clayton, they crossed a wooden bridge and then followed a crushed gravel trail. After only a few ten's of yards, Clayton left the trail and stepped through some weeds and onto a decrepit boardwalk. This broken-down split-log walk had treacherous footing and was overgrown with grass and brush. It only went about forty yards, then abruptly ended.

A fallen tree blocked the way, but Clayton scrambled over it and then they were in deep brush. Graham was amazed at how quickly they had left civilization; there was no way to tell that the town was only a quarter-mile away. A faint trail weaved through trees, but was disused; fallen branches and swampy patches obscured it in many places.

Occasionally they crossed a road, either dirt or paved, and the howl of dirt bikes echoed in the distance, but they saw no houses or other people. Clayton skipped over logs and splashed through trickles of streams and mud, but did not even look back to see how Graham was coming along.

Sometimes, he would get far ahead and Graham would momentarily lose sight of him, but, breathing hard, Graham would pick up the pace and catch up. In places, the mosquitoes swarmed so thick they were blinding, but the massive doses of DEET seemed to keep most of them off. There were a few bloody smears on his arms where his sleeves had ridden up—where Graham had swatted them.

Lili's voice echoed in his ears.

They probably won't kill you, but they will make you wish you were dead.

Graham sent private thanks in her direction. Without her coaching, he would have been completely unprotected.

You might get outfitted with a comfortable pair of boots, Clayton had suggested.

Asshole.

Along the way, while gasping for breath, he wondered about the plan. Clayton was not carrying enough equipment for an overnight stay. Graham hoped there was a lodge or something where they could spend the night. Something with a hot shower and soft bed, but somehow he doubted it. As they climbed and walked through the trees, Graham got more and more tired. They'd landed about three o'clock, so it couldn't be too bad; there were only a few hours until darkness fell.

"How're you doing back there?" Clayton asked, while skipping across a small gully.

"Just fine," Graham said. "These Scottish legs were made for walking."

"Good. We'd better pick up our speed a bit or we won't make the first camp before night hits."

"You're the one setting the pace," Clayton replied, while trying not to break a leg on a tangled clump of roots.

Clayton laughed.

"It appears I've already underestimated you, my friend. Still, there's a long way to go between here and there," he said, while briskly moving through a patch of huckleberries.

Robert Kinsley

Pay phones were not easy to find—and the first two were out of service. The first one had a missing handset; its decapitated cord looked—disturbingly—like a severed spine. The second seemed to be intact, though it was covered with graffiti and rude messages scratched into its plastic panels. It did not emit a dial tone.

At a telephone kiosk at the Alderwood Mall, he impatiently waited for one of the stations to open.

There, a pudgy, bleached-blonde, fourteen year-old Hispanic girl with a tubular roll of baby fat oozing over the top of her lowrider jeans dexterously thumbed messages into her cell phone while cradling the phone's receiver against her shoulder. In the phone, she flexed chats about a four-twenty mack-up with her butterface sister's marinated boyfriend and how unkrunky gay her social studies class was and about getting faded with her jinky camo boyz and finally—the need to score cheddar from her silverback geezer.

He moved quickly and grabbed the phone before an evil-looking black kid, wearing flowing nylon athletic warm-ups and hair pulled back severely into cornrows, could take the station. The warm earpiece was oily, so Robert wiped it down with his shirt sleeve before he could tolerate placing it against his ear. After feeding in quarters, he made the call and listened to the screechy ring tone.

"Yes?"

"A friend gave me this number. I'm calling because I want to do some environmental fieldwork. I'm a third year student at—"

"No biography. Is there a phonebook?"

Robert looked. There was a ragged phonebook—it looked like most of the pages had been torn out.

"Yes," he said.

"Open it at random and tell me the first name you see."

"Uh, Gaspard," Robert said.

"Very good, Gaspard. My name is Ajax. Are you a cop, Gaspard? An undercover pud?"

"No."

"Doesn't mean anything, but I always like to ask. You still have to prove yourself. Frag a Hummer and Mobog. I'll give you a day or two, then call back."

"I'm sorry, I don't know what you mean?"

"Tocotox. Later."

The line went dead and Robert was left staring at the receiver.

The black kid walked up and held out his hand for the phone.

"Excuse me," Robert said, "do you know the slang word...tocotox?"

"Sure, wonderbread, it's too complicated to explain." The kid smiled and looked a lot less evil, in spite of a gold inlay on one of his front teeth. The kid turned his back and swiped a phone card in the reader.

"What?" Robert mumbled. "I need a drink."

He wandered down the mall and stepped into a martini bar. Two elegant girls, wearing identical short red dresses and black pumps, sat at the counter. They looked him over and did an inventory. It seemed as if they could instantly calculate a man's net present value and earning potential, but Robert's imagination could have been overheated. He ordered a cranberry martini, sat at a booth and made notes on a paper coaster.

Tocotox. Frag a Hummer. Mobog.

Why don't people use plain English to communicate?

He realized that the black kid had literally answered his question. Tocotox was a contraction of *too complicated to explain*. Could *Frag a Hummer* simply mean find one of the obscene over-sized urban assault vehicles and destroy it?

When the waiter brought his second martini, Robbie said, "Excuse me, do you know what a Mobog is?"

"That's a photographic website where guys upload pictures—usually of their dicks—from their digital cameras."

Robert nodded. While alcohol surged through his veins, the message became clear. He should, as a rite of passage, in the next forty-eight hours, blow up someone's Hummer, take pictures and upload them to the Mobog website.

After his third martini, this plan seemed like a very good one.

He ordered a pair of martinis for the girls at the bar and decided to find out if they'd be impressed with his upscale Boston accent—laid on thick.

CHAPTER SIX

Willie and Maria

AFTER THE LAST hot shower she would enjoy for a while, Maria supervised the transport of their luggage and supplies onto the dock. The air was crisp and cool and a hint of breeze riffled the lake's surface. Willie stood on the beach and stared into the woods.

They had asked Chief Sam Joe to pick them up at ten o'clock sharp, but he was notoriously unwilling to be pinned down to an exact time. When he did float into view, he stopped and idled his big engine while talking to the Provincial park ranger for a half hour while Maria arranged and rearranged their belongings. She decided to walk to the market to replace a forgotten hairclip. When she returned Chief Sam had loaded the boat and Willie sat in the rear with a hand trailing in the water.

"My Lady. Where you been? Chief Sam Joe has a pressing appointment and can't be late."

Maria kissed Joe on the cheek. "You'll have a pressing appointment with the back of my hand if you don't stop it," she said.

"Professor Walters? You still haven't busted-in this squaw? You come see Sam Joe if you need any help. Heap big-skookum sleeping bag mojo."

Chief Sam Joe's real name was Chester MacGregor and he was a retired Computer Science professor from the University of Victoria. He was weathered from sun and wind, but could pass for an Indian only via an uneducated examination. He owned a few cabins on lease land and augmented his retirement income by renting out these cabins to summer people. Sam Joe and Willie had written a book together in the early 80's that sold about three-hundred copies, but was widely cited in subsequent research papers. If there was a wider audience for a book titled *The Post Capitalist Manifesto: Underground Currencies, Electronic Transactions and Barter*, they would have both been wealthy men.

"Shut your damned trap and drive."

"Yes, ma-am," Chief Sam Joe said, giving her an insolent nautical salute as he turned to the steering wheel and revved up the Glastron's V8 engine. Maria settled in the back and arranged Willie's arm across her shoulders to ward off the windchill. She handed him a maple bar and he chewed on it unconsciously. She watched him eat, flicked at a morsel of maple glaze lodged in his wispy beard and thought about days gone by.

She'd been back a school for a few weeks—working hard to catch up on her studies and prepare for mid-term testing—when a piece of paper was placed on her library workstation.

"What's this?" she whispered.

"You're in trouble now. Professor Walters wants to see you in his office."

It was no use, she couldn't concentrate; her eyes kept returning to the Professor's note. Eventually, she gave up studying, closed her books and gathered her papers. The Professor was occupied, so she leaned against the hallway wall and listened to him talk to his students.

"Oil prices have not changed much over time, though there are fluctuations due to spikes in demand and artificial restrictions on supply caused by onerous environmental regulations. If you want to see windfall profits, allow the oil companies to collect as much profit as the government collects in gasoline taxes. Or, restrict the government collections to the petrol company profits and not just gross sales and you'll surely hear some squealing pigs then."

"Professor, please." The student's voice was strained, as if he was talking to a willful child who would not listen. "Surely you've noticed what we're paying for a gallon of gasoline? The oil companies—"

"The oil companies are publicly-owned, for-profit institutions. Crude oil is an international commodity, no different than steel, aluminum, copper, gold or rubber. The price of jute went up by twenty-five percent in four months, Thai rice went up twenty-three percent in a year and tapioca starch out of Bangkok increased thirty-one percent. Were these price increases caused by evil Saudi oil barons or corrupt oil companies? I don't require you to accept my analysis, but I do insist you use your mind—don't just regurgitate stupid clichés from George Soros, John Galbraith, Thomas Friedman or whoever else is filling your heads with junk economics. If I tell you the price of gasoline hasn't changed much, and you know you're spending more dollars at the pump, then how can this be?"

"Because the Professor is wrong?" one of the students suggested tentatively.

"Perhaps the Professor *is* wrong. It could happen. However, humor me and offer another explanation."

"Um, because the buying power of my dollar has declined," the other student offered.

"Yes, thank you very much, the dollar has been devalued. Figuratively speaking in this age of electronic transactions, the printing presses have been working overtime to print hundred dollar bills. Why do you think that is? Now, get out of here and get to work on your papers. They are due on Friday. Don't come around asking for a postponement. Good day to you."

Maria poked her head around the edge of the door.

"Students," the Professor complained, "will be the death of me. Are they getting dumber every year or is it just me? We're in big trouble if it's just the Asian and Indian students who grasp basic concepts and are willing to work their asses off. Come in, dear."

Settling on the guest chair, she smoothed her skirt. He remained standing with his back turned as he stared out his dusty blinds through a dirty window to the blustery day outside.

"I don't see how this can possibly work. First of all, it's only been a few months, since...well, since she passed. I need more time to grieve. Plus, it's such a tired cliché, the pretty young grad student and the lonely, lecherous old professor. I'm too old and eccentric for you. I had a bad case of mumps as a young boy so I'm sterile. There is no chance of giving you children. I'm black and you're brown. I was raised on a hog farm in Arkansas and you're a spoiled brat from a rich Mexican family. You're Catholic and I'm an unrepentant atheist. I don't even know if you can cook or how well you keep house. It all seems impossible."

"Excuse me, Professor, but what are you talking about? Have you lost your mind? I have a boyfriend."

"Perhaps I *have* lost my mind," he said, turning and running his hand over his kinky hair. Walking over, he tilted her head back with a large plump hand so he could look into her eyes. "Your father called me."

"Oh," Maria said. Her shoulders slumped and all the air left her body. She felt like an empty balloon. Her eyes filled with tears. "He had no right."

"I agree, but regardless, he called me. He swore if I broke your heart, he'd hire Juarez thugs and break my back. He's a rather direct man who cares for you very deeply. As do I, Maria. I need another six months or so to come to grips with the loss of my wife. Until then, my judgment is unreliable and suspect. My animal logic is broken. I ask you to give me time to heal. If, after all those months, your boyfriend reappears from France and rekindles your emotions, or some other young man wins your interest, then nothing is lost. We'll still be good friends. Can you give me six months before we take the next step?"

"Yes," she said, rising and enveloping him in her arms. She buried her head in the crook of his shoulder. "Yes, I will wait," she said, before turning and rushing, tearfully, out of the room.

She stared at the green hills they passed. The chilly wind made her shiver as they passed through the channel between Echo Island and the mainland.

"Sasquatch Provincial Park, right there," the Professor said. "Watch carefully, maybe you'll see something."

She punched him in the arm. "You say that every time we pass this place. Stop it."

"Did you buy anymore of those maple bars?" the Chief asked, grinning.

"If it will shut you up, you can have as many as you want," Maria said, while opening the bakery bag.

Clayton Powell and Graham Wallace

There was a trail, but it was washed out in places and difficult to detect in the rocky sections. Sometimes Clayton stopped and punched buttons on a nifty little electronic device; Graham assumed it had GPS and mapping capability.

"There," Clayton said, pointing.

A green bundle hung from a dead lodgepole pine tree. The stand of trees was reddish and sickly-looking.

"Help me cut this thing down." With a curved clasp knife, Clayton hacked at the straps and the bundle crashed to the forest floor. Graham, panting and sweaty, set his walking sticks against a tree and leaned over with his hands on his knees. Lifting his head slightly, he gazed out over the terrain. They were on the edge of a hillock; below a small lake glittered in the late afternoon sun. Mosquitoes immediately started attacking and after futilely waving them away for a minute, Graham dug in his backpack and sprayed a fresh dose of repellent on his neck and arms.

"Gather some rocks. Let's make a fire pit," Clayton said.

It took a few minutes to assemble a pit from jagged chunks of lava rock and granite. All the while Clayton chatted on a satellite phone and hauled equipment out of the bundle. Graham overheard parts of the conversation; Clayton had apparently won a bet.

"Yeah, he's doing well; apparently the report that he has no backwoods experience was wrong. However, this was the easy day. We'll see how he does tomorrow. All is well, I'll check in later."

With that, he folded up the phone and stuffed it away in a pocket.

"What's with all these dead trees?" Graham asked.

"Mountain pine beetle," Clayton said in a tone that implied he'd just explained everything. "Help me break up this coal." They hammered at a block of coal with rocks and arranged the fragments in the fire pit. Clayton activated a starter that looked like a flare and buried it in the coal. Soon, the pale fire caught and the pit began emitting a surprisingly intense heat.

Looking around at the endless hilltops and isolation, Graham asked, "How did that bundle get in the tree?"

"It was roped down from a helicopter."

"How did you know where to find it?"

"It transmits. I tracked it with my GPS locator. Are you going to work your jaws or help me assemble our camp?" He looked over foil-wrapped packages. "Do you want broccoli or mixed-vegetable soup?"

"Veggie."

"Wrong answer. I want the veggie soup, so you're getting the broccoli."

"Why the hell did you ask me, then?"

"There was a fifty-fifty chance you'd get it right and then I'd appear fair. Set them on the edge of the fire to warm them up." He tossed Graham a plastic bottle of water and laid out the camping equipment.

"We have fishing line if you want protein with your dinner."

"I'm too damned tired to mess with it."

"Me, too," Clayton said, grinning. He tossed Graham a long plastic-wrapped package.

"This one is yours," he said. After unwrapping it, Graham exposed a black longbow and a quiver of arrows. Clayton's was fancier, made from colorful laminated hardwoods. Clayton pointed into the water. "See if you can hit that log out there," he said, drawing the bow back smoothly.

He loosed an arrow and it arced through the air and hit the log with a solid thunk. Graham fumbled for a moment before managing to get his arrow flying. He was able to hit the lake, but it was far from the floating log.

"Hmph," Clayton grunted. "You suck. Let's eat."

Gingerly, Graham fished the hot food packets off the rocks. The broccoli soup was pungent with garlic, and the package included cornbread and a big hunk of blueberry pie. It was not completely heated through, but after a few bites, Graham discovered he was hungry. He shoveled food in his mouth.

Looking over Graham's meal, Clayton said, "I'll trade you apple cobbler for your pie."

"Fuck off," Graham replied while holding his dinner out of reach.

After hovering a long time on the horizon, the sun set. Clouds were illuminated from within with rose-colored light. Arranging a bundle as a cushion against a rock, Clayton leaned back. He tossed a cigar to Graham.

"This will help keep the bugs away," he said, while leaning over and igniting the stogie in the fire.

Graham felt as if he'd been beaten. His joints were loose and every muscle complained of abuse. Still, with a full belly, puffing on a cigar and watching the stars emerge from the darkening sky—he felt a sense of well-being. They watched a sleek beaver, towing a branch, glide through the shallow water of the lake. Owls hooted and seemed to be talking to each other.

"I'll give you five-hundred dollars if you can hit that beaver."

"No, thanks," Graham replied. "The only thing missing is an after-dinner drink—some brandy or something," he mused.

"When you're right, you're right," Clayton said. He rooted through a bag and produced a pair of tiny bottles. "Martell Cordon Bleu is probably wasted on a guy like you, but I insist on being a gracious host."

They tapped their little bottles together and sipped. It was fully dark when Clayton stirred. He turned on a blinding solid state lantern and arranged his sleeping bag. He filled an air mattress with a CO_2 tank that looked like a fire extinguisher. Graham watched carefully and followed his example. Soon he had mosquito netting deployed and his air mattress filled. Enveloped in the warm sleeping bag, he felt like he was in heaven.

"Care to share what we're in for tomorrow?" Graham said.

"I think I shall not," Clayton replied, grinning like a jackal as he extinguished the lantern.

Robert Kinsley

Slowly, Robert achieved consciousness. The girls, wearing only their red panties, sat at the kitchenette table and giggled. They fed each other blueberries plucked from a huge stack of mutilated pancakes.

Slowly, fractured memories from the previous night came back. He'd done serious American Express card abuse starting at the Space Needle restaurant and ending in the W Hotel bar. He shuddered to think what the W would charge him for the room service pancakes the girls were picking at. His parents would come unglued when they got the bill; there were at least $3,000 in charges, basically for the dubious pleasure of watching the girls have sex with themselves. Neither girl seemed very interested in serving his male desires, no matter how much plastic money he was spending. He had wanted a rainbow lipstick party and he'd gotten a perfunctory hand job and an excruciating headache.

"Do you ladies keep aspirin in your silly little expensive handbags?"

"The W thinks of everything. There is some in the bathroom, sweetie," the girl with brown roots said. Robert couldn't keep track of their names; they were Bambi, Brandi, Britney, Bree, Babs or some damned thing, so he thought of them according to the roots growing out of their blond hair: brown and black.

"Could you bring me some, please? And water."

"We're busy, get it yourself, honey," black roots said.

Robert groaned as he sat up in the tangled bedding.

"I'm going to take a shit and jump in the shower. I'd really appreciate if you girls were long gone when I come out."

"We have more room service coming," black roots explained patiently.

"The last one out of the room gets stuck with the bill," Robert said.

"He's kind of a mean one, isn't he?" brown roots pouted.

Feeling the aspirin burn holes in his gastric system, he let the shower pour hot water over his head. He brushed his teeth with the W toothbrush and felt nearly human when he walked out of the steamy bathroom.

The girls were gone, but spitefully; they'd dumped the left-over pancakes on his slacks, then poured syrup and orange juice on top of the nasty mess. Angry, he washed the pants out in the bathtub and dried them with the hairdryer. All the while, he considered how to destroy a Hummer.

If he could get some Lithium metal powder, he could make a really hot fire, but he didn't know where to get the powder. It was really dangerous anyway, a small amount of water or even high humidity would set the stuff off. He decided there was no reason to get fancy.

Buy some gloves, a six-gallon plastic gas container and a road flare—that would do the trick. He thought the plan through. He would rent a midsize car, preferably white, wait until dark, then drive around until he found an unsupervised Hummer somewhere; they were commonplace in Microsoft-millionaire-yuppie-land. Smash a window with a hardware store hammer, take the top off the gas can, throw it inside followed by a flare, upload a few pictures with a prepaid camera phone and call it done.

The plan worked flawlessly.

He wore dark glasses, leather gloves and a stocking cap, doctored the rental car license plate with pieces of electrical tape to alter the numbers, and found a Hummer parked sideways so it wouldn't get scratched in the back corner of a shopping center parking lot. He torched it and grabbed the snapshot of the flaming SUV. Soon, he pulled onto the main drag, immersed his car in traffic, and was well away from the scene in less than five minutes.

It was so much fun; he wondered why everyone didn't do it.

CHAPTER SEVEN

Willie and Maria

CHIEF SAM JOE beached the boat on small section of gravelly bank. He jumped off and tied the painter to their dock. After climbing a steep stairway, he lowered a lifting platform—a crude, home-made elevator—via a complex rope and pulley system. Maria and Willie loaded their supplies and gear on the platform and Chief Sam Joe laboriously pulled it up.

The cabin was built on a rocky outcrop—the front deck protruded precariously over the sapphire water. An adventurous diver could jump into the frigid water. Willie threatened to swan dive over the side, but he never did.

Inside, the floor was strewn with field mouse turds and dust. After wrapping a bandana over his face to protect against the hanta virus, Chief Sam Joe vigorously swept out the place while Maria put away canned goods. Willie baited a hook and flung out his fishing line, rested the pole into a holder, and reopened the thick book he was reading. Except for smoke from a campfire down lake a few miles, there were no other visible human signs. The isolation was nearly complete.

To ward off the chill, Chief Sam Joe started a fire in the woodstove. No one said much as Maria opened a large can of beef stew and heated it over a blue propane flame. On the deck, she served the men stew, buttered French bread and Molson's beer. She loaded up a net bag with the remaining beer and diet sodas, and lowered the bundle on a nylon rope into the lake to keep it cold.

They sat on wooden deck chairs, looked out over the water and ate their lunch while an annoying formation of jet skis buzzed by at high speed. The high-pitched whine bored into their heads like dental drills.

Chief Sam Joe shrugged.

"Can't have everything," he said in a resigned voice.

Willie stuffed tobacco into his pipe and handed the leather pouch across Maria for the Chief. They puffed on their pipes while Maria used exaggerated gestures to dispel the smoke.

"There's a reason we vacation up here in the fresh air instead of in a diesel power plant," she said.

"Did you hear something, Chief?" Willie asked.

"Just the northwind whistling through the trees," the Chief replied.

After the Chief used a footpump to inflate their air bed, he looked around the place to see what might have been forgotten.

"That's about it, I think," he said.

"Did you check the outhouse for possums? I don't want another rude surprise out there," Maria said.

"I checked, it's all clear."

"I guess you earned a beer for the road."

"You truly are an angel of mercy. See ya'all."

They waved as the Chief's boat churned around the end of Long Island and disappeared. In silence, they stared across the water at the forest that lined the far shoreline. A bald eagle soared by—screeching and scanning the water's surface.

"Why do we ever leave this place?" Willie said.

"Because of the big mortgage payment back home."

"I love you, baby," Willie said.

"I love you back, more," Maria responded.

"I said it first, so yours doesn't count."

Willie tamped fresh tobacco in his pipe. Ignored, his book slipped off his lap and splayed on the deck. After going inside to hide from the brisk wind, Maria watched the Professor through the windows as she washed the kitchen counters with a rag.

Her thoughts drifted backward in time.

It became a habit. Each afternoon, from the Hub cafeteria, she brought him a cup of peppermint tea with a large dollop of honey. She couldn't tell if he really liked it or if he just humored her. Sometimes they would talk and sometimes they would just sip the tea and look at each other.

One day, with the wind whistling and agitating the trees outside his office, the Professor spoke.

"All right, what about religion? If God exists, he's no friend of mine. You should have met my little niece, a beautiful little girl, dead at the age of three from bladder cancer. Kalisha. She had eyes like precious jewels and a keen sense of humor. 'How did Benjamin Franklin feel when he flew his kite in a lightning storm and discovered electricity? Shocked!' She must have told me that silly joke a hundred times. She couldn't say electricity, so it came out as 'trishity. Ben Fanklin. God took time out of his busy schedule torturing Christian missionaries in Indonesia to reach down and afflict this beautiful little girl with an evil disease. I'm sorry, but it's easier for me to believe in the cold randomness of the universe than an all-powerful and cruel God sitting on his golden throne up in heaven. You could never love me, a man with such cynicism."

"I have doubts, too, but I can't bring myself to embrace nihilism."

"At least you didn't say 'the lord works in mysterious ways'. I would have tossed you out of this office and slammed the door on your pretty ass. It would have been all over for us. Alright, I will make a confession. I'm not a nihilist either; there must be a reason for all this complexity. It can't just be a million years of evolution without some cosmic purpose. We must be evolving toward something." He shook his index finger at her. "But don't get any wild ideas about converting me. I'd be a lot happier man if I could relax and place everything on the shoulders of some supreme being, but I can't take the leap of faith and suspend what my intellect tells me. Church? TV Preachers?

Prophesy? Organized religion? It's all bullshit. Hucksters and used car salesmen. If you don't mind, I prefer to skip the retail outlets and get my religion on a factory-direct basis."

"But you believe there is some central purpose?"

"Yes, but it's the pinnacle of arrogance and conceit to imagine we'll ever know what it is. So, are you okay with this personal philosophy?"

"Yes. The Gods of love work in mysterious ways."

Willie glared at her, searching her face for mockery and disrespect.

"I'll let that one pass," he said. "What about your parents?"

"My dad read one of your books. He's a fan."

"Which one?"

"I think it was *Slapped by the Invisible Hand*[5]."

"Ah, the book that got me thrown out of the NAACP. He must be one of the three hundred that read it."

"You're such a damned phony. Your publisher sold eighteen thousand copies of that book. It remains, by far, their largest-selling title. The damned thing turned a nice profit. Don't bullshit me; I talked to the publisher when I special-ordered my copy."

"Yes, but only three hundred read it," Willie said.

"You're a liar."

"There's no data, so I'm estimating, not lying."

"A distinction without a difference, liar."

"Hmmph. Am I going to lose every argument if we become a couple?"

Maria smirked. "Only if you're half as smart as you think you are," she said.

"Hmmph," the Professor grunted.

She wondered how long she'd been drying the coffee cup in her hands. Perhaps the Professor's autism *was* communicable. The wind whistled in the corners of the cabin and rattled the windows. She threw another

---

[5] *Slapped by the Invisible Hand: Replacing the Iron Chains of Slavery with the Voluntary Chains of Dependence, Socialism and Welfare,* Dr. William Walters, Professor of Economics, The University of Washington, published by Clear Title Books, Ypsilanti, Michigan.

log into the wood stove. She felt small in the great outdoors, like an ant crawling across a vast white table top.

Poking her head out the back door, she debated making a run to the outhouse. Black shadows haunted gaps between the fir trees.

There's something out there, watching, she thought irrationally.

Her skin felt prickly, as if electrified. In her brow, she felt the pressure of an impending headache.

My bladder can hold out for a couple of more hours.

Clayton Powell and Graham Wallace

Clayton pissed against a dying tree; his urine steamed in the cool morning air. The sun was not yet over the horizon. Graham had to pee too; otherwise he planned to stay in the warm sleeping bag all day. Shivering and walking hesitantly on sore feet, he joined Clayton to irrigate the landscape. As Graham zipped up his pants, Clayton broke down the camp—stuffing things at random into a net bag. They threw the bag up into the fork of a tree.

"What's the deal?" Graham said.

"My staff will pick it up later."

"Won't we need all that stuff?"

"Nope."

"Where are we?"

"This is one of the Flat Lakes. There are about twenty-five of them. We're not far from Highway 97 as the crow flies, but we're not crows, are we? If you want to bail out, just walk east. Eventually you'll hit the highway and you can hitch a ride."

"I'm not bailing."

"As you wish. Let's choke down some trail mix and instant coffee and hit it."

Clayton slipped his longbow into a loop on his quiver and zipped up his parka. He patted insect repellent onto his neck and wrists.

The asshole didn't offer to share.

Graham glanced at his watch as they started off—it was only seven. They'd walked about four hours the day before and could, theoretically, walk fourteen hours before the light gave out. Yesterday's terrain was mostly flat; they'd walked up and down hills, but nothing too steep or too long. The view ahead looked rougher.

Could be a long goddamned day.

It was hard to shoulder his pack and start moving, but after twenty minutes, his legs and back were warmed up and he felt looser and refreshed.

"Do you want me to lead?" Graham asked.

Clayton stopped and gave him a critical look.

"I can pick up the pace if I'm going too slowly for you."

"I'm not complaining."

"Good, then save your breath. And keep a lookout, there are grizzly bears around. Here's some free advice—don't stand between me and the bear."

"Thanks for the suggestion."

"Think nothing of it," Clayton said, while turning and attacking the trail as it wound through the woods between two swampy lake sections. He was clearly walking faster now.

I need to learn to keep my fat mouth shut.

Occasionally, they followed gravel roads and narrow ATV trails as they traveled a westerly course. Beyond a few chainsaws and motorcycles that could be heard far in the distance, they were all alone. He was getting seriously tired when Clayton called for a break—in the shade of a massive lava-rock outcropping. Graham's leaden feet tripped on the smallest roots and stray branches. Glancing at his watch, he saw that it wasn't quite ten o'clock. He watched Clayton from the corner of his eye to see if he was winded; though Clayton's skin was flushed, he didn't seem affected by the hike so far.

"That was a pleasant warm-up stroll," Graham commented, while trying to appear casual while sipping desperately-needed water from his bottle. He pulled a chocolate power bar from his jacket pocket and munched.

"Tough guy, huh?" replied Clayton. "Don't worry, by the end of the day we'll begin to see what you're made of."

Graham did not like the sound of this…not even a little.

"Bring it on, baby," he said.

"You're a mouthy sonuvabitch, aren't you? *Sometimes* I find that amusing."

His tone implied this was not one of those times.

"Care for a bite of my power bar?" Graham said.

"Kiss my hairy white ass," Clayton said.

Graham unlaced his shoes, and wiggled his toes and rubbed his feet. As the REI clerk claimed, the gel-filled hiking shoes were comfortable, but Graham still had tender spots on the balls of his feet. He pulled moleskin tape from his pack and covered the sore areas.

"You thought to bring moleskin," Clayton said.

"Never leave home without it," Graham replied even though he'd never heard of the stuff a week prior. He made an internal promise to promote Lili or marry her or something when he got back. Without her help, he'd be one big miserable mosquito-eaten blister by now. Having recovered somewhat, he took note of his surroundings. The rock face stretched high and curved away so he could not see the summit.

"Which way around are we going?"

Clayton laughed. "We're going over." Shouldering his pack, he stood up. "Are you ready, tough guy?"

If I go east far enough, I'll hit the highway where I can hitch a ride.

"What are we waiting for?" Graham said.

They walked a hundred meters along the base of the cliff, hopping over talus and boulders. When Clayton stopped, Graham nearly bowled him over. A rope ladder that appeared to be made from high-test fishing line snaked up the rock face. Graham gazed up and felt dizzy; the earth seemed spongy and unstable.

"I really don't care for heights," he said.

"Then I strongly suggest you don't look down," Clayton said mildly as he started climbing. "Give me some room. Don't climb up my ass, alright?" he called down.

Graham was frustrated.

I told him I can't tolerate heights and he pulls this stunt. What good does a fifty-million-dollar contract do for me if I fall off this cliff and get mashed into hamburger? There's no way I'm climbing this fucking stupid little kite-string ladder.

Slinging his walking sticks across his back with leather cords, he made up his mind to head toward the highway.

Feet, take me east.

He noticed he'd started climbing. He looked down and was ten feet off the rocky surface. Fighting vertigo, he desperately clasped a ladder cross member.

I wasn't supposed to climb.

I can't do this.

He decided to climb down slowly, but found his feet and arms taking him *up* instead.

I'm losing my mind. Am I not in control of my body?

He thought of Clayton at the top, calling in on his satellite telephone to collect on a wager. A seed of anger flared in the pit of his stomach.

We'll see how funny he thinks it is when I fall off this fucking rock and spray my brains across Canada.

Then he realized the absurdity of his thought.

Clayton doesn't give a shit if I fall to my death.

He'd probably laugh himself silly while collecting on the bet.

As he got angrier, he realized that he didn't care if he fell or not.

Screw this ladder, this rock, this countryside, the contract and above all, screw you, rich boy. Clayton Powell. Asshole.

When he pulled himself to the top, his arms were rubbery and his whole body had no strength, as if he was two-hundred pounds of jiggling gelatin.

A jellyfish, that's what I am. Useless mush.

He collapsed over an outcropping and gasped like a beached salmon.

Isn't there any air at this altitude?

He heaved and a sloppy chocolate power bar mess erupted from his stomach.

"That's attractive," Clayton commented.

Graham slipped into a sitting position and wiped his beard.

"Is there even the slightest chance we'll end this trip as friends?"

Clayton laughed. "That's not what this is about," he said. "Take a few minutes to catch your breath, then we need to get moving. We're behind schedule."

"Fuck your schedule," Graham said.

"Suit yourself. However, you're sleeping raw in the wild if you don't get to the next station. That would be uncomfortable. Dangerous, perhaps. We get to the stations, that's where our meals, water and sleeping accommodations are. Haven't you figured that out by now?"

Graham got off the rock, then turned around and sat down. He rinsed his mouth with water and spat. His stomach was still roiling and he was angry. Then he noticed how close he was to the edge of the cliff and how the rope ladder trailed away into space. He had an instant of unsteadiness as he imagined falling, then it receded.

Clayton may very well be trying to kill me, but I don't need to make it easy.

Clayton released the ladder from some spikes driven into rock and tossed it over the edge.

"What's the deal?" Graham asked.

"It cost a bundle to stage this hike. I'm not giving away any freebies. Besides, some kid could get hurt, then where would I be?"

Graham took a drink of his water and stood on the ridge looking out over the Flat Lakes.

"Yeah, I get it," he said. "Are we going to lollygag up here all day? Move your ass."

Clayton looked at him with an inscrutable expression. He stood slowly and gathered up his bow, quiver and backpack.

"Yes, you're absolutely right. Let's roll."

Robert Kinsley

After tearing off the black tape that disguised the license plate number, Robert returned the rental car to the airport and picked up his car from the parking garage. He drove to the Alderwood Mall to use the same payphone. It was unoccupied. He dialed the call.

"This is Gaspard. I uploaded the picture to Mobog, did you see it?"

"Yes and we're very impressed. Good job."

"Now that I've passed the test, when can we meet?"

"That's amusing, Gaspard. We're never going to meet. It's not safe. You'll take your assignments over the phone, just like we're doing now. Hey, you're not calling from the same payphone are you?"

"Yes, I am."

"Well, hang up and find another one. Never use the same one twice, got it?"

There was a click on the line and Robert was left staring at the dead receiver.

Robert found a payphone outside a 7-Eleven. He asked the clerk for change and she wordlessly pointed to a hand-written sign that said *No change with no purchase.*

Exasperated, he bought a bottle of water and a pack of gum.

After feeding the phone, the connection was made.

"This is Gaspard," he said.

"We have a mission at a Wal-Mart construction site. More night work. Are you up for it?"

"Sure," Robert replied.

"Spend some of your daddy's money on gloves, bolt-cutters and a sledge hammer. Pay cash; don't use a credit card, okay? The rendezvous point is the corner of 125th and Thorne. Don't stop if you think you might be followed. Peace out, soldier."

Robert, feeling adrenaline surging in his veins, stared at the dead phone receiver.

At eleven o'clock, with the sun long set, the highway was still busy.

Robert parked on the shoulder in line with several other vehicles. A woman, dressed all in black, waved for him to follow a trail through the woods. They came out on another road and piled into a large van. They introduced themselves. Thistle and Willow looked like twins—short, heavy-set young women with multiple piercings and multi-colored hair bound up by bandanas. Coho was a lanky young man wearing a black Mohawk, heavy boots and steel chains looped around his neck and wrists.

The driver, wearing a grungy cowboy hat pulled down so far on his forehead that his eyes were barely visible, turned and said, "Snake."

"I'm Gaspard," Robert said.

The woman in black, apparently the leader of the mission, said, "Raven."

Raven was about forty and had wisps of gray hair escaping from under her stocking cap. Her wrinkled skin was tanned like leather. She spoke with a loud, raspy voice.

"The guard is a friend of the Fellowship. We need to cut the chains to unlock the gate to cover for him. We'll wrap him in duct tape, but go easy, just a black eye should be enough to keep him out of trouble. Got it?"

There were nods around the van.

She continued.

"We're allowing thirty minutes. I'll give one whistle for the five minute warning and with two whistles, head back to the van immediately. Snake will hit the van's horn if the pigs come. If that happens, scatter in the woods."

Crossing their arms, they clasped hands. Awkwardly, Robert replicated the motion and completed the ring.

"We beseech you, Dagda the Holly King and Danu the Planet Mother, to bless our Forest Fellowship and ward off inchoate corporate evils aligned against us."

"In her name," they chanted. They watched Robert until, hesitantly, he said it too.

"In her name."

With headlights off, they drove a final quarter mile on a rough gravel track and stopped before a gate. They piled out and Robert attacked the chain with his boltcutters. Once inside, they efficiently turned the guard into a mummy with several rolls of duct tape.

Raven pointed at Robert.

"You do it," she said.

Robert, after tugging on his leather gloves, shrugged, hauled back and bashed the guard in the eye. The man toppled over like a deadfall.

"You could have pulled that a little more," Raven said. "Are you all right?" she asked the guard.

Wincing, he nodded. "It hurts," he said.

She looked accusingly at Robert.

"I saved some for you if you want it," he said, waving a fist at her.

"No time to tussle," she said. "Let's loose the angry wolves of mayhem."

They cut hydraulic hoses and poured corn syrup into fuel tanks. They tipped over portable toilets. Robert watched a gleeful Coho run a whining cordless drill into a stack of joists and laminated beams. Raven spray-painted pentangles on concrete tilt-up panels while Robert flattened the tires of grader with a borrowed ice axe. Walking by, Thistle asked if she could borrow his sledge hammer. When Robert nodded, she began smashing the windshields of a group of service vehicles. Robert sweated while hacking through a coil of fiber optic cables with the axe—when the first whistle sounded.

Could it really be twenty-five minutes already? We just got here.

He drifted back toward the van and along the way, lent his shoulder to the women pushing a pickup truck into an excavated pit. It cascaded fifty feet into the hole and landed with a satisfying crunch as the double whistle blasts sounded. They ran back through the gate and jumped in the van. Robert carried the boltcutters, but Raven grabbed them and tossed them into the weeds.

"We don't carry evidence out with us," she said as the van reversed up the gravel road through a canopy of overhanging trees.

In minutes, the van pulled off the road and they hiked through the woods back to their cars.

They huddled just for an instant on the road's shoulder.

"In the name of the holy wheel," they chanted.

"Yes, in the name of the holy wheel," Robert echoed, "whatever the fuck that means."

"Now scatter," Raven said, with a lingering and enigmatic look into Robert's eyes.

"You," she said.

"What?" Robert asked.

"I sensed the true spirit of mayhem in you, but you'd better learn to show the old gods some respect. It's a mistake to fraternize, but these wildings get my blood up. Back home, I have wine. Would you like to come to my place? I am the tranquility and the quickening."

She was covered in bulky black clothes, so it was impossible to tell if she was fat or thin. Nearly old enough to be his mother, her dark eyes glittered—reptile-like—in the dim light.

"Sure, why not?" Robert said.

"Then follow me," she said.

CHAPTER EIGHT

Willie and Maria

MARIA HATED TO disturb him when he was finally writing and not just reading. His forgotten books were scattered across the deck like carcasses, with pages rippling in the intermittent wind coming off the water. When he wasn't chewing the ends off his pencils or sharpening the leads into perfect points, he scribbled longhand on yellow legal tablets. However, she'd stalled long enough; it was past time for dinner. In a cast iron skillet on the propane stove, she pan-fried Italian sausages with a sweet onion—and steamed a batch of rice in a large iron pot.

"I think a red wine would be better with the sausages, but we have white if you prefer."

Willie—lost in his thoughts—did not respond, but he sipped when she placed a glass of Merlot in his hand.

"How's the book coming along?" she said.

Willie took off his glasses and rubbed his eyes. He claimed to be working on a new textbook called *The Social Consequences of Wealth—Trivial Lives Consumed by Trivial Pursuits* for Harvard University Press. They had paid him a $1,000 advance and the book was already a year past due, but Maria had read his manuscript while he slept and knew he was actually working on a mystery novel with the working title *The Long Sunset*. Under the pseudonym Edgar Blades, he'd sold 65,000 copies of two previous titles; they were minor hits and the latest had been mentioned as a Chester Himes Mystery Award candidate.

"Not so bad," Willie replied. "Did you know the Japanese phrase for parasite singles is *parasaito shinguru* and NEET stands for Not in Employment, Education or Training? Many NEETs are parasitic singles that have given up. This is a demographic wave, a huge mass of young dependent people with lots of free time and expendible income. The sociology is fascinating."

"Stop it, you're full of crap. You're writing about the continuing adventures of Mickey Blood."

"I knew it. You've been reading the manuscript. You know I hate that."

"No, you don't, you love it."

Willie stuffed a slice of sausage in his mouth and washed it down with a sip of wine.

"Well, since you're so damned snoopy, what do you think?" he asked with exaggerated casualness.

"I think—if you write another mystery where the bad guy turns out to be a government bureaucrat, people will get sick to death of your formula."

"Well, Miss Can't-keep-her-nose-out-of-my-private-business, it happens that the bad guy is an insurance agent this time."

"That's a relief. You've found a completely different over-stuffed bureaucratic villain this time. Hurray."

Willie laughed. "I'm not making people buy these books, they just do. I didn't hear you complaining when I used my last royalty check to pay off the Murano."

"You know I'm your biggest fan."

"Yes, I know, dear." With a muffled thump, something fell on the roof of the cabin and rolled off. "Now the squirrels are critics too," he commented.

"Maybe the Harvard Press people sent him over."

Willie laughed and finished his wine.

"Might I have some more, Mrs. Walters?"

"Yes, Professor Walters, you may," she said formally as she refilled his glass.

After dark, under the light of a hanging lantern, Willie sat in an antique leather-bound recliner and read the newspapers Chief Sam Joe had left behind. One of the papers was a tabloid—*The Planetary Observer*—with a crudely-Photoshopped cover picture of the president shaking hands with a vampire.

"Hey, babe, take a look at this," Willie said.

Maria looked up from her embroidery project.

"The Pope is an alien?"

"No, it's Bigfoot."

"Oh, Lord, not this again. Okay, what about it?"

"The guy is from Dogwood Valley. That's nearby."

Maria set aside her sewing and picked up the newspaper. The photograph showed a man kneeling by a barbed wire fence pointing at large, widely-spaced tracks.

Bigfoot Stole my Chickens the headline announced in lurid black letters.

"So?"

"Dogwood Valley is not so very far away."

"You said that, but what are you getting at?"

"Maybe I'd like to go talk to him."

Maria groaned.

"I sense another of your crazy ideas brewing. What is it with you and Sasquatch?"

Willie grinned. "The existence of Bigfoot does not seem so absurd to me—we're discovering new species all the time. There's a legitimate science…cryptozoology. Also, maybe I'm bored with writing about serial killers and gangsters and I'm looking for something else to do."

"Then work on your Harvard Press book."

"No one has written the Great North American Sasquatch novel yet. I feel the tug of destiny."

"Good lord, Willie, when I think you've achieved the pinnacle of madness, you…"

"You sure are sexy when you're trying to be practical."

"I guess I'm done with my embroidery for the night," she said, sensing—and appreciating—his mood for love.

After sex, Maria lay in bed looking at the ceiling—listening to the wind rustle through the pines. With Willie's seed seeping, she collected the energy to make the trip out back to the outhouse. Willie was unconscious and his breathing was quietly rythmic. If she was a man, she would blissfully scratch her balls and mindlessly piss off the back deck instead of trekking to sit on the cold outhouse seat.

Some differences between the sexes are simply cruel and unfair.

On the edge of sleep, her mind drifted back in time.

The designated smoking area was a gazebo around the back of the building by the air conditioning condensers. The ground was littered with fast food drink cups and cigarette butts. Willie puffed on his pipe and massaged a sore knee. Rain spattered on the roof.

"I suppose we should talk about sex," he commented.

"What about it?" Maria asked. "I'm all for it in the right circumstances."

"It's been a while. I'm not exactly sure all my equipment still works. At my advanced age, it's unlikely that I could keep up with, much less satisfy, a young healthy woman. Such as yourself, for example."

"I'm not worried about it."

"Maybe not now, but one day a virile, young electrician or milkman will whisper in your ear, and then where are we? Sure, you'd feel a little guilty, but let's be realistic, the fires of passion don't burn in my loins like they used to. At the same time, you're young and inevitably full of womanly desires and expectations."

"A milkman? Where do you get these ludicrous ideas?"

"Women like to sit at home and have men bring them things. It's a genetic imprint—an evolutionary imperative. They can't help it."

Maria slugged him in the arm. "That's the rudest thing you've ever said to me. You're a pig if you believe that. Besides, they make little blue pills to help men with their problems. We'll buy a few cases and stock up. Look, do we have to talk about everything? Can't we just explore and discover things as we go along? Work things out? I don't want to agonize over every detail."

"I'm just trying to cover the bases."

"Well, stop it. You're annoying me."

"Annoying women is one of my core competencies, my dear," Willie said.

She laughed.

Clayton Powell and Graham Wallace

Clayton stumbled once and bruised his knee on an outcropping of rock. Under layers of clothing, he could feel the joint puffing up—swelling. He needed to be more careful with his footing, but it was impossible, as he could barely lift his legs. The only thing that kept him going was rage—a furious boiling hatred of Clayton and his manipulation and games. It was after one o'clock when Clayton called for a break.

"Go see if you can bag a rabbit or squirrel or something," Clayton said, while preparing a small fire pit.

"With what? A rock?"

"With your bow, numbnuts. We need protein or we're not going to make it."

"Fuck you," Graham said as he unshouldered his pack and collapsed against a log.

"Suit yourself," Clayton said. "If I bag it, you're going to gut it, skin it and do the cooking. I'm not carrying your ass on this trip."

With the fire catching, Clayton took up the bow and walked into a little clearing where he stood silently and watched a patch of trees. Graham heard a chattering as Clayton smoothly drew back an arrow and then loosed it.

"Ha! Got it," Clayton said.

He walked into the woods and retrieved the arrow and a limp, bloody squirrel pinned against the tree. Walking back, he threw the squirrel on Graham's lap.

"I'm not fucking around with this," Graham complained.

"I'm leaving you behind if you don't pull your weight. Test me on that if you want. Skin it and try not to nick the gall bladder or you'll taint the meat."

"Skin it with what?"

"I'll bet whoever made up that pack for you didn't send you up here without a good knife."

Unable to stop himself, Graham grinned.

Another thing I need to thank Lili for.

He rooted through the backpack until he found the Gerber clasp knife. He held up the squirrel and tried to decide how to proceed.

"To skin it, slide the blade under the fur and loosen it, and then yank the hide off."

Graham took a deep breath and hefted the small, still-warm body. The knife was scary-sharp. He hacked off the head and tail, tossed the unwanted pieces away and was left with a small carcass holding a few ounces of meat on the legs and back.

"Seems like a lot of work for such a little bit of meat," he said.

"Slit the belly and scoop out the guts. And bury all the waste or we'll be up to our ears in scavengers."

Graham sat with the bloody mess on his lap and looked to Clayton for guidance.

"Wash it and stab it on this spit," Clayton said, handing over a green branch he'd stripped and sharpened. Graham rinsed the carcass and his hands with water from his plastic bottle, and speared the body. Clayton took it from him.

"Okay, I'll cook," he said, holding the meat over the little fire.

Graham did an inventory. His knee was swollen but his feet, though sore, were holding up. Every muscle in his body complained and he wanted to fall into a feather bed and sleep for a decade or two. He chewed trail mix, sipped water and watched the squirrel brown and drip grease into the flame. He resisted, but the smell of the meat searing over the flame was appetizing. Clayton gingerly sliced off a hot strip and chewed it slowly.

"It's tough and could use salt and pepper, but otherwise, it's not too bad."

"Alright, you fuck, give me some," Graham said.

Part of his mind wondered what he was doing, but another part, intoxicated by the smell, was eager to be fed. The meat was gamy and stringy, but good. He held out his hand for another piece. There was protein in the trail mix, but it wasn't the same as meat, Graham had to admit. He gazed over the landscape. They were on the top of a small rise and the hills, visible in stripes through the trees, stretched into the distance. Clayton tossed him an orange. Together, they pulled off and fed the skins to the fire.

"We have a long stretch of bad road ahead of us before we camp for the night," Clayton said as he trimmed the end off a cigar.

Graham gestured for Clayton to hand one over.

"These lovely things are wasted on you," Clayton complained.

"Shut up and be a more gracious host," Graham said, while rolling the tip in the fire to get it going.

"Keep your eyes open. It would be great to bag a bighorn sheep for dinner. It's not likely—we'll probably end up with a greasy possum," Clayton said.

"Yum, my favorite," Graham said, while wondering whether he actually knew what a possum was.

Some sort of nasty rodent.

"Bullshit, you were born in Orange County. You wouldn't know a possum from a nutria, jerk."

"You don't know me. I got this far, didn't I?"

"In the next day or so, we'll take the full measure of how tough you are," Clayton commented.

Graham felt an angry stirring in his Scottish blood.

"How about a side bet?"

"We're already wagering a fifty-million-dollar contract."

"How about that pretty Hummer?"

"Against what?"

"My Porsche Carrera GT."

"I figured you were leasing that thing. It's yours to bet?"

Graham, wondering what fresh madness had overtaken him, nodded. "Yes, I own it—free and clear."

Clayton pulled a voice recorder out of a packet in his jacket.

"Say it," he said.

"I hereby wager my Porsche Carrera against Powell's Hummer that I make it to Harrison Hot Springs. Alive."

"And I accept the bet," Clayton said into the recorder before turning it off and slipping it back in a pocket. "Tonight's camp is not coming to us. If we're going to get there, we'd better move it," he said, while kicking dirt onto the fire. He smoothly picked up his backpack and quiver.

"Give me a hand up," Graham asked, holding out his hand.

"Huh, that's funny," Clayton said.

In seconds, Clayton was at the edge of the clearing—moving quickly. He was completely out of sight by the time Graham struggled to his feet and wriggled into the arm straps of his pack. It was scary how fast he was isolated and alone. With a surge of adrenaline, he ignored the stiffness of his complaining muscles and hustled after Clayton.

Robert Kinsley

Raven lived in a condominium complex that bordered a slough. It was somewhat run down and beat-up—older cars filled the parking lot—but there were green trees and well-tended shrubbery to soften the lower-middle-class ambiance.

"This is more upscale than I pictured for you," Robert said.

"I lived for three years in a yurt," Raven said defensively. "I get a Section 8 rent subsidy, otherwise, I'd be living on the street again. Don't you think housing is a basic human right?"

Sure, along with the basic right for poor people to buy cheap Chinese shit at Wal-Mart.

"Sure," he said, while trying to picture her naked body underneath her bulky clothes. After checking her mailbox at a kiosk, she led him up two flights of stairs to her unit. She threw her mail on an end table and Robert glanced at the envelopes, which included a couple of credit card bills and promotional flyers from Planned Parenthood and the Sierra Club. She tossed off her jacket and slipped off her boots.

"Oh, it feels good to get out of those things," she said. She decanted wine from a box into plastic juice glasses and handed him one.

"Chablis," she said. "I hope that's okay."

It tasted better than he expected, but maybe he was just thirsty and craving alcohol. He walked to the window—which had a great view of the parking lot—and looked over a small shrine with black candles, silver pentangles, incense holders, quartz crystals and a tangled collection of small animal bones, either birds or rodents, he couldn't tell. A dagger lay on a piece of black velvet. A pair of large black circles seemed to be dyed into the pale carpeting.

He turned and watched Raven shrug out of her clothes. Under her black turtleneck sweater and tights, she wore a red bra and panties. She was older than he thought and her body had stretch marks and loose flesh, but overall her figure was full and desirable. He felt a stirring in his loins as her looked her over.

"I hope you're cool with this—I'm a silver-spirit Wiccan," she said, as if she hoped this would explain everything.

"Sorry, I'm completely ignorant of witches and covens and stuff."

"Oh, shit, you're going to get the wrong idea. My pagan religion does not allow my body to be penetrated by others, but we can still be experientially sensual and have some fun. I'll be your May Queen if you'll be my Green Man. All loving acts of spirit and pleasure are my rituals, do you see?"

"No," Robert said.

Raven's shoulders slumped. "Okay, the basic rules are you can't touch me and I can't touch you. Otherwise, do as you will. Do you understand? You can't touch me. If you can't make that promise, then you need to leave now. I'm serious."

"No touching at all?"

"Not physically, though our spirits will mingle and merge. You stay in your circle and I'll stay in mine. Do you promise?"

Promise what?

"Yes, sure, I can give that a try."

"Thank you. Some people can't open their minds to the power of isolation. Our souls will fuck, but we'll maintain our earthbound virginal purity as we offer our bodies to the chalice and the athamé. Go ahead—strip off your clothes and I'll get the implements."

Robert tossed dregs of wine back in his throat and helped himself to a refill. Raven appeared from a backroom with a silver tray. Among other things, the tray held a pipe shaped like an owl with the stem emitting from its tail. She'd pulled her hair back with a red ribbon.

"Still dressed?" she said. "Let's smoke some herb, that will loosen you up."

She stuffed a thick green wad into the pipe and fired it up with a butane lighter. "It's a genetic hybrid of ganja, opium and Saint John's Wort. You're not used to it, so you'd better go easy at first."

Robert took the pipe and sucked a dose deep into his lungs.

"Whoa, big boy, too much, I think. Get your pants off and we'll get started. First, pick one of the tools. Don't touch it, just point at the one you want me to use."

Robert's mind was already altered by the drug. His consciousness seemed expanded beyond the confines of his skull. At the periphery of his vision, little colored splashes washed the room and he heard an ethereal, echoing popping sound, like popcorn kernels in God's cosmic microwave. He looked over the items on the silver platter. An array of dildos—a large ribbed black one, an ivory one apparently carved from an elephant's tusk and a shiny tubular one curved like a boomerang.

"Dumbo," Robert whispered.

"Ah, that's funny. The ivory—a very good choice. Now get your clothes off. We're in this together right? Don't leave me standing alone with my all-naturals hanging about."

Robert struggled with his buttons and zippers. His fingers seemed to be expanding and contracting. A heat developed in his belly and spread to his limbs while warm, friendly eyes blinked in the walls and furniture. Somehow, he achieved nakedness. His erect penis quivered like an electric eel in the cool air.

Raven took off her bra and panties and settled on the carpet in her prayer circle. As she puffed on the pipe, she gestured for Robert to get in his circle. The room was filled with coiling strands of smoke and beams of prismatic light. Her black pubic hair was carefully trimmed and she had large brown circles of areola around tiny black nipples.

Robert stared as if he'd never seen a naked woman before; his eyes explored her mysterious swollen folds and bulges. She prepared the curved ivory as if buttering a corncob; it glistened with fragrant oil squeezed from a plastic tube. Robert's senses were scrambled. He smelled the soft glow emanating from the ivory, his eyes were filled with the lavender scent of the incense and his skin throbbed with the sound of imagined wind chimes. She ran the ivory down her body and it left a slimy trail like a slug. The trail reminded him of runes and he heard someone chanting…

From the Goddess, come we all
And return, we shall, into her
Like the rain to the leaf
Like the leaf to the tree
Like the tree to the earth
Like the earth to the Goddess
Return we shall, into her.

He watched her writhe and bare her teeth in pain or passion. At the same time, she watched him stroke himself and this further inflamed him. He didn't see her lips move, but someone said, "Unleash the seed, Robert."

Like spurts of sparks, the energy flowed out of him.

In his dream, he chased the May Queen deep into dark-green woods—through curtains of moss and fern. He didn't want to wake up, but Raven shook his shoulder and would not leave him alone. His face was buried in the carpet and his mouth was filled with acid-paste. She handed him a sweating bottle of cold water. He gulped it in freezing swallows. She was dressed in a fluffy yellow bathrobe and her hair was wet and swept back from her face.

"You're a mess, Robert. Take a shower, and then go home, okay?"

"What was in that pipe?" he asked.

"We believe bioengineering can help us get closer to the womb of the Earth Mother," she said.

Robert's skin was sticky and he could smell the sour scent of biochemical waste in his sweat. In her shower, he washed himself with her all-natural strawberry body wash and organic avocado shampoo. He stood under the hot stream until the hot water ran low and the water began to flow cool. He dressed and ran her brush through his hair. Outside, she'd gathered up his clothing. Pressing the bundle in his arms, she ushered him toward the door.

He tried to kiss her but she avoided his lips.

"No intimate touching," she said.

"We could hardly have been more intimate a few hours ago."

"That's the point. Don't you see it?"

"No. When can we do this again?"

"Never. There is only one first time, of course."

"I mean, when will the second time come to be?"

She sighed.

"We'll have to see about that, Robert," she said.

CHAPTER NINE

Willie and Maria

MARIA, WALKING AROUND the cabin in a fluffy white bathrobe and fuzzy slippers, started a pot of coffee on the propane stove. Outside, the air was still cool. She shivered—still cold from her walk to the outhouse.

Willie tossed and turned in bed while she leafed through his manuscript. He wrote parallel stories and somehow weaved them together in a coherent mosaic, but she could not figure out how he did it; it never made sense until he was done and the themes coalesced and linked, like his odd watercolor paintings.

In this story, a handsome insurance agent was framed for a series of murders by an evil ex-wife. In addition, the story included a bizarre first-person narrative of a Native American college student investigating a secret government cold fusion experiment.

The overall effect was maddening, but he could be playing with her—knowing she read along without his permission. The other two novels had come out well and there was even talk of optioning a screenplay to the writer/director of a couple of edgy LA-noir detective movies. After all his years of writing award-winning, poorly-selling socioeconomic-philosophical non-fiction, the idea that he might make his fortune writing sleazy detective novels made her laugh.

"And what, my dear, do you find amusing?" Willie asked.

He stood in the doorway in his boxer shorts scratching the thin fuzz on his chin.

"You. You make me laugh. This new story makes absolutely no sense. I think you throw oddball ideas around just to mess with my head."

"Oh, you are just missing an important part—the part that, due to my incredible literary genius, ties the whole thing together organically and inevitably," he said, waving a sheaf of yellow pages at her. She jumped up and reached out, but he walked back in the bedroom and locked them in his briefcase. "I don't think you've figured out the combination yet, so they should be safe."

She spoke with false anger.

"You're a sneaky bastard."

"Now, dear, that's no way to start a fine morning. Pour me a cup of coffee, will you? I need to make a run out back."

"Don't piss off the porch. That's gross."

"Nature, my dear, it's the way of nature. You'd do it too, if nature built squatters that way. Clearly, this is more evidence that standers are superior to squatters in the natural order."

"Well, you smug old man, you can *stand* in the kitchen and pour your own damned coffee."

He grinned over his shoulder as he walked out the back door. She opened a tin of Vienna sausages and began heating them.

Mixed with dehydrated eggs and grilled onions, they aren't so bad.

Relenting in her mock anger, she poured him a large mug of coffee and stirred in powdered creamer and sugar.

When he came back, she handed him his mug.

"Here's your cappuccino, your majesty," she said.

"Thank you, my sweet," he replied.

She could tell his mind was elsewhere as he sipped his coffee and stared out over the water.

He proposed at the Salish Lodge at Snoqualmie Falls—twenty-five miles east of Seattle. Their table was next to the window and they had a great view of the magnificent, thundering torrent. Permanent rainbows hovered in the mist as sunlight poured through broken clouds. For weeks she had a sense he was going to ask, so she was unsurprised when, after dinner, as they were enjoying snifters of Crown Royal, he produced a little box tied with a ribbon.

"Is this something shiny and expensive?" she said.

"Of course," he replied.

"Is there a certain question attached to this little box?"

"Yes, my dear, there certainly is."

"Well, the answer is *yes*.

"Don't you want to make sure I picked a ring you'll like? What if it's a cheap plastic mood ring or a Captain Crunch secret decoder ring? What if it's old and hideous like me?"

"You aren't so old. You act like you have one foot in the grave."

"My life insurance is a lot more expensive the last few years," he said. "The insurance companies know what's what."

"To goddamned hell with them."

"Well, open it; I need to see if I wasted my money."

The ring was a wide hunk of scalloped gold. He slipped it on her finger and it fit snugly...perfectly.

"No diamond?"

"The idea of the diamond as an investment is a fraud. The only reason they are expensive is because the Dutch and Russian cartels artificially restrict the supply. They promote sentimental value to kill the resale market. Diamonds are forever, my ass. Gold, on the other hand, has intrinsic value, at least it has had for thousands of years—and I don't see anything that will change in the next few hundred. The history of the wedding ring is interesting. Women wore them as a mark of ownership and a symbol of their fetters. In Roman times, the ring was a binding legal agreement. The Egyptians saw the never-ending band as supernatural and placed it on the third finger because they believed it contained a vein, called vena amoris, which led directly to the heart. So, do you approve?"

"Of the lecture, no. Of the ring, yes. It's lovely. How did you figure out my size?"

"I borrowed a ring sizing thingy from a jeweler and measured one of your rings."

"Ring sizing thingy. How precise, Professor. Well, your evil scheme worked, it fits. Now we just need to set a date. Let's not agonize over this, let's just go to Reno and get a quickie license and drive-through ceremony," she suggested.

"No, my family would skin me alive. It doesn't have to be elaborate, but we should invite a few people. Shall we give them thirty days to clear a spot on their schedule?"

"Fine with me."

"So let it be written, so let it be done."

"You stole that from an old movie."

"Yul Brynner playing Rameses in the Ten Commandments. Sue me."

He leaned over the table and they shared a tender kiss.

From behind, Willie wrapped his arms around her. They listened to a woodpecker hammer on a dying tree as a cautious chipmunk grabbed crumbs from the deck. Blinding beams of sunlight reflected from wind-swept ripples on the lake. Sausages sizzled in the frying pan.

"What were you thinking?" she said.

"About my romantic marriage proposal. Remember? Snoqualmie Falls?"

"Of course I remember. I held my breath and hoped you'd ask."

"I don't know how it's possible, but you get more beautiful every day."

"So, you love me completely and would do anything for me?"

"Of course."

"Good, then you'll show me what you're writing."

"Ha, nice try, sneaky broad."

"At least give me a hint. I can't stand it. You know I'm your biggest fan."

"You're my biggest critic and my most genuine pain in the butt, but you made me coffee, so perhaps I will indulge you. Promise, one hint and that's all? Then you'll leave me alone?"

"Yes, damn you. If that's all you're offering, yes."

"Bigfoot."

"Bigfoot? The secret connecting thread in your novel is Bigfoot? Are you making a weird joke? Have you completely lost your mind?"

"You said you'd leave me alone."

"I lied. I guess this explains your recent obsession with Bigfoot. Now you *have* to show me those pages."

Willie reached around her and used a fork to spear a Vienna sausage.

"Nope," he said, "they are not ready for an audience yet. You'll have to learn the virtue of patience."

"Well, tough guy, maybe you'd like to learn the virtue of waiting patiently for sexual intercourse?"

Willie laughed and slipped his hands inside her bathrobe.

"As if you could resist my masterful skill in the bedroom. In fact, we don't seem to be busy, so why don't we slip out of these robes and see what comes up?"

"No. I'm angry with you."

"Really?" Willie said, while running his hands down her belly and over her thighs.

She turned off the propane flame and turned to face him. Her robe slipped off her shoulders into a pile on the floorboard.

"All right, Signore Casanova, you're right. I'm yours."

Clayton Powell and Graham Wallace

The day became an endless misery. They scrambled up hillsides, clambered over fallen logs and waded though swampy bogs and streams. Each step increased Graham's nightmare of pain. He wanted to collapse into a boneless pile and simply die, but something kept him moving.

Sometimes it was raw fury at Clayton for leading him in this green madness, sometimes it was the thought of impressing Lili with his determination, and sometimes it was Scottish pride that seeped out of his bones. He'd lost track of how many times he'd fallen. While crossing a brook, water had overflowed the top of his left boot and he could feel the softened skin on his heel slipping and sliding.

At the edge of a marshy meadow, Clayton called a halt. He unslung his bow and notched an arrow.

"Quiet, oaf," he said.

Graham leaned against a hemlock and panted. He tried to see what Clayton had spotted. A dappled fawn eased into view but slipped into the brush when Graham threw a rock. Clayton loosed his arrow anyway, but it shattered ineffectually on a stony outcropping.

"Hey, asshole, what are you doing? They are tender and delicious when they are that young."

"That was just a baby, can't be legal."

"Do you see any forest rangers around? If you interfere with my hunt again, I'll hamstring you and leave you for the carrion birds. They'll eat your eyes first and your bones will be scattered from here to Kamloops."

"Your threats are getting tedious. Are we walking or working our jawbones? Camp is not going to come to us, is it?" Graham said, leaning against the tree and trying to look rested and casual while his body screamed for mercy.

Clayton looked over Graham from head to toe. Graham was mud-spattered. A clump of moss was tangled in his beard. He gripped the walking sticks as if they were crutches.

"You're a stubborn son-of-a-bitch, aren't you? We only have a few miles left for the day," Clayton said, relenting. "We can take a short breather, I guess."

A few miles? I'm not going to make it another ten feet.

"Sure, if you need a break, that's fine with me," Graham said.

He pulled off his boots and stretched his socks in a patch of sun to dry. He had a blister the size of a silver dollar on the heel of his left foot, but, thankfully, it had not popped. Clayton walked around the meadow, leaning over and picking things out of the shadows. He showed Graham a handful of shriveled-looking mushrooms.

"Morels," he said. "They would have been great with that fawn, roasted," he said. "You can't be a good businessman unless you're willing to make a hard decision. A self-made rich man may seem like a nice guy, but I guarantee you, inside, there is ruthlessness. There's no place for a soft heart in the marketplace. That's why you're here, so I can take your measure, and I have to say, so far, I'm unimpressed. Flank of fawn, you can't find better eating than that." He handed Graham a handful of pale orange berries. "Salmon berries," he said. "Try some, they're good."

"Let me see you eat some first," Graham said.

Clayton laughed and showed a handful, then popped them—one-by-one—into his mouth.

"That foot looks nasty and painful. I can call on the satellite phone and get a chopper set down here in this clearing and have you out of here in a couple of hours if you're ready to call it quits. You'll be eating steak and drinking Canadian beer by nightfall, no problem."

"This blister is nothing. I'm good to go. In fact, I'm just starting to get warmed up and in an outdoorsy mood. I don't want to rob myself of all this fresh air and natural stuff."

"You are full of shit. You know nothing about the outdoors. You couldn't tell a trillium from queen cup lily."

"I'm a software engineer, not a florist. Besides, you didn't think I'd get this far and yet, here I am."

"You make a valid point," Clayton mused. "I may—indeed—have slightly underestimated you. But, there is a long way between here and there. Of that, I assure you."

Starting with a few impossible miles.

He didn't like the tone of Clayton's voice and wondered what evil the next few days would hold. He imagined the reception he would get back at the office if he took the escape by helicopter. He'd show off his blisters and bruises and no one would blame him for telling Clayton to shove his contract up his butt. Not to his face anyway, but maybe that would be the beginning of the end.

His managers would conspire and gossip. His better programmers would circulate their resumes and take lucrative offers at other companies. His reputation would dissolve like piles of dogshit melting in the rain. He shook his head to dissipate the morbid, infantile image. He opened his pack and pulled out a package of beef jerky. He wasn't hungry, but he knew he needed to eat something to recover any semblance of strength. As he chewed the leathery meat, he realized that he *did* have an appetite. He assembled a meal of smoked fish and trail mix.

"What is that? Cod?" Clayton said.

"Yeah, I guess," Graham said, peering at the package. He tossed a strip to Clayton, who took off his hat and settled in a sunny patch.

"I love it out here," Clayton commented, while tearing dried whitefish with his teeth. "There is nothing like the raw cruelty of nature to strip away the layers of bullshit and expose the central core of things. I'd go nuts if I had to spend all my time in the city."

"Yeah, whatever," Graham said. He wiggled his toes and waved away a cloud of hovering mosquitoes. After applying a few more strips of moleskin, he was ready to go. He pulled on dry socks and slipped his sore feet back into the boots. His back had stiffened and he could barely stand up.

"I don't have all day to stand around here waiting for you, pussy," he said.

Clayton laughed—a short bark like a seal.

"Fine, let's do it to it," Clayton said.

After ten minutes of walking, they found a muddy track and followed it. It wound around a group of sandstone outcroppings and then fell away into a valley. Through the trees a river flowed, deep and green.

"What's this?" Graham asked.

"Fraser River," Clayton replied.

"How are we going to get over it?"

"You'll see," Clayton responded with a crooked grin as he walked down the trail toward the water. Graham scrambled to keep up.

Robert Kinsley

Robert lay in bed and realized he had absolutely no reason, other than a complaining bladder, to get up. He had slept soundly and it seemed like maybe days had passed but there was no way to know without rising. He did an inventory. His skin felt swollen. His head throbbed and seemed stuffed with itchy, pink-fiberglass insulation.

The urge to urinate was overwhelming; he'd pee in the bed or get up, so he got up.

He thought of Raven and the way the candlelight illuminated and accented her womanly mysteries. It was, by far, his oddest sexual experience, even putting to shame the adventures he was most proud of, like diddling two cocaine-addled sisters in a limousine and screwing a fat virgin, whose name he didn't know, on the floor of the science lab during a high school dance.

Raven turned my head completely around.

Oddly, he wanted to see her again. The bizarre scene in her living room generated an addictive sexual intimacy. He wondered if he could find her place and what she'd say if he turned up her doorstep with flowers and hot paper cups of cardamom chai tea.

Sighing, he decided she'd slam the door in his face.

He drove his car to the nearest Tully's Coffee. Ordering a triple Sulawesis espresso Con Panna, he tried to pay with the American Express gold card, but it was declined. The Platinum World Points MasterCard was also declined and Robert began to panic.

Was his dad cutting him off?

Was the party at the W Hotel the final straw?

"They must not have posted my payment yet," he said, while smiling wanly and digging deeper into his wallet to produce an old Visa card.

"You'll want to get this renewed, it's almost expired," the smiling cashier pointed out.

She ran it through the machine and it was accepted. Robert breathed an internal sigh of relief and tried to look casual.

"Can I get some cash back on that?" he asked.

"Sorry, sir, that's against store policy," she said, while handing him back his card.

He rarely thought about money. His family was not filthy rich, but they were comfortable and had agreed to pay his tuition and living expenses while he went to college.

What would he do if they cancelled the cards and cut off his allowance? How did other people get money? Get a job, he supposed, but that would take time and employers didn't pay right away. Most jobs paid shit-wages anyway. When no one appeared to be looking, he sorted through the receipts in his wallet and did an inventory of his cash.

He wasn't completely broke—he had twenty-six dollars, but that wouldn't last long. This was not fair; his family shouldn't make him worry like this until he was at least twenty-four. There were payments due on the cell phone, the apartment, the rental car, and he had to have walking-around money for essentials like food and martinis.

It couldn't be avoided.

He'd have to call back home and see what was going on.

After finishing his tea, he sat in the car and, using his cell phone, made the call. His little sister answered.

"Hi, Sarah, it's Robert."

"Hey, Robbie, you are in bodacious trouble."

"Hello, Sarah. I love you too. What's going on around there?"

She lowered her voice. "Daddy is really pissed. He's been talking to the credit card companies all morning. He says he has to sell mutual funds to pay your bills. What's a mutual fund and what're you doing out there?"

"It must be identity theft."

"Don't try that one, they have your signatures. What's an escort service?"

"I'm not your health education teacher, look it up on the Internet. I have to go."

"No. Daddy wants to talk to you, he'll kill me if I don't—"

Her voice was cut off.

"Hello, Robert."

"Hi, Dad, it's Robbie."

"Don't *Robbie* me, Robert. What the hell do you think you're doing? I got a call from a very unpleasant man named Big Dick who told me if I did a chargeback on credit card charges for your lap dances, he'd send people out here and bust me up. This is not good. Have you completely gone crazy? I'm a patient man. I remember being young once too, but this is simply too much."

"I can explain—"

"Big Dick said he'd fuck your sister up the ass. Can you explain that? We were patient when you crashed the cars and got Polly Simpson pregnant. I wanted to shut you down a long time ago, but your mother talked me out of it. Now she's taking pills and sleeping all day. This simply has to stop."

"Dad, please. I learned a valuable lesson."

"That's what you said when you got arrested selling pot to the Little League kids. You've gone too far this time; we're washing our hands of you."

"I need money to survive out here, Dad."

"Do what I did. Get a job."

"I thought of that, Dad, and it sounds easy, but it's hard out in the world these days. All the good jobs are out-sourced to India, so what can I do? McJobs pay nothing."

"I cancelled all the cards except the Citibank card which has two thousand in available credit. When you max that one out, you're done."

"Don't do this, Dad."

"I should have done it a long time ago. The way I figure it, you owe this family over thirty-three thousand dollars and that does not include the college tuition bills. I don't think we'll be speaking again for a while, but I'll pay the cell phone bill so your mom can call you. Otherwise, we're all done, do you understand?"

"That's not fair."

"Thank you for pointing that out. Anything else?"

"No, I guess not."

His dad disconnected and Robert sat, staring at the dead phone.

Two thousand dollars.

If I watch my spending, it will hold me for a few weeks.

He really scared me for a minute—I thought I was in real trouble.

He looked through his wallet and found the Citibank card. Rubbing a smudge off the hologram, he kissed it.

Realizing he was hungry, he walked across the parking lot to the McDonalds and charged a Big Mac meal. Super-sized—with a strawberry sundae for dessert.

CHAPTER TEN

Willie and Maria

WILLIE, ON THE deck, wrapped cocoon-like in a bathrobe, smoked his pipe and pretended to write. From Maria's vantage point, it seemed as if he spent more time staring at the water than actually applying the pencil to paper.

Uncharacteristically idle, Maria felt at a loss; the breakfast dishes were clean and she'd swept the floor and made the bed. She could work on *her* book, but she felt restless and unmotivated.

"Hey, babe," she called out.

"Yes, dear?"

"I'm going to walk the loop and get some fresh air. Do you want to put on your shoes and come along?"

He never did, but she always asked anyway.

"No, you go ahead. I'm fine."

She blew him a kiss and laced up her boots. The trail to the outhouse was well-beaten, but, beyond and up the steep hill, it was overgrown. She clambered a hundred yards when, startled, she saw a bobcat carrying a limp rabbit in its jaws. It glanced at her incuriously before disappearing into the brush.

A red-tailed hawk soared overhead, scanning the ground. Breathing hard, she hiked through a sparse stand of wind-warped junipers to achieve the summit where she flopped on a granite boulder.

The view of the lake was breathtaking; the blue water stretched north and south as far as she could see. Across the water, pale blue smoke from a distant campfire threaded through the trees. A group of energetic Chickadees pecked among pine needles for bugs while a chipmunk evaluated her potential for providing loot. He eventually lost interest and devoted his attention to dismantling a pine cone.

As wind rustled the tree branches, she closed her eyes, pulled her hair away from her face and let the sun soak into her olive skin. It was probably her imagination, but she thought she could smell the faint odor of Willie's pipe tobacco carried on the breeze.

Looking over the water, she recited the names of the ridges she could remember.

Mount Clarke, Nursery and Granger Peaks.

A flotilla of kayakers, intermittently visible through the trees, paddled in and out of sight as they hugged the shoreline; their laughter hovered on the edge of audibility. The world was in balance. In harmony. She heard a branch break and turned. From behind, something big moved in the trees. A headache flared behind her eyes.

A litany of dangerous animals flashed through her mind. Wolves and cougars, for example, could be very aggressive. She carried mace; she searched through her pockets and made sure it was handy. A patch of huckleberries rustled and she saw the head of a small black bear poke through. He didn't stay long. When he disappeared, she took a deep breath and relaxed.

It was silly to be scared; it would be highly unlikely to be attacked, but it would be stupid to be unconscious and ignorant of the potential danger.

Releasing her grip on the mace, she pulled out a plastic bag of blanched almonds. She tossed one to the chipmunk.

"You'd protect me, wouldn't you?" she said.

In response, the chipmunk chittered and ran away.

She leaned back against a twisted stump and let her mind drift backwards.

It became overwhelming, so she bolted.

The wedding invitations were printed, the Pastor's and church's schedules were coordinated, people made flight plans, she picked out a dress and set an appointment for hair styling and nail work at the beauty salon. It was the florist who finally drove her over the edge. Roses or gladiolas for the buffet tables, an orchid or plumeria corsage, and what type of bouquet for the maid of honor?

Too damned many decisions.

And, what was she doing, marrying this old man?

The gap between their ages stretched like a crevice. Though in her early thirties, she often felt awkward—as if she was still a gawky teenager. He was in great shape for a man in his sixties, but his hands trembled and sometimes moisture appeared in the corners of his mouth. A premonition of drool, she was sure.

In a remote section of the UW parking lot, she pounded on the steering wheel of her Honda Accord and wailed. She was nearly spent—wiping away tears—when she turned her head and found his face in the side window.

She wiped away an oval of fog to frame his face. Inexplicably, he wore a wide, foolish grin.

The idea of starting the car and driving off flashed through her mind, but instead she hit the button to open the window.

"Dare I ask how you found me?" she said.

"The security guard recognized your car and called one of my grad students, who then called me. No big mystery. Are you nearly through with your hysterics?"

"No, I still want to break something…something like your big, dumb face. I feel like I'm losing control—my whole life is caught in a giant, cosmic sausage grinder. I could have married the French law student. At thirty, he already has a house on Mercer Island and a BMW convertible."

"Of course, dear, what was his name? I've forgotten."

"I'm trying to make a serious point about my life."

"And I'm trying to make a point too, dear. His name was Lorenzo and you've already forgotten it. Otherwise you would have said his name instead of calling him the French law student. Please correct me if I'm wrong."

She gripped the steering wheel so tightly that her knuckles turned skeletal.

"I suppose your so-called unassailable logic is supposed to rinse away my irrational fears and lead me a grand epiphany...illuminating the idyllic perfection our life together will be."

"I really love your creative vocabulary, but you shouldn't end your sentences with prepositions. It's uncouth, dear."

"Is that what I have to look forward to? A lifetime of you belittling my emotions and correcting my grammar?"

"Sometimes I'll get wrapped up in my work and ignore you completely, if that helps," the Professor said. "Shall I call the Pastor and tell him the crisis is over and the wedding is back on?"

"Someone called the Pastor?"

"His niece owns the flower shop, dear, did you forget that too? Are you getting senile?"

She wiped her eyes with the heels of her hands.

"Yes. I think my little breakdown is over, thanks."

"And dear?"

"Yes?"

"Screw the damned flowers. Who really cares?"

"The Pastor's niece cares a lot."

"Then let her pick the dog-blasted bridal bouquet, okay?"

Maria felt strange—detached from her body. Floating. As if seeing herself from other eyes. Eyes watching from deep within the green forest. There was a tidal pull at her blood.

She wondered if she was having a mini-stroke. It didn't hurt, but it felt odd. Somehow, she knew it...something in the woods, in a cold, calculating manner, watched, weighed and measured her.

She rotated her body and stared defiantly back.

Show yourself, ghosts.

Clayton Powell and Graham Wallace

The river flowed by swiftly and, to Graham, looked dangerous. They slowly traversed a treacherous bluff along the edge of the surging green torrent. Clayton settled on a boulder and took a drink of water from a plastic bottle. Graham was beyond exhaustion; he leaned on the rock and tried to scratch at an itch on his sweaty back. His feet felt flayed.

"All right, genius," Graham said. "What are we going to do now? Swim for it?"

"Ever been in a kayak?" Clayton said.

Kayak?

A quick vision of flipping over in a canoe flashed through Graham's mind. At summer camp when he was thirteen. The other kids had laughed and laughed.

How much is a kayak like a canoe? Too damned much.

"Where are we getting a kayak?" he said.

Clayton pointed. Upstream and up the hill, hidden by foliage, two bright-orange kayaks dangled from an overhanging limb.

"Now?" Graham asked.

"Yes, now," Clayton said.

They lowered the kayaks and sorted through the equipment stuffed inside. The kayaks had flat bottoms, but seemed way too narrow for stability.

"I don't see personal flotation devices," Graham commented.

"Life jackets are for pussies," Clayton replied with a thin smile.

For a few moments, Graham cursed Lili and J-C. They should have thought of this.

J-C had probably kayaked across the Atlantic with a pint of fresh water, dislocated shoulders and a spear gun. Surely he could have provided guidance for using a kayak in river rapids.

Graham grudgingly acknowledged that without J-C's training and the little conditioning they'd had time for, there was no way he'd have made it halfway to wherever they were now.

"I confess, I don't know anything about kayaks. Can you give me a few hints?"

"Don't make any sudden movements and keep the dry side up," Clayton said, as he shoved off and was captured by the swift current. Smoothly, he paddled on alternate sides. "See you on the other side," he called out over his shoulder.

Taking a deep breath, Graham held onto a branch and tried to get his balance. He faced upstream, which did not bode well for his prospects, but he shifted his weight and tried not to panic.

Other side. All I have to do is make it to the other side.

He released the branch and almost immediately capsized as the current dragged him backwards. Paddling furiously, he turned the nose of the kayak downstream and felt triumphant until an eddy grabbed the hull and very nearly tipped him over. The far shore was only fifty yards away, but it seemed like a mile. Traveling swiftly, Graham came around a bend and saw Clayton paddling urgently across the current.

Clayton stopped paddling so vigorously when he saw Graham watching. This created a tickle in Graham's mind. He couldn't hear anything over the rush of water, but he imagined something roaring downstream. Something deadly and perilous. All of the sudden, Graham simply knew there was a waterfall or something equally deadly coming up. He cursed himself for not realizing this earlier.

He dipped his port-side paddle deeply and hauled toward the far shore. All his aches and pains were forgotten as he put his shoulders into the effort. Ahead, Clayton beached his kayak on a stretch of gravelly bank and hauled it onto the shore. Only twenty yards away, Graham swept by and watched Clayton shout at him and point downstream.

Sure, warn me now, asshole.

He waved casually and rested until he was out of sight, then dug in deeply with the paddle. The channel narrowed and the water picked up speed.

Graham decided to bail out; he aimed toward a deadfall and managed to get the kayak wedged into its branches. Breathing heavily, he hauled himself out and crawled like a baby along the dead tree toward shore. Looking downstream, he tried to imagine what was waiting.

On shore, he irrationally grabbed a handful of gravel and rubbed his face in it. He took an inventory; he was wet, but still had his pack and his walking staffs and he was in one piece. He stood on a boulder and tried to see farther downstream, but it was hopeless—the trees were too tangled and the track of the river too convoluted. It could be his imagination, but he thought the river roared more loudly and that there seemed to be a roiling, misty void the water rushed into.

Probably a thousand foot drop onto jagged rocks. Rocks like teeth.

He noticed he still had gravel squeezed tightly in his fist. He threw it in the water and laughed.

Surviving is a real pleasure.

He struggled upstream through brambles and brush until he found Clayton heating a saucepan of soup over a butane stove. Hidden, Graham watched him test the soup and wondered what he was thinking.

"Did you make enough soup for two?" Graham asked loudly as he pushed through a last patch of sword ferns.

Clayton started and spilled soup on his lap.

"Make your own damned soup," he said, wiping at the mess.

"Of course," Graham replied.

Robert Kinsley

Bored, Robert clicked between channels on the TV—switching between *Jackass*, a new reality show called *MILFs*[6] *in Paradise* and a swimsuit competition called *Under the Veil, Babes in Baghdad*. There was a tap on the door and he glanced at his watch. The pizza guy had made

---

[6] Mothers I'd Like to Fondle, or something like that.

record time, only fifteen minutes. Robert grabbed his wallet and walked to the door.

Outside, it wasn't the pizza guy. Snake and Coho crowded into his entry, pushing him aside.

"What?" Robert sputtered.

"Get dressed, yuppie-boy. We're going on a mission," Coho said.

Snake used the remote to turn off the TV.

"Wear dark colors," he said.

They piled into Snake's old station wagon and Robert watched with longing as the pizza delivery guy passed them in the parking lot.

"Let's at least grab the pizza," he suggested.

"Shut up," Coho said.

They stopped at a Lowe's and Robert bought new boltcutters with his Visa card.

"You're going to want to get this card renewed soon. It expires the end of the month," the clerk said helpfully.

"Thanks, I know," Robert replied.

After driving up Aurora Avenue, they pulled into a service driveway hidden by ivy and fir trees on the north side of Woodland Park Zoo.

"What are we doing at the Zoo?" Robert asked.

Coho and Snake ignored him as they drove through a gate with the chain hanging loosely. Snake turned the car around and switched off the engine among a group of old cars. They pulled on ski masks.

"What's the mission?"

"You'll see," Coho hissed as he pulled over-stuffed duffle bags out of the backseat of the car.

They walked through another gate and entered a low concrete building. Inside, the lights were off, but the scene was intermittently illuminated with shrouded flashlights. Robert could see several people lined up against the wall—tied up and gagged and surrounded by eco-terrorists dressed in black. Recognizing Raven, Robert walked over to listen to her as she spoke to a group. She gestured at a collection of rifles leaning against the wall.

"Use your best guess as to weight; we want to use about twenty cubic centimeters of the drug per hundred pounds of animal. Be careful, you'll kill the animals if you use too much—make sure you don't hit the same animal twice."

Looking more closely, Robert recognized the rifles.

"Tranquilizer guns?" he said.

Raven laughed. "Not when they're filled with methamphetamine," she said. "Remember, we want to hit the grizzly bears first, then the African lions, and then the Bengal tigers. Robert, you make sure the cages are open—then stay out of the way. The animals are going to be very angry. We want to be out of here in ten minutes on my mark, is everyone ready?" She scanned the milling black-clad group. "Go," she said.

"What are we doing?" Robert asked.

"You're in charge of animal liberation. Crack open the padlocks with your boltcutters. There's no time to dawdle," she said, while pushing him toward the doorway.

Roaming the compound, Robert cut the locks on every gate he saw—and threw them open. He didn't see any animals, but he heard glass breaking and muffled shouting. With his arms quivering from the effort of the cutting, he was standing on a concrete walkway, resting, when a pair of activists sprinted by.

Robert recognized one of them.

"Hi, Pitbull," he said.

"Run, you idiot," Pitbull said.

Robert heard claws skittering on the concrete. Something massive came fast. Robert ran. He followed the pair as they dashed through a doorway. Peeking through the wire-reinforced glass, they watched a large, auburn-colored bear lope by. The bear looked at them as it passed and it could have been Robert's imagination, but its eyes seemed to be glowing red. It disappeared down the pathway. A single blast of a horn echoed.

"That's the signal," Pitbull said. "Time to clear out."

They did not see any more animals but something feral screamed in the distance. Robert jumped in the backseat of Coho's station wagon.

"Did you hear that?" Robert asked.

"Hit it," Snake said. Coho started the engine and they were soon off the zoo grounds. Snake drove south on Highway 99 while Coho diddled with the radio, scanning talk radio channels. They crossed the bridge to West Seattle and parked at the Alki Beach Park. They hiked up to a run-down house where the lights were blazing and TVs were blaring. A girl, dressed in military fatigues, pressed a jelly jar of wine into Robert's hand and kissed him on the cheek.

"Welcome, warrior," she said.

There was commotion in the living room.

"What channel?" someone shouted.

"Five," came the reply and soon several TVs were set to the same channel. Pushing through a crowd, Robert was able to see a screen.

"Shut up and listen," a woman bellowed. Robert recognized Raven's voice, but he couldn't see her.

A reporter stood by the Woodland Park Zoo sign. Police cars and ambulances were visible in the background. The reporter was speaking.

"Thank you, Chet. We're live at the Woodland Park Zoo where there are reports of animals loose on the street. We have not confirmed this, but it appears some children were killed at a day care. Do we have that footage, Chet? A parent had a video camera and we have some of the unedited video. I'm not sure what we'll see."

The jerky video had been taken through a car window. A large striped tiger carried a toddler. With a vigorous shake of its head, it ripped the child's arm off.

"We'd better not show any more," the reporter said as the scene changed back to the studio. "We have very disturbing video; we apologize for what you just saw. It appears that many large animals escaped—we have reports of multiple fatalities, including, as you saw, some children." There were sharp noises in the background. "I believe we're hearing gunfire. I'm told the police have shot a bear on the running trail at Green Lake. Folks, it's mayhem out here. We're trying to figure out what happened, but to repeat, large, predatory animals have escaped from the Woodland Park Zoo and we have reports of human fatalities. Let's see if we can get a report. Officer? Can we talk to you for a moment? Do you have any idea how the animals escaped?"

The police officer looked annoyed.

"Please step back," she said. "We're trying to get a handle on the situation and you're in the way. Please step beyond the yellow tape and let us figure things out."

"We have callers telling us about fatalities at a childcare facility. Can you confirm these reports?"

"Asshole," the officer said through gritted teeth.

"Obviously, emotions run high here at Woodland Park Zoo, where wild animals have escaped and are mauling children. Police advise you to stay away from the area. Highway 99 is closed and traffic is snarled. We're hearing gunfire and assume the police are shooting the animals, but this information is unconfirmed. Chet, back to you in the studio as our coverage of the Seattle Zoo Rampage continues."

"Thank you, Simon, we'll get back with you in a few minutes. After a commercial message, we have an interview with the Mayor's press secretary and interviews with eyewitnesses. Please stay with us for continuous coverage of the on-going tragedy at the Woodland Park Zoo."

Robert saw Raven push through the crowd toward the kitchen. He followed. She drank from a gallon jug of cheap burgundy. It dribbled down her chin. He leaned against the counter and accepted the jug. After taking a deep drink, he handed the jug back.

"Did you imagine something like this would happen?" he asked.

"Well, when you shoot large carnivores with methamphetamine—you hope something interesting comes of it."

"Too bad they're shooting the tigers."

"Wouldn't you prefer that to the living hell of a zoo with endless, stupid school kids staring at you all day? Nevermind that, you have to decide now. Do you want to go to Mexico or Canada?"

"Excuse me?"

"After this, we can't stay here. A group is flying to Puerto Vallarta and a group driving to Canada. Which do you prefer?"

"Where are you going?"

Raven sighed.

"I'm traveling on my own. Some friends offered me the use of a cabin up in British Columbia."

"Can I come with you?"

She rubbed her eyes so vigorously that they squeaked.

"I'm not sure that's a good idea."

"When are we leaving?"

After taking a final sip of wine, she looked around the filthy kitchen.

She looked deflated and beaten.

"Now," she said.

CHAPTER ELEVEN

Willie and Maria

WILLIE SAT ON the deck, nearly motionless. As Maria watched through the window, the wind teased his collar. His eyes were open and occasionally he puffed on his pipe, so she knew he was just deep in thought, rather than immersed in one of his spells. Leaning over the edge of the deck, she pulled in the rope to draw up their cache of cold beer. With the heel of her hand she banged a bottle against the deck rail. The top popped off; she handed the dripping bottle to Willie.

"I remember when you'd break one for every one you opened," Willie commented. "Damned near cut your hand off before you acquired the skill."

"Practice makes perfect," she said, while efficiently opening a bottle for herself.

She flopped down on a deckchair and held out her bottle in a toast.

"Cheers," she said.

"Back at you," he replied.

They looked over the lake and drank in comfortable silence.

"Up on the bluff, I felt like something was watching me." After a second's hesitation, Willie picked up his tablet and scribbled with hurried urgency as if he was afraid he'd forget something. "Not this again. You're not going to start writing down everything I say."

"No," Willie said, distracted.

"Liar. Did you hear me? Something watched me from the woods."

"I heard you. Of course you were being watched. Marmots, squirrels, jays, crows, they all have eyes and they watch. You probably had dozens of pairs of eyes all over you. Now that I think about it, maybe I'm jealous. You should be for me only." He cocked his head to listen. "Think that's the Chief?"

"I don't know. Why is the Chief coming?"

"I told you, dear. I'm going to go talk to the Bigfoot guy over in Dogwood Valley. Are you coming along?"

"No, I'll stay around here. Pick up some canned peaches in Harrison, will you?"

"Fine, but you stay away from my manuscript."

"I don't care a whit about Bigfoot and your insane crypto-zoological fantasy."

"Good," Willie said, grinning.

Maria waved from the deck as Willie and Chief Sam Joe motored out of sight. Once they were safely gone, she immediately tried different combinations on his briefcase—starting with variations on her birthday and their wedding date.

Chief Sam Joe's ex-wife's sister's boy, Hubert, dropped Willie off at the farm.

"A couple of hours will do it?" Hubert asked.

"Sure," Willie responded, looking up the gravel driveway at the house.

As he walked up the driveway, a group of dogs ran up and sniffed his legs. He stopped to look at a section of barbed wire fencing and compared it to the tabloid picture folded in his pocket. He shook his head, but continued up the driveway. On the porch, a tall man with gray hair pulled back into a pony tail stood waiting. He extended his hand.

"You're the man who wants to talk about Squatch?"

"That's me," replied Willie.

"Pleased to meetcha. I'm Albert." They sat on the porch and Albert poured lemonade from a large glass pitcher. "I hope you don't mind, the lemonade is from a can. Frozen. It's not as good as fresh-squeezed, but I'm too lazy to mess with real lemons anymore, so we make do with the fake stuff."

Willie sipped and put the glass down.

"I don't want to be rude, but speaking of fake stuff, I think this picture was taken by your fence down the driveway," Willie said, handing over the rumpled tabloid photograph.

Albert laughed heartily.

"Yes, of course," he said. "'Bigfoot stole my chickens'. They came up with that. I send the pictures—they write the stories and dream up the overheated headlines. Fifty dollars. Fifty U. S. dollars. That's good money around here for a half-hour of work. The tabloids buy a couple of pictures a year. I made up giant plywood feet. It's not as easy as you'd think to get a good imprint in the snow and I nearly froze my ass off. I earned my money that time, yes, sir, I did, eh? I can show you the plywood feet. They're rigged up so they can be worn like snow shoes. Perhaps you'd give 'em a spin?"

Willie shook his head, disappointed.

"I'm sorry I wasted your time," he said, rising.

The old man laughed and sipped from his lemonade. He wiped his mouth.

"Hey, don't get the wrong idea. Just because I take fake pictures of Bigfoot tracks don't mean there ain't no real Bigfoot, am I right, eh? That's logic, right?"

"Uh, pardon me?"

"Just sit for a minute; I want to show you something."

Albert walked into the house and Willie heard him rustling through papers. His muffled voice drifted from inside.

"Honey, where did you put—oh, here it is, I have it."

Reappearing, Albert dropped a bundle on Willie's lap; an object wrapped in a dirty towel.

"What's this?" Willie asked.

"Go ahead. Take a look, it won't bite you."

Willie unwrapped the towel and a gray lump fell on his lap. He picked it up and examined it…a small skull with a thick mass of bone over the eye sockets.

"Mutant?" he asked.

"No. Undeniable proof Bigfoot exists," Albert said.

Clayton Powell and Graham Wallace

Graham stretched his sodden socks on a branch in the sun to dry and examined the soles of his damaged feet. One of the blisters had popped and the skin was inflamed. He tried not to look at it while he taped it up tightly.

"You seem to have a lot of useful stuff in that pack. What else do you have?" Clayton asked.

"None of your damned business," Graham responded.

Clayton laughed. "Sure, have it your way."

"Do you mind giving me an idea where we are?"

"Fraser Plateau. You've been introduced to the Fraser River. I can estimate the GPS coordinates, if that is helpful. Otherwise, I think that's about it."

"What's down-river you forgot to warn me about?"

"You'll see soon enough. A bit of a gorge, that's all. We're headed that way as soon as you get off your ass. We have a ways to go before we stop for the night."

Graham sorted through his backpack and found a spare set of dry socks. He made a mental note to stop being upset about the astronomical cost of the pack.

"You packed spare socks—that's good," Clayton observed.

"You told me to, didn't you?" Graham said.

"No, I don't think so. I would have remembered that, I think."

Graham pulled on his boots and tried not to let pain show on his face. His left foot felt flayed and shredded.

"Shall we quit lollygagging and get rolling?" Graham said. "We don't have all day to laze around, am I right?"

"No, you're right about that," Clayton said, while shouldering his pack.

After hiking along the river a hundred yards, they came across the orange kayak still entangled in the deadfall.

"Lucky that snag was there, eh?" Clayton commented, speaking loudly against the white noise clamor of the river.

"Sure, I guess so," Graham said with artificial innocence.

Robert Kinsley

After waiting nearly an hour at the border crossing, Robert grew more and more nervous. He mopped his forehead with a shirt sleeve and chewed his fingernails.

"What do we say when we're crossing over?" he said.

"Don't say anything. I'll do the talking."

Finally, it was their turn.

"What is the purpose of your visit?" the customs officer asked, while typing their license plate number into his computer terminal.

"We're just going up for the weekend," Raven said.

"You're both U.S. citizens? Carrying any firearms or merchandise for sale? Any fresh produce?" he asked, without waiting for a reply.

"We're on our honeymoon," Robert said, leaning over Raven.

This got the officer's attention. "Honeymooners, eh? That's lovely. When were you married?"

Raven squeezed Robert's thigh—hard—to shut him up, but he spoke anyway.

"Last week, sir."

She glared at him with malice, and then produced a sweet smile before turning back to the officer.

"Congratulations. Big wedding?" the officer asked, looking over the battered old Ford. Raven moved her hand out of sight and hoped the officer did not notice she was not wearing a wedding ring.

"Thank you. No, not a big wedding, just a civil ceremony."

"Where are you headed?"

"We rented a cabin near Yale."

"Sylvester Stallone filmed the first Rambo movie near there. At Hope. Yale is beyond Hope. That's a local joke, get it? Beyond Hope. During the goldrush, Yale was the largest city north of San Francisco and west of Chicago, but now the population is something like seventeen. Literally. Did you know? Sylvester Stallone is little, bitty guy. Five-foot-eight."

"I didn't know all that," Raven said. "It's interesting."

Making a decision, the officer waved them on.

"Enjoy yourselves out there," he said.

Raven stewed, but did not speak for a few miles as they drove north on Highway 15.

"What was that about?"

"I was making small talk. No big deal."

"We were clear until you opened your mouth. Now he'll remember mismatched newlyweds in a piece of crap car. You're an idiot."

"Sorry."

"I don't want to hear it," she replied, through clenched jaws. "I'm going to drop you off when we get to Chilliwack. You can go your own way from there."

"No, you'll have to drag me out of the car. I won't leave. We need to stick together. We're on the run like Bonnie and Clyde."

"That worked out so well for them," Raven said.

"You don't want to invoke negative spiritual energy, am I right? The Goddess will watch over us, but we have to align our soul-fields for greater power in mutual oneness."

"You don't know what the hell you're talking about. The ways of the Goddess are complex and should not be mocked."

"But, I'm right. We should stay together."

"I'll think about it," she said.

Robert watched the scenery through the window as they passed through small towns and farms on Highway 1—the first section of the Trans-Canada Highway. Tension in the car increased as they approached the Chilliwack exits, but Raven maintained her cruise-control speed and soon they raced toward the dark mountains standing like fortress walls around the Fraser River Valley.

"You won't regret this decision," Robert said.

"I already do," Raven said.

CHAPTER TWELVE

Willie and Maria

SITTING ON THE deck with Willie's briefcase on her lap, she slowed down. Every few minutes she'd think of a new combination to try, but the lock—stubbornly—stayed closed. Soon she drifted and napped and dreamed of four-number combinations; this is how Willie found her after Chief Sam Joe dropped him off. When she sat up and stretched, she found Willie beside her—drinking a cup of coffee.

He smiled.

"Couldn't figure it out?"

"You're an evil man," Maria said. "I dreamed of something watching me again."

"That twas I," Willie said, leering.

"You know what I mean. Something out in the woods, not my dirty-minded old husband."

"Hormones. Listen, I have something to show you."

He took the briefcase and dropped the towel-wrapped bundle on her lap. "You're the doctor—tell me what this is."

"I have the degree, but I didn't do my residency. I wish you'd stop calling me Doctor."

"You have a PhD, so you earned the title. Are you going to look at this thing or not? I don't have all day to argue."

"Yes, you do."

"Just look at the thing."

"Is this something from the Bigfoot-guy? Did you find him?"

Willie, exasperated, pointed at the bundle and flapped his hands to urge her to hurry up.

"Just relax," she said, "I know this is going to be something stupid."

She unrolled the towel and hefted the small skull, examining it. She sat up in her chair and looked it over carefully.

"Cause of death due to impact on the head, perhaps a fall?" she said.

"What about the bone mass over the eyes? What do you make of that?"

"I'm getting there. Hold on and let me do my thing, okay?" Rotating the skull slowly in her hands, she stared at each section intently. "I'm not an anthropologist, but I'd say this is not Homo sapiens. This is some sort of offshoot of Homo erectus, not human like us. Or, it could just be a horrible deformity—that's the most likely explanation."

"What about the bone mass?"

"Okay, I'm looking at it," she said impatiently. "These holes are like channels. They loop back and forth. They seem too regular to be random. Where have I seen something similar? Sort of like coils of wire in an inductor, but that's dumb. I've never seen anything like this. It's fascinating."

"That's what I was trying to tell you. Right here in our hands, we have evidentiary proof of the existence of Bigfoot. This is big."

"No, we don't. Stop it. This is probably a skull from a deformed chimp or something equally obvious. Let's not fly off the handle with irrational speculation."

Something worked at the back of her mind. For some unknown reason, Willie knew Morse Code. She'd seen his FCC technician's card somewhere.

What if he converted dots and dashes into a binary code? Gotta be four digits. What about MA for Maria? If dashes were ones and dots were zeroes? That would be 1101.

She set the skull aside and picked up the briefcase. She thumbed in the number and was rewarded with a satisfying click. She released the latch and popped open the briefcase.

"Aha," she said.

"No, you don't," Willie complained, grabbing the case from her grasp. "You're evil and horrible...a diabolical woman."

While they wrestled with the briefcase, Maria flashed back to their wedding day.

The church was lit by candles which flickered when gusty wind, pouring through open doors and windows, swept through the hall. She wore a simple white dress and he was resplendent in a black tuxedo. The Pastor, tall and wide as a bear, grinned at them with white teeth gleaming.

"Professor, you may kiss your bride," he said.

After lifting her veil, Willie pressed his lips gently against hers. They walked away from the altar and she was hugged and kissed on the cheeks by her mother and father and the plump ladies of Willie's family. His deceased wife's sister, a huge black woman encased in a long dress like an overstuffed sausage, whispered in her ear.

"I know Victoria looks down on you and smiles. Take care of her man for her, dear."

This thought resonated in Maria's mind.

Victoria looks down on you...

Suddenly cold and shivering, Maria gazed back at the woods encircling the little cabin. She felt small against the massive wilderness.

Watching.

There was definitely something watching. Not with evil intent, but with piercing, penetrating curiosity. She felt pressure in her forehead.

Headache coming.

"Let's move inside," she said.

Clayton Powell and Graham Wallace

Graham leaned over his walking sticks and tried to take weight off his sore foot. Clayton pointed at the entangled kayak and leaned close to shout over the noise of the river.

"Those things are expensive. Go out there and haul it in."

Graham looked at the bobbing, throbbing deadfall stretched precariously into the surging current.

"You first," he said.

Clayton shrugged and, careful in his footing, began hiking further downriver.

After several hundred more yards, they passed a bend in the river and the channel narrowed. The water, roaring and white, raced over boulders and between steep walls of rock. Clayton leaned over and shouted into Graham's ear, but the cacophony was too much. Graham could not understand him.

In response, he gestured rudely at Clayton with his middle finger. Clayton grinned and continued picking his way downstream. The river widened and spread into a barely-moving, deep pool. The noise abated—just wind in the trees and a gentle babble of water flowing over smooth rocks.

A little more alert to his surroundings, Graham spotted two more kayaks hanging in the trees—along with bulky bundles wrapped in nets. He found the ropes and lowered the bundles.

"We're camping here for the night," Clayton said redundantly.

"No shit," Graham replied.

Soon they had a butane stove heating water. Clayton had tossed out a fishing line. After relieving himself in a clump of bushes, Graham, sipping a hot cup of tea, squatted beside Clayton who sat comfortably on an unfurled camp stool.

"I suppose you hoped to fish my body out of the water right about here," Graham commented, while waving away a buzzing cloud of mosquitoes.

"I don't know what you're talking about," Clayton said innocently, while flicking the end of his pole.

"You can lift my kilt and kiss my pimply white Scottish ass."

"I'm not sure I appreciate your attitude," Clayton said with a toothy grin. At that instant, the end of the pole jerked. "If you don't cheer up, I won't share my trout with you," he said, reeling in the line.

Within a half hour, Clayton had caught three moderately-large brook trout. He gutted them and rinsed them out in the water. Graham was determined not to eat any, but the filets sizzling over the stove with olive oil, garlic, leeks and freeze-dried green pepper smelled good—and he was starving. He held out his plate and Clayton scooped on large portions with the spatula. From deep within one of the bundles, Clayton produced a bottle of wine and a corkscrew. He made a toast.

"It's good to be alive."

"It's good to be rich," Graham commented wryly, while savoring the wine. "You really know how to *rough* it. What's the plan?"

"We'll drift downriver for the next fifty kilometers or so, then cut over cross-country at Leon Creek toward Bridge River."

"Are there any more adventures like...?" Graham said, gesturing upriver.

Clayton laughed. "No. There are several dodgy places where we'll have to portage or hike and pick up new kayaks, but nothing exciting like the chasm. I'll say," he said, pointing his wineglass at Graham, "that I'm mighty impressed you made it this far."

"Just lucky."

"Don't discount luck—it's every successful businessman's best friend." Clayton gestured with his plastic wine glass and toasted. "To calm waters and good fortune."

"Sure."

They leaned back and watched the water flow. Clayton removed a cigar from a glass tube. He wetted it with saliva, nipped off the end and lit it with the stove's butane flame.

"Got another of those?"

"You don't smoke. Besides, these are Cubanos and wasted on the unwashed."

Graham held out his hand impatiently. "Stop whining and hand one over. At least it will keep the bugs at bay."

"That's an expensive repellent."

"Shut the hell up, you can afford it."

Still grumbling, Clayton found one in the pack. After lighting up and coughing a little, Graham thought the cigar tasted like dung, but he did not give Clayton the pleasure of knowing that. It repelled the bugs—he could still hear them buzzing, but they did not hover directly in his face.

"Delicious," Graham said, inspecting the glowing coal.

"You're killing me," Clayton complained.

"Blow me," Graham replied.

With a battery-operated air pump, they inflated air mattresses and prepared for the impending night. Graham noticed Clayton had left the soiled frying pan near his bedding. Graham plunged it in the river and scrubbed out the left-over fish with a handful of sand.

"Nice try, jerk," he commented.

"I was going to get around to cleaning that," Clayton said, wounded.

"Sure you were…after a bear ate my head." Graham looked around, and then pulled his bedding into a protected area under the shadow of a large rock.

"What was wrong with where I put you? That was a very nice, comfortable spot."

"I don't know. You like it so much, you sleep there. I'll sleep over here."

"Paranoia is an unattractive quality for a prospective business partner."

"That's too damned bad," Graham replied.

After rummaging around in his backpack, Graham found JC's stash of mosquito netting—he set it up to drape over spidery plastic frames. Once the mosquitoes inside the netting had been killed, the rest weren't quite so maddening, though they still buzzed mercilessly. The noise filled Graham's head like tinnitus. Buried in his sleeping bag, Graham looked at the stars overhead. They were bright. The Milky Way splashed a glowing arc across the sky.

Graham admired the view for about five seconds before falling fast asleep.

Robert Kinsley

After a twist through Hope, the highway turned north. Robert asked if they could stop for lunch, but Raven ignored him. The Fraser River, a solid, steely green-gray under low clouds, twisted and churned. The highway followed its meandering course.

After a few miles, Raven slowed the car and traffic surged around them. She abruptly turned onto a sloppy track and the car sprayed mud while climbing a steep, overgrown roadway. At the end they found a mossy log cabin. A tree, with root ball exposed, leaned against one side. The cabin looked like it had been abandoned for years.

"Are you sure this is the place?" Robert asked.

"Yes, we're here," replied Raven.

The floorboards of the porch were spongy and rotten. The front door was secured with a large rusty padlock.

"What do we do now?" Robert asked.

"We didn't have time to dump the boltcutter. Get it and make yourself useful," Raven said.

"Oh yeah, sorry."

Robert cut through the lock and they pushed inside. The place was decorated with hanging cobwebs and scattered mouse turds. A branch protruded through a broken window.

"There is a motel back in Hope. Swiss Chalets," Robert said wistfully.

"Shut up and sweep the place while I make a run to the store for supplies," Raven said firmly, while dropping a bundle on the floor. "How much cash do you have?"

"Almost twenty dollars."

Raven sighed. "That's all? Fine, hand it over."

Sweating profusely, Robert wiped his forehead with a dirty cloth. He'd swept out both floors—the main room and the bedroom loft. Upstairs, there was no mattress, but there was a raised wooden platform for the bed. The roof seemed to be holding up okay—there were only a couple of damp areas where coffee cans were set out to catch drips. After cleaning, the cabin looked a lot better, but it was far from clean or comfortable. Through the dirty loft window, he could see patches of the river through the trees and hear traffic sweep by on the highway. Outside, he heard a loud grinding noise which startled him.

Standing on the porch, he watched a large dumptruck filled with firewood back up. The driver wore filthy overalls and a hat advertising the Kamloops Blazers.

"Raven's place?" the man asked.

Robert nodded.

The man climbed back in the cab and the truck bed groaned. Robert had to step back to avoid being hit by firewood cascading out the back. When the bed was empty, the driver came back and secured the rear flap.

"Are you going to stack it on the porch for us?" Robert asked.

"Stacking's extra. Stack it yourself."

With a blast of blue exhaust, the truck was soon gone, leaving Robert to despair over the size of the huge pile. Sighing, he started stacking the wood.

When Raven finally appeared, most of the wood was on the porch, but his stacking was precarious. Too tired to move, he watched as she hauled plastic bags and string-wrapped bundles from the car into the cabin.

After her last load, she stood in front of him with her arms akimbo.

"When you're done stacking, chop up some kindling and I'll get a fire going."

"Chop kindling with what?"

She stared at him for a moment like he was worthless, then walked around the back of the cabin. When she came back, she carried a rusty hatchet which she placed on the porch.

"Okay, I'll do it. Did you buy any beer?"

Her only answer was the cabin door slamming firmly.

Muttering, he continued stacking firewood.

It was completely dark when he finished working. He carried in a huge bundle of kindling and dropped it by the stove. He could smell something cooking. She'd bought Sterno and heated beef stew in its can. It smelled heavenly.

She sat in the dark on a cheap folding chair.

"We made the Vancouver Sun," she said, offering him the newspaper. "Seven people died."

She lit a trio of candles and started work on building a fire in the woodstove. Robert read the bold-print headline.

Zoo Massacre in Seattle

"Seven people?" he said.

"Five of them were little kids."

"What did you expect to happen when we let the animals out?"

"I don't know," she said. "Chaos and excitement. It didn't occur to me the Bengals would maul children."

"How do you feel?" Robert said.

"Sick. Sad for them."

"The kids were casualties of war. Collateral damage. Who cares about spoiled, urban snot-noses?"

"The Bengals, you idiot," she said. "They killed them all and one of the grizzlies too. It's a tragedy—those big cats are nobility."

"Well, we live to carry on the battle."

"They'll find us, it's just a matter of time. With seven people dead? They'll break heads and smash down doors until they find us."

"Until then, here we are in our own private paradise."

The fire caught the rumpled newspaper and soon the kindling crackled and popped. The stove door would not completely close and though most of the smoke went up the chimney, the cabin was soon filled with stray roiling tendrils. After idly scanning the news story, Robert handed back the paper.

"Who cares? I'm starving; let's have at that delicious stew. You never did say. Did you buy any beer?"

Raven was moody and quiet while serving him stew in a paper bowl and apple juice in a plastic cup. She set to work repairing the broken window with duct tape and cardboard. Upstairs, she unrolled a foam pad and made up the bed. With great satisfaction, he watched her arrange the pillows; the cabin was too small for anything but complete and total intimacy.

"Is there anything to read?" he asked.

She tossed down a tattered paperback. *Keeping the Rabble in Line* by Noam Chomsky.

He studied the cover. "I've tried to read his stuff, but it's too…"

She poked her head over the loft railing.

"Too what?" she asked in a threatening tone.

He fumbled for the right word.

"Advanced," he said.

She considered his response, and was mollified.

"There's a Harry Potter somewhere," she said. "J-K really understands the seductive power and mystique of the occult."

After a moment of searching through her things, she dropped the book down to him.

"Perfect," Robert said, while pulling his chair closer to the candles. "Would it be asking too much? We're out here together; can't we try regular sex instead of that no-touching stuff?"

She exhaled until she seemed completely deflated.

"I suppose," she said, while looking down at him from the loft, "if that's what you want. There'll be little else to do around here."

"Sweet," he said.

With a paper cup of water, he wet a sliver of soap and rubbed it on his cheeks.

"What are you doing?" she said.

"I thought I'd shave."

"It would be better if you let your beard grow out. Tomorrow, I'll drive up to Lillooet and get my hair cut and dyed blonde. They will get us, but we don't have to make it easy. Do you understand?"

"Yes," he replied, while rubbing the soap off his stubbly cheeks with a paper towel.

He climbed the stairs; she stood naked in the candlelight. He stared—frozen in surprise. She cupped her breasts and wiggled them.

"Boobs, and here's my thatch," she said, gesturing. "The usual, standard equipment for a woman. No big deal. Go ahead and look, I don't care."

He was excited by the way the flickering light and shadows danced on her body.

"Can you see well enough?" She moved closer to the candles. "All this has nothing to do with who I am as a person, but you're a guy and guys don't care. You're vile, simpleminded creatures. Sometimes I wish the great mother had not decided you are required. Perhaps in our next stage of evolution..."

She turned around and patted her butt. "Here's my ass. I have a pooper between my cheeks just like you, whoopee." She rotated until she faced him again. "You've seen it all before, okay? Enough? Look as much as you want. Do you want me to spread my legs? Are you into gynecology, female plumbing? Some guys are, some aren't. Freud had wise comments, but we can explore that later. Nipples. Pubic hair. Come closer. When you're done looking, you can screw me, but please make it quick. I'm really tired and want to get some sleep."

CHAPTER THIRTEEN

Willie and Maria

WILLIE PRETENDED TO work on his manuscript while watching Maria take digital photographs of the little skull. She arranged the gas lantern and took shot after shot; the flash filled the darkened cabin like lightning. Willie was silent, but Maria answered his unasked query.

"I'm thinking."

"Eventually you're going to have to stop thinking and explore some hypotheses…offer up speculation and present possible conclusions for consideration."

"No, I don't."

"Yes, you do," Willie insisted. "Oh, I almost forgot, there was something else." He fished around in his pants pocket and brought out an egg-shaped rock. It was small, like an oblong marble with a glassy gray texture. Maria examined it under the light.

"What is it?"

"The Bigfoot-guy said it's a diamond, but I don't know."

"I saw uncut diamonds when I visited Johannesburg. They looked a little like this, but it can't be. Something this big would be worth a lot of money. He wouldn't just give it away, right?"

"You need to stop asking questions and offer alternative solutions or give in and embrace the obvious fact that Bigfoot exists."

"No, I don't. I'm on vacation."

"Yes, you do."

"Why are you repeating yourself? You can be very annoying. What exactly did the guy say?"

Willie rubbed his forehead and put aside his manuscript.

"He admitted faking the tabloid photographs, but said there really are Sasquatches in the mountains, lots of them. They live underground and don't like to be bothered. He said they are stranger creatures than we can imagine—intelligent but savage. When you see them, you're supposed to give them the skull."

"When *I* see them? How did I get mixed up in this?"

"For some reason he wouldn't explain, I shouldn't see them. Maybe they don't like black men? I don't know."

"I don't like this. How did I get injected into this conversation? I won't have anything to do with this madness. Don't talk about me with delusional and dangerous people. What were you thinking?"

"He asked to see your picture, so I showed him."

Maria was furious. She glared at her husband.

"Don't grin at me. I'm very angry with you."

Willie held up his hands in defense.

"I know. Don't bite my head off."

"I don't understand how I came into the conversation."

"He knew about you. We've been coming up here for a few years—people talk. You're a beautiful woman…men notice. Married to an old black guy, that stirs up gossip. I don't know how he knew, but he did. It wasn't my doing."

Maria relented. "Okay, I'm sorry. It was bad enough when you started going crazy with all this Bigfoot nonsense, now I'm mixed in somehow. It makes me uncomfortable. Do your thing, but leave me out of it, please."

"I don't think it's all nonsense."

"Really, William? With all of our technology and all the people running around in the hills and no scientific evidence of an alternative hominid? If they existed, there would be plenty of proof by now. We can read license plates with satellite imagery and there are no photographs except clear fakes in cheap tabloids along with vampire-bat-boys and silver-skinned aliens? Hunters and trappers in these mountains for several hundred years and nobody hauled a Sasquatch home in the back of their pickup truck? No Bigfoot head mounted over a fireplace someplace with the elk and the caribou? This is beneath you, Willie. It's illogical and stupid."

"Have I told you how lovely you are when you're all riled up?"

"All those great arguments and you're still unconvinced?"

Willie sighed. "I think there's something out there and my curiosity is piqued. Let's not agonize over this any more tonight, okay? Let's get some sleep and see how things look in the morning."

Tired, Maria nodded. Later, buried under their down comforter, she listened to Willie breathe and the wind rustling the trees.

With her mind racing, she got up and stood on the deck—clutching her bathrobe to her chest and freezing in the chill. An owl hooted and a distant pack of coyotes whined. In the faint light of the halfmoon, rubbing her forehead, she watched a beaver swim by with a long branch gripped in its jaws. Shivering and cold to the bone, she went back to bed. It took a long time, but as she warmed up, she fell asleep.

Clayton Powell and Graham Wallace

Stiff and chilled, Graham woke to the sound and scent of sizzling sausages. After pissing, he poked through the ice chest and pulled out a plastic jug of orange juice. He squatted next to Clayton.

"It sure would be a pain if we had to carry all the supplies."

"Tell me about it," Clayton said. "The next drop is a long way off, so enjoy this fresh food while you can," he said, while breaking eggs into the frying pan. "Hey, use a cup. Don't drink out of the community juice jug. That's unsanitary."

Graham shook his head and took another deep draught.

"You don't need to have any if you're so damned fussy," he said, wiping his chin.

"Pig," Clayton replied, looking skeptically at the offered jug. With a sour expression, he wiped the top and drank.

After breakfast, Graham launched a kayak and practiced paddling around the pool. He rocked the craft and got a feel for the balance—it was pleasant once he felt in control. His muscles loosened and he was happy. On shore, he noticed Clayton had unpacked life jackets.

"*Now* we have life jackets?"

Clayton shrugged. "There's a bit of white water between here and there. Follow my lead and keep the bow pointed downstream—stay off the rocks and you'll be fine."

They repacked the camp site and pulled the bundle back up the tree.

"Someone will fly in and pick all this up?" Graham asked.

"Of course," Clayton said.

"Tell me, if I quit or don't make it," Graham said, while gesturing up the river at the rapids, "would you continue on your own?"

Clayton laughed. "Of course not. You're not the only nerd who wants my contract. I have several other companions on call. I'd miss your fine company, but I'd fly someone in and we'd carry on. No big deal."

"I don't think I believe you."

"Ah, shit, you caught me. But, I do have a couple of friends who love the back country. I'd make a call—someone would come out. It's not safe to be out here alone even if I do have a satellite phone, you know?"

"Yes, I do know," Graham said.

After stuffing their packs into the kayaks, they launched. They scraped bottom leaving the pool, but were able to float out into a deeper channel. Slave to the current, they alternately drifted through quiet areas and roller-coastered through swiftly-flowing sections. Graham was filled with sheer terror in the first few rough segments, but quickly got used to them.

He watched how Clayton navigated and tried to emulate the strategies as closely as possible. Between rapids, he found floating under the canopy of trees very pleasant. The peaceful harmony was intoxicating. The muscles of his shoulders burned, but there were easy stretches to rest and recover. The sun was high overhead when Clayton grounded his kayak and stood on the shore stretching his back and walking off the stiffness in his legs.

"That was cool," Graham said.

"I'm pleased you approve," Clayton said. After digging around in his pack, he brought out a bag of trail mix and venison jerky. "Lunchtime."

Graham found a rock in a patch of sunlight and sat down. Upstream, he noticed a doe and a pair of fawns watching cautiously before lowering their heads to drink. Graham didn't think Clayton would reach for his bow, but he did not point out the wildlife anyway, just in case.

Clayton stacked the kayaks and laced them together with rope.

"Portage?" Graham asked.

"Yep," was Clayton's reply.

They started off uphill with Clayton leading. Rope, tied to the bows of the kayaks, was slung over his shoulder. Graham brought up the rear and carried the stern (and heavier, he suspected) ends. Eventually the trail straightened and they followed the edge of a rocky ridgeline. The river churned and boiled below and at one point completely disappeared under a bridge of lava-like rock. They stopped to look.

"That would have been interesting to navigate in a kayak."

Clayton grinned in response.

After an hour of picking their way, they found themselves back on the shoreline. The water, deep and glowing green under the bright sky, flowed swiftly through high cliff walls. Clayton unlaced the kayaks.

"No nasty surprises?" Graham asked, while trying to see downriver as far as he could.

"No, we're good," Clayton replied.

He seemed to be paying closer attention to the straps on his life vest, so Graham did the same.

"Don't bullshit me, what's down there?"

"You'll see," Clayton said over his shoulder as he launched.

Robert Kinsley

When he woke, Robert's eyes were gummy and his mouth tasted foul. He urgently needed to urinate, so he pulled on his jeans. The cabin was cool, but he felt heat radiating from the woodstove. Overnight, Raven had stoked the fire. He leaned over the railing. She rolled out a small patch of carpet on the floor and knelt, naked and chanting, with her eyes closed, wearing wisps of dried moss arranged on her head. The carpet was embroidered with a large circle and faint symbols.

"What are you doing?"

"I'm asking the forest spirits for protection and guidance—permission to live in their domain. It wouldn't hurt to open your one-dimensional western plastic mind and honor the tree forces."

"Sure, soon as I take a piss, I'll jump right on that," Robert said. "Hey, I forgot. We can smoke a joint when I get back. I have organic pot. It will give us something to do."

Raven's shoulders slumped. She flopped back on her elbows with her legs splayed.

"You had Cannabis on you when we crossed the border? And you didn't tell me? Do you know what they would have done to us?"

"The Canucks don't care; it's practically legal up here."

"That doesn't mean they like us bringing it over the border. You are a completely clueless and stupid person."

"Well, someone woke up in a grumpy mood this morning, didn't she?"

He pulled on his tennis shoes and walked out back. The outhouse was functional after Raven chased the spiders out with a broom, but only barely, and Robert would not go in unless it was an absolute necessity. He picked a tree and let his urine flow. It steamed in the cool morning air and the relief was immense. He looked around—the trees were thick and the forest was dark. A bird chattered and he could hear something rustle in the underbrush.

When he came back inside, she had pulled on a pair of jeans, but was still topless. He came up behind her and grasped a breast in each hand. She was heating water for oatmeal in the leftover stew can.

"Did you mention something about some weed?" she said.

"I'll be right back."

Standing in the kitchen and leaning against the rough-cut counter, Robert lit the joint with the Sterno flame and, gentleman-like, offered her the first toke. Stirring the porridge, she took a deep, practiced drag. They alternated until nothing was left but a stub, which Robert dismantled and sprinkled on their breakfast.

"That's really good shit," she said.

"It's ironic, BC Bud, grown in a hothouse near Horseshoe Bay, exported with great risk to Seattle, then brought back by you and me into Canada."

This struck Raven as very funny. Leaning with her hands on her knees and her breasts jiggling, she hooted uproariously. After the laughing spell dissipated, she faced him, wrapped her arms around his shoulders and rubbed herself against him.

"You're the funniest," she said.

"Is there any brown sugar for the oatmeal?"

She tilted her head back and looked at him as if he'd had gone daft.

"Are you insane? Of course there is," she said.

They passed the spoon back and forth, sharing the oatmeal until it was gone. Robert scraped the last remnants from the tin can and gallantly offered it to her. She accepted it with her mouth wide open and her eyes clamped shut.

"Perfect," Robert said, rubbing his belly with satisfaction.

"Yes, completely lovely, eh, as the hockey-heads would say."

It was Robert's turn to laugh. "Hockey-heads."

"Take off your pants and join me on my prayer rug."

"Sure," Robert said, peeling.

She put the folding chair in the center of the rug and moved it around until she was happy with its position and alignment. Guiding, she sat him down.

"Okay, I'm going to sit on your lap and let you penetrate me, but I want you to try, very hard, not to move. Just join in me and try to feel the center of my female essence. Can you do that?"

"I can try."

The cheap chair creaked with the strain of their collective weights. Raven, with her knees up, settled on him and made small adjustments with her pelvis until they were completely locked together. Robert made every effort to remain still, not wanting to ruin the mood. After a few minutes, she tightened and released her vaginal muscles.

"Can you feel that?" she asked.

"Oh, yes, I certainly can," he replied, now worried about coming too soon.

"Good. We should talk about killing ourselves. I don't think we should let the Canadian Mounties take us alive."

"Do we need to talk about that right now?"

"Yes. I bought hemp rope. We should get it ready, one end for your neck and the other for mine. If we die at the same time, then there is a chance we'll be united in the spirit world. We can complete the magic circle of life—it doesn't have to be an ugly thing. Do you understand?"

Robert's penis throbbed involuntarily.

"Yes, I understand," he said.

"Then we have a pact?"

"Yes," he said, on the edge of orgasm.

"Then don't hold back, let your ejaculate flower."

"Uhhgn," he grunted, as his world dissolved into light.

After Raven cleaned herself she rejoined Robert on the prayer rug. He lay on his back—drowsy and drifting. She stroked the thin hair on his chest.

"That wasn't very nice of you to keep your dope a secret."

"I was always going to share. I forgot I had it, that's all. I'm sorry."

"I have a small confession."

"Okay, I'm ready. What is it?"

"Upstairs, I have a half-liter of Mescal. One-hundred-percent Agave."

Suddenly alert, Robert raised himself on an elbow and leaned over her.

"Hot damn, woman, go get it."

CHAPTER FOURTEEN

Willie and Maria

UNCHARACTERISTICALLY, WILLIE WAS up first; he started Maria's breakfast. She woke to the smell of frying ham. Her belly gurgled with hungry anticipation. She kissed the back of his neck before making the trek out back to the outhouse. On her return, Willie handed her a steaming cup of coffee. They sat around the breakfast table, quietly eating and looking out the windows. After washing the dishes, Willie tamped tobacco into his pipe. Wordlessly, Maria pointed toward the porch.

"I know," he said.

She was cold, so she layered a heavy jacket over a wool sweater before joining her husband outside.

"So?" Willie asked.

"So what?" she replied, feigning ignorance.

He puffed on his pipe and waited her out.

"I'll make a few notes and call a few friends when we're back in town. Maybe *Science* or *Nature* will pay a few dollars for a magazine article; we could certainly use the money. Are you happy now?"

"I'm always happy when I'm alone with you, my dear," he said.

"Don't try sweet-talk on me. I'm onto you and your smooth bullshit, Mister."

"Yes, dear."

They spent the morning working. Maria stared at the little skull and made sketches with questions and notes on its features. The teeth seemed to be filed into sharpened points; the effect was subtle, but eerie, once she noticed. The only similar thing she'd seen was in National Geographic photographs of a cannibal tribe in Borneo.

I hope the comparison is imaginary.

Growing tired of inactivity, she stood.

"I'm going for a walk, care to join me?"

"No, I'm fine here. Have fun," Willie replied while distractedly scratching his head with his pencil.

The diamond rested on papers stirred by the wind.

She kissed his forehead and laced up her boots.

"Back soon," she said.

At her customary resting place at the top of the ridge, she pulled the skull from her pocket. Rolling it around in her palms like a worry stone, she leaned back and stared into the sky. An airplane, probably destined for Calgary or Edmonton, reminded her that civilization was not so very far away. She took some small comfort in that as her thoughts drifted.

They honeymooned in Tahiti—spending ten leisurely days in a grotesquely expensive, but very pleasant thatch-roofed hut. The water, rolling in gentle waves under their feet, was hypnotic and soothing. Exhausted from the long flight and the time zone changes, they slept almost sixteen hours before making love for the first time in their soft, comfortable bed.

She knew full well that a woman did not marry an older man to get energetic sex; Maria didn't have high expectations of her husband. However, he was attentive and gentle. There were no orgasmic fireworks, but she appreciated his noble efforts.

They spent their days riding the ferry system with the locals and shopping at the markets and trinket stands. Renting a car on Bora Bora, they toured the island, making an obligatory stop at Bloody Mary's where they drank a few too many Daiquiris fortified with 151-proof rum. The owner's daughter insisted on driving them to the ferry terminal and made sure they boarded safely—waving from the shore before returning the rental car for them.

Willie spent nearly an entire day reviewing his finances with her. He was not a wealthy man, but had a few off-shore investments and enjoyed a reasonable salary from his tenured position at the University of Washington.

"Do we have to do this on our honeymoon?" Maria complained.

"At my age, tomorrow might be too late. It's important to me to know you're taken care of if anything happens. You need to be prepared to take over my extensive estate."

"I'll kill you myself if you keep up this morbid talk."

"Then I'm glad I left a letter with my lawyer. If anything mysterious happens to me, the police will be looking at you very, very carefully." He waved a warning finger in her face. "Don't be thinking you'll get away with anything."

"If I do kill you, it won't be at all mysterious. Please come to bed."

"You didn't disclose you are a nymphomaniac. All you care about is stealing my vital fluids. It's a sad thing."

Braless, she peeled off her blouse. "Come get milked dry, big boy."

Too soon, it was time to return to their real lives. As the plane banked and they got a final glimpse of the string of islands, Maria impulsively grabbed Willie's head and kissed it.

"The phrase *my true love* does not capture everything I feel for you," she whispered.

"The phrase *you made me lose my place* does not capture how irritated I am that you disturbed my reading," he replied with fake offense.

"Screw you, Mister," she said, punching him on the arm.

"It's never enough for you, is it? You always want more. Hussy."

"That's right, old man," she said, laughing at him.

Stiff, Maria realized she'd dozed off. She dabbed at a strand of drool with the back of her hand and looked back into the woods.

Something watched—she was absolutely sure of it. Filled with unexplained irritation, she stood up and stretched her back and legs, then ran. At first the trees were sparse and the terrain was easy—she rapidly dodged branches and leaped over roots.

Ahead, there was a shadow…something small and lithe flitting in the shadows. At first, she could only tell what it was not. It ran on two legs, unlike most everything else in the mountains, so it was not a deer or a coyote. As she went deeper into the woods, the going got worse.

She had to stop to climb over rotting logs and skirt thorny bushes. She'd nearly decided to stop and go back when, fifty yards away, she saw the creature looking back at her with its face fully illuminated in a swath of sunlight. It was not human. It slipped into shadow and was gone. Wiping sweat from her brow, she considered her options, and decided to press ahead.

Her progress slowed to walking speed. She'd lost track of time, but felt she'd been in the woods for at least an hour. Far ahead, there was the sound of a rockslide and a howl of pain. Vectoring on the sound she climbed a cliff and stood looking over a ravine. There was a splash of blood on the rubble—and a twisted figure writhing below. It was an unattractive humanoid creature and she had to admit it was absolutely true…it had very large feet.

A breeze carried a strong musky odor that made her eyes water. She plotted a strategy for getting down the rock face.

Clayton Powell and Graham Wallace

Rock walls towered over them and the water rumbled and raged in a steep channel. Graham could not estimate their speed, but it was fast, perhaps something greater than twenty miles per hour. After a mile of this, the cliffs opened up into a bowl and the river widened.

Clayton paddled furiously toward the right side. There was no obvious exit; the edges of the bowl were nearly vertical. Graham, determined not to be left behind, paddled as hard as he could. The water disappeared into a roiling and roaring mist. It was a waterfall, a huge one, and they were both going to die.

Graham's heart spasmed in his chest and his life unrolled before his clenched-shut eyes. Born in Seattle and died in British Columbia—with little to show for his effort in-between.

Bury whatever is left of my body anywhere. I don't care.

He forced his eyes open. There was no escape. Clayton still paddled as if the devil was after him, so Graham paddled furiously too. He recognized that he *was* furious—angry and disgusted. He didn't like heights and didn't want his life to end like this. He pushed everything out of his head and paddled until the kayak launched into space.

Instead of freefall, he crashed into Clayton's kayak and they seemed to be floating.

What the fuck?

The netting was sheer and nearly transparent—suspended between a boulder and a huge tree. His Tam o'Shanter fell away into the gorge.

"Whooh," Clayton shouted. "That was excellent."

Looking down, Graham watched the water drop into space; the termination pool was at least one hundred and twenty feet below them. The net dangled and stretched—the effect was surreal and Graham was still terrified, but also angry at being jerked around. Wrapped in the net like a spider's prey, he wriggled out of his kayak and tried to hit Clayton with his paddle, but the net swayed and he missed.

"Hey, man, knock it off," Clayton said.

With a scared look, Clayton dragged himself along the netting—pulling his kayak along behind. When he reached the tree the net was attached to, he dropped his kayak in a landing zone and climbed down a rope ladder. Following, Graham was slower.

Finally, with both feet on the ground, Graham gasped for breath and took inventory. He seemed to be alive. Noticing he still clutched the paddle, he swung from the hip like going for a home run but Clayton dodged.

"Stop it. What's your problem?" Clayton said with his voice raised against the cacophony of the waterfall. "The net is carbon nanotube; it wasn't going to break. That was just about the coolest thing ever. And the look on your face? Awesome. Class Three-plus white water, it doesn't get any better."

Stalking with the paddle, Graham shouted.

"I've had enough of your games. I'm going to kill you before you kill me."

Clayton hid behind a tree. Graham, tiring of the game and breathing in ragged gasps, dropped the paddle and sank to his knees.

Cautiously, Clayton came out from behind the tree.

"Are you done?"

"Hear me this one time, shit-bird. If there is one more of these…" Graham fumbled for the word while waving at the waterfall, "hazards, and you don't tell me everything before we get there, then I'm going to kill you and eat your fucking heart, do you understand? I'm not kidding. Got me on this?"

Clayton held his hands up. "You don't have to get all womanly and emotional."

Graham got to his feet. "You'd better agree or I swear on Hadrian's Wall, you're going over the side right now."

Defensive, Clayton raised his hands. "Yes, I agree. No more surprises. You earned it, no problem. Just chill and enjoy the rush. Can't you feel it? It's great to be alive."

"Go fuck yourself. Not only did you nearly kill me, but you made me lose my hat," Graham said bitterly. He flopped on a log and watched the frail netting drift in the breeze over the water. If he'd missed the channel and had gone over the falls to the left of the boulder, he'd be soggy hamburger. The life jacket would make it easy to retrieve his lifeless body—perhaps that was the point.

After rooting through his pack, Clayton handed Graham a bottle of Scottish ale.

"Take it, it's a peace offering. You deserve it. Imported from Glasgow, I thought you might like it."

Graham grabbed it rudely and stared at the top. Clayton offered an opener, but Graham waved it away. He pulled his Leatherman multitool from a pocket in his Utilikilt and found the bottle opener. Flipping the top into the pine needles, he tipped the bottle back and lustily guzzled the dark, cool beer.

With exaggerated politeness, Clayton offered a cigar and a flame to light it. Smoking, Graham leaned his back against the log. His muscles ached and he was still deeply pissed off, but, on reflection, had to admit, as the remnants of sheer terror receded, surviving what had seemed like certain death *was* pretty cool.

Robert Kinsley

The Mescal burned all the way down his throat and created a solar heat in his belly. With the creaking woodstove stoked, they sat cross-legged—naked and sweating—on the swath of dirty carpet and handed the bottle back and forth. She asked questions about Harvard and he told her everything he could remember. He'd spent most of the time either partying or recovering from partying, so his exciting tales were a little repetitive and tedious, but smoke and drink lowered the threshold of boredom. They giggled for almost two hours.

When the bottle was half empty, Raven set it aside. "Let's save some for tomorrow," she suggested. Then, in spite of Robert's jokes, her mood turned dark.

"I can't get the images out of my head. The majestic Bengal tigers, murdered coldly by the Fascist pig-people. Now they'll kill us and we'll be dead too."

"I thought we're going to kill ourselves."

Raven was instantly angry. "It wouldn't be necessary if they'd just leave us alone. We should be folk heroes, martyrs. Maybe, someday, we'll have our faces on t-shirts and there will be lots of websites in our memory, but that does us no good up here, now."

"We're a long way from anywhere. Maybe they won't find us."

"They have Snake and Snake knows about this cabin. He may hold out for a while against the gulag-masters, but he'll tell them. The plastic pig-people have no souls; they'll hurt him until he tells. I know how they work—the machine will work relentlessly against us until we're crushed. We have to be ready; do you know how to tie a slipknot?"

She retrieved the hemp rope and laid the coil between them.

"Hemp holds the spirit of the Green Man in every strand. Let's pray over it."

She closed her eyes and chanted.

From the soul of the weed
From the soil and the seed
From the fire and the passion
The hemp's spirit is freed.

She cut the rope to length and fashioned the slip knots. She threw one end over the main beam of the cabin's roof and the ends dangled. She sat back down and stared at the loops oscillating in the air.

"Okay, you get it? When the war machine comes up the driveway, we don't hesitate or wait. We run, meet here and put the loops around our necks. They say a man's penis gets erect when he hangs. You'd like to die that way, wouldn't you? In me? Joined with me?"

He thought the whole thing sounded great.

Except for the stupid, pointless dying part of the plan.

He nodded.

"Yes, that sounds fabulous," he said, trying to visualize how the scene would look on a t-shirt. "Why can't we just keep running? I don't have any cash, but my credit card is still good. We could go to Alaska; no one would ever find us up there."

She sighed. "The car will never make it, the clutch is slipping. If I nurse it, it will go another thousand miles, that's it."

"Isn't that enough? Anchorage can't be that far."

She shook her head sadly. "One day you'll have to get a map and actually look. Until then, just trust me, we are where we are going to be."

"I have enough credit limit left on credit card to fix the clutch."

"You can't use your credit card; they'll be onto us in a few hours. Face it, we're home," she said. "I'm going to brew tea, would you like a cup?"

"It's not made of hemp, is it?"

"No, silly, cheap black tea is all we can afford. We have honey to sweeten it."

"Okay."

She returned to the rug and handed him a foam cup.

"I really prefer to be naked, will it bother you? With the stove stoked up, it's warm enough."

"I think I can handle it," he replied.

CHAPTER FIFTEEN

Maria

AS SHE DESCENDED, the scent grew stronger; it was like tear gas (her mind flashed back to a campus protest and a disheveled group of anti-war agitators being hauled off by the police. All she had wanted to do was get to her advanced anatomy class, but instead she'd gotten a diluted lungful of pepper spray) and her eyes were weeping and red.

She tried to avoid rubbing her eyes, which would only make the irritation worse. At the bottom of the cliff, the creature's leg was broken—he was trapped by scattered stones. He struggled feebly. It *was* a 'he'; his penis flopped as he thrashed about. His head wound bled on the talus. His hairy feet were leathery on the bottom and she studied his odd bulging forehead. He looked disturbingly like a werewolf from an absurd cheap movie. She reached out to touch his forehead, but he growled and snapped at her viciously with yellow teeth.

"Okay, have it your way," she muttered. Looking around, she found a rock to sit on. "Maybe you'll behave yourself once you're unconscious."

She watched the creature writhe for a few minutes. Finally, it gave up. Somehow, she could tell the fight was gone and it would accept her help. Grunting with exertion, she moved rocks around and freed the creature. She wrapped a bandana around its head to staunch the bleeding and made a crude splint for its leg with sticks and the elastic scrunchies she used to tie back her long hair.

Picking him up, she was surprised at how light he was; it was as if he was hollow. She looked up the rock face and began mapping out a path, but the creature hissed in complaint until she got the message he wanted to go deeper in the woods. The image of a cave hovered at the edge of her mind; it was crazy, but as she put her head close to his, this image seemed more vivid.

This is nuts—my overheated imagination is making me stupid.

She had a vision of Willie's face—his response if she told him she was getting telepathic images from an adolescent Bigfoot. He'd laugh and she'd never live it down.

If we find a cave like the one pictured in my mind, I'm going to scream and scream and never stop.

She shook her head to dispel the ludicrous notion.

Guiding her with hisses of disapproval and gurgles indicating agreement, she entered the forest. There was a trail of sorts, convoluted and faint, but much better than struggling through the wild terrain. She thought for one moment, while resting, that the creature might try to bite her again, but she gave it a stern look and visualized smacking it on its bandaged head, and the thought went away.

That settles it. Officially, clinically, undeniably—I'm insane.

She really felt crazy when, after weaving through a tangle of deadfall trees, they found the cave entrance. It was exactly as she'd visualized it. She tried to rationalize.

Bigfoot would have to live in a cave to avoid discovery, right? And caves, they are just holes in the ground. How many variations can there be? This must be my deluded subconscious mind running in overdrive.

Still, the way the trees framed the scene and the ragged shape of the cave's mouth left her feeling disoriented and detached. It could not be real, but there it was—undeniably before her eyes.

The opening was larger than it first appeared; she had no trouble entering while standing upright. The foul odor was nauseating. She thought she might vomit, but continued inside. It was not completely dark—the walls glowed with a faint white light, like the radioactive glow of watch hands. Also, it was warm and the air was humid. After a few yards of following a twisting and well-worn pathway, the cave opened into a huge room. At first, as her eyes adjusted to the dim light, it seemed empty. But there was movement, everywhere movement.

The creature wriggled in her arms and she gently put him down. She expected some sort of sign of gratitude, but he crawled away without even a glance over his shoulder. She stood and looked around. It must be imagination, but she felt like her mind was under attack, as if being probed by hundreds of filthy prodding fingers. Ugly and rude fingers, stirring a headache and stabbing at her brain to make it worse.

"Stop it," she shouted.

The sound echoed in the chamber and the prodding eased, but immediately started again. She became aware that someone was talking—a small, dark figure who approached from a gloomy corner. The garble began to make sense.

"A friend, finally a friend to gossip with, to talk to, with fresh news from the outside. What an unexpected pleasure. Of course, we knew you were coming but we did not know when, this year, last year, next year, some year, yes, of course, we knew."

It was a man, small and thin in frame, but with normal-sized dirty feet. He laughed as he caught her checking.

"It's just me, Elmer, welcoming you to the tribe. Come and sit and talk we shall, you and I."

His hair was tangled in dreadlocks and he wore a scraggly beard and the remnants of a rotting pair of blue jeans. Pulling her hand, he led her toward a corner of the chamber.

Clayton Powell and Graham Wallace

After a rest, they unloaded the kayaks and put on their packs. Clayton pushed his kayak to the edge and launched it into space. Grunting with exertion, Graham did the same and watched the craft rotate through the air and splashdown far below.

They followed a wisp of trail and found a rope ladder anchored to the top section of cliff. Without hesitation, Clayton started climbing and Graham followed. Idly, Graham noticed the height did not seem to bother him as much.

After my near-death experiences, perhaps my fear of heights is cured?

At the bottom, the water spread out and slowed, collecting in a series of deep pools that cascaded cheerfully over large rocks. Trapped by eddies, the kayaks bobbed and drifted in circles. Using the paddles, they snagged the kayaks and pulled them to shore. Graham got a glimpse of something colorful: his tam was caught on a deadfall limb on the other side.

He grabbed Clayton's shoulder and pointed.

"Great, you found your hat."

"Go out there and get it," Graham said.

"Get it yourself," Clayton replied.

Graham raised his paddle threateningly.

"Don't fuck with me, Powell."

"All right. Don't be pre-menstrual. I'll do it."

While Graham sat and watched, Clayton took off his jacket, shoes and socks and picked his way across the rocks. There was a section where he had to swim; he jumped in and splashed across a deep channel. From rocks on the other side, he was able to reach out and get the hat; he stood and waved it in the air in victory. He was downstream and had to swim farther coming back, but eventually, soggy and dripping, he hiked back from far downriver.

With a flourish, he handed it over.

"Your hat, sir," he said.

Graham wrung it out and put it on a rock to dry.

"Not too much further before we camp for the night," Clayton said.

"We'll rest here a while first," Graham said in a tone that allowed no argument.

"Good idea," Clayton replied, while mopping at his wet hair with a bandana.

They found a spot where a log lay against a boulder. By using the lifejackets as cushions for their butts, it made for comfortable seating.

"Got any more of those cigars?" Graham asked.

"One left," came the reply.

"Hand it over," Graham said, gesturing.

"It's my last one."

"Then break it in half."

"It would be a sacrilege to break a beautiful Cuban Romeo y Julieta cigar in half."

"Then hand it over whole, jerk-off."

With a look of disgust, Clayton produced a big clasp knife, hacked the cigar in half and offered up a piece.

"You cut, I choose," Graham said, pointing at the other half.

"Okay," Clayton said. "I liked you better when you were hopeless."

"Too damned bad," Graham said, puffing smoke. "Let's talk about the rest of the day. What other death-traps are set for me?"

"I swear. There's one potentially tricky part later in our trip. Otherwise, its smooth sailing."

"Tricky? I don't like the sound of that. What's the deal?"

"I'll tell you, don't worry. When we get there I'll tell you everything. For now, let's relax and enjoy the rest of the day."

It was hard to get their tired muscles working again after their break, but, as the sun descended into the trees and the air took on a chill, they packed everything and prepared to move out. Graham pulled on his nearly-dry Tam o'Shanter and they continued downstream, alternating with jumping between rocks of the shoreline and short jaunts through the woods that hugged the river, all the while hauling their kayaks.

The campsite was located in a pebbly bend in the river under a canopy of trees. Graham strolled around the area looking for anything dangerous, but it seemed safe, even idyllic.

Perfect.

A breeze kept the bugs to a minimum, which they appreciated. The large camp bundle, suspended in a tree, included firewood and kindling. With river rocks, Clayton made a fire ring and soon had a blaze going. By the time dinner was ready, bottles of beer, cooling in the river, had attained a perfect temperature. All was at peace in the world.

They leaned back against their packs and smoked cigars from a refreshed stash. Afterward, Graham grabbed a camp shovel and found a place in the woods to lift his kilt and enjoy a leisurely voiding of his bowels. He buried his waste and returned to the campsite.

Laying on their air mattresses and looking at the stars through the trees, they talked about work. While Clayton pontificated about a corporate take-over, consummated over a marathon game of poker, Graham drifted into sleep.

Clayton's babble mixed with the soothing sound of the river flowing by.

Robert Kinsley

On the hard bed, they screwed before falling asleep. Again, in the morning, Raven willingly and passively spread her legs, but she did not otherwise participate. Robert enjoyed the release, but was already bored with her.

Besides, she smelled rank. The cabin was cozy enough, but there were no facilities for bathing. Except for a few visits to his favorite tree to piss, he lay in bed until nearly noon reading the Harry Potter book. Raven pulled on her jeans and a t-shirt and went to the store for newspapers.

"Another kid died," she announced when she came back. "And now, we're officially international eco-terrorists."

"Cool, I like the sound of that."

"It's not good. They can use international provisions of the Patriot Act against us. Torture. Detainment. Unlimited power of subpoena. Medical histories and library record searches. I should never have let Coho spraypaint those slogans; the pictures are in the newspaper. The cops think we're part of the Animal Liberation Front and they've caught everyone but us. We're next, I can feel it. They are getting closer."

"I thought you preferred to be naked," Robert said.

She gave him a look of contempt as she peeled off her shirt.

"Throw another log on the fire," she said.

Watching her putter around the house, Robert considered asking her for sex. It had only been a few hours, but he felt a tickle of desire. His member was partially swollen.

"Come over here and take a look at this," he suggested.

She walked over. "Look at what?"

"My manhood."

"You're a freaking idiot," she said, turning back to her work in the kitchen.

He finished rereading the comics in the newspaper while she worked in the kitchen. After a couple of hours of labor, she stood before him.

"I met a friend of a friend when I went to town..." she said.

"You know people around here?" he asked.

"I visited up here a lot. Most of my family is Canadian," she said, impatiently. "Didn't you know?"

"No."

She shook her head in despair. "Your ignorance is beside the point I'm trying to make. I met someone in town, and he gave me a gift."

"Okay, that's nice. I still can't get over the idea you're Canadian."

"I'm a U.S. citizen. Please try to focus; I'm trying to tell you something."

"Okay."

"I have mushrooms and I made an elixir. Mescal and mushrooms. It will connect us with the spirit world and maybe, just maybe, prepare us for our journey. I really hope the transition will advance your awareness and move you around the grand cosmic wheel. You desperately need more depth and clarity. You can't see beyond the material world into the majestic passion play of eternal soul-space."

"Hell, yes, let's get high and explore space. The eternal holy space between your thighs."

Raven sighed. "Hate is a trap, but it wouldn't be wasted on you. I don't know why the Goddess put us together. A penance I suppose. I can only trust there is a reason beyond my comprehension." She handed him a cup. "It will taste bad. Drink it slowly and don't vomit it back up. It won't work if you can't keep it down."

"I have experience with strong drink—one of my buddies at school had a pint of Everclear—pure medical-grade grain alcohol. That stuff will knock you on your ass and put you in touch with the spirit world, take my word for it."

He took the warm drink and tossed it back.

Choking, he said, "Oh, my God, that's gross. Is it made from lizard guts and warthog afterbirth? I'm going to be sick."

"I warned you. Hold that down or there is no more intercourse." She sipped her drink and tried not to grimace, but she couldn't help it. "You're right, it tastes like offal, but we're not drinking it for the taste." She sipped the mixture until it was gone.

"My guts feel like they're rupturing," Robert complained. "You poisoned me."

"Please shut up."

"I'm going to be sick. My guts are churning. You killed me and I'm dying."

"Try to relax. You're not going to die unless you really piss me off and I kill you," she said, while rubbing her own swollen belly. "I hate the way you talk. Please suffer in silence."

Robert writhed on the patch of carpet. His body temperature oscillated—at first he was very cold, then, from something that felt like flaming coals deep in his gut, he was hot, burning, inflamed.

"I can't hold it in. I'm going to throw up."

"No, you're not. Hold on, we're almost there."

CHAPTER SIXTEEN

Maria

THE MAN'S CORNER was padded with fur; he arranged things to make a spot for her to sit. The stench was intense—her eyes would not stop watering and her headache built on itself from her frontal lobe and the brain stem, both throbbing.

"Of course, you're uncomfortable," Elmer said. "Let me see what I can do."

He stood outside of his corner, bellowing shrilly and beating on a drum. The echoing noise in the cavern was painful to Maria's ears.

How will this help?

However, when he was done, her headache eased. She felt more normal. The effect was mysterious—she'd never had a headache that came and went so quickly or felt so intense. Her mind worked on the implications.

What is going on?

"Let me know when they start coming back at you. They don't like the drum and I'll beat on it again if you want. Come to think of it, I don't like the drum either. This place is like a cathedral—the sound reflects and can drive a man mad. Please tell me of the outside. Who is president now? What wars are brewing and what wars are subsiding? Disease, floods, hurricanes, earthquakes and mass murder? You know what I miss? Pepsi Cola, did you bring any? Sometimes I crave it so much that I think I'll go berserk. A cold soda with ice would be so heavenly, that's what I miss the most, isn't that strange? I'm talking too much, I'll shut up and let you speak, please forgive me, it's been years, what year is it outside? I lost track. Please, go ahead; you must think I'm very rude."

"Are you a prisoner?"

The man laughed. "Oh, what you must think, very bizarre, all this, am I right? No, I am not a prisoner, not at all, I can leave anytime, but they wouldn't let me return if I did, not that I care that much about these horrible, god-forsaken creatures. They are disgusting, but fascinating all the same, alien and odd. Why do I stay? This is my place now, here with them, but one day, I'll go get myself a cold Pepsi Cola, with the bubbles, right? And ice, in a big cup. You can still get this, right? Please tell me, that's one thing I really miss, I'd take an RC Cola, even a Coca Cola, but that's kind of sour, I really like the sweet ones, a giant Pepsi with a straw, I'd trade a limb for one right now. Can you still get them?"

"Yes, no problem, you can get a Pepsi as big as you want. All I have in my bag is a bottle of water, but you're welcome to it."

"Water? No, we have plenty of water here. Where are my manners? Are you hungry? There is plenty of food if you can stand the taste, mainly grubs and bone marrow made into a paste and dried, nasty stuff, but filling and nutritious. They eat each other, did I say that? The children they don't want, when they are about six, they kill them and eat them. It seems cruel, but that's their way, one-hundred-and-twenty-seven, that's all the adults they allow. I don't know why that many, no more and no less, but that's the way they do it. They hate the way we reproduce without limit; it offends them and makes them angry. We shouldn't judge their way, it works for them, they are an ancient race, from before the ice cycles, so who are we to criticize? The way we wage war and manipulate the environment, they think of us a pure undisciplined evil on the face of the earth, that's the truth. But, I'm talking too much again, I apologize. Speak, I really want to hear about things. Please speak."

"Um, where should I begin? The war with Saudi Arabia did not go well for us. The Islamic government turned out to be worse than the royal families and the puppet government we installed lasted only a year. Seven hundred thousand people died in India and Southeast Asia when the tectonic plate shifted, another hundred thousand in the Philippines when the tsunami wiped out Manila. There must be good news. We partnered with South Korea and put a colony on Mars. More and more, robots are everywhere, helping the disabled and doing our physical labor. Global warming led to great wheat fields in Siberia and northern Canada. Do you want good news or bad news? The Iraqi fundamentalists exploded a bomb in Baghdad; there is no more Baghdad, just radioactive glass, a huge patch in the desert twenty miles across. Is this what you want?"

"Yes, thank you, who is the president? Clinton is still the leader of the UN? Is there still a UN? Tiger is still playing golf? I don't care, all the details, whatever you can think of, I'm starving for it, did I ask, are you hungry, thirsty, do you need to relieve yourself, are you warm, cold, do you need a blanket? Should I beat the drum? I must remember my manners, I really must. Now I'll stop, you can talk, please. Don't allow me to interrupt. Go ahead."

"I need to know some things from you. I don't understand this place. How did you get here? Tell me about these creatures."

"Ah, yes, of course, you'd be curious, I remember when I first found them…I was lost in the woods and the snows came all of a sudden. It was only October, global warming my ass, not that year, the winter came on hard and fast. Did anyone look for me? Probably, but it was hopeless, I'll bet a lot of people died in the wild that year. Where was I? Yes, I found the cave and they didn't want me around, but they didn't turn me out either. I found this corner and I stayed and I watched them and I learned their ways. I don't like them, they are cruel, did I say that already? They worship old Gods and eat their young—it makes me sick to say it, but we shouldn't judge them on our terms, these are a different race, much older than we are, many tens of thousands of years old, living underground around thermal vents, volcanic vents, you know? Warm places underground. That's where they live, how many colonies? I don't know, not many, maybe ten or twenty? Who can say? Always one-hundred-and-twenty-seven adults per colony, that I know. Why one-hundred-and-twenty-seven? I can't say, but they worship old gods and one-hundred-and-twenty-seven is the number. What can I tell you? They adapted to the world and all of its hazards. We're the endangered species, not them."

"Why have they not been found?"

"That's not so hard—they live underground. They watch us and they know us. They even know when the satellites are overhead. They know about cameras and thermal sensors, and sometimes when a hiker or hunter is found dead in the woods? The hiker saw something and was killed. They eat their dead, even the bones, so there is no evidence left behind. There's so few of them, they have been hiding from us for thousands of years, it's not so hard."

"They didn't kill me."

"Oh, you don't understand that? That's easy, of course, they wouldn't kill you. I'll explain—no problem. Did I ask, are you hungry? It tastes very bad, but it's food. It will keep you alive and healthy, though it's terrible. Don't think about where it came from. I never get used to it, but I eat it. It's all we have, can I get you some? Are you thirsty?"

Clayton Powell and Graham Wallace

In the morning, Graham got up first and stoked up the fire. Dry splits of firewood, ignited by hot coals, were soon blazing. Clayton stretched and yawned.

"You fell asleep, where did I leave off? I had a pair of threes, but I was getting a sense Oliver was bluffing, he had nothing, so I…"

"I don't care about your poker game. Let's talk about the plan for the day. Where are we going and what will we encounter? What nasty surprises are coming? I'm sick of your games."

Clayton unzipped his sleeping bag and sat up, scratching his groin.

"Don't be tedious; I already told you, everything is smooth and easy for a few days. We'll kayak some and hike some. No big deal, I promise. I haven't lied to you yet, have I?"

"No, no lies, but you have a habit of leaving out things that might get me killed. We're done with that, read me?"

"Yes, I understand. Can we drop the subject? Let's call a truce and eat breakfast. It looks like we're going to be business partners—you'll get your precious contract, all right? Let's relax and enjoy ourselves."

"Just remember, I'm watching you."

"Hey, I have beer. How about a breakfast beer, on me. Okay, partner?"

Graham looked at Clayton and considered.

"Okay," he said.

They broke camp about ten o'clock with the direct sunlight streaming over the treeline. Starting out, they did a portage for a mile or so over mostly flat terrain. The river was wide and shallow; there were too many shallow areas to bother with the kayaks. Graham was tired of walking through swampy bogs and was happy when they reached a spot suitable for floating the kayaks. The flow of water was more concentrated as the river wound through a small canyon.

"What's coming up?" Graham asked.

"Easy, you've seen the hard water, nothing but Class Two sections, and only short sections at that. It's nothing after the good rapids we shot yesterday. Child's play."

"No bullshit."

"No bullshit. I wish you'd get over yourself. You're in one piece, so what are you complaining about? Smooth sailing ahead, you'll love it. Relax and enjoy the scenery."

Clayton's life jacket straps hung loosely, so Graham believed him this time. They launched and floated. It was serene and mild except for a few adrenaline-drenched dashes through rough channels, as Clayton had said. Mostly, Graham drifted and paddled on auto-pilot, watching the trees flow by and the clouds floating overhead. They passed a moose standing in the shade, and its head rotated as they went past, otherwise, it did not move. Graham gave it more clearance than Clayton. The massive beast had to weigh at least a thousand pounds.

The miles passed and the sun touched the treetops when Clayton pointed to a landing spot on the west shore.

Over his shoulder, he said, "You're going to love tonight's camp, it's really awesome."

"No surprises," Graham said sternly.

"No *bad* surprises. This one you'll appreciate."

Robert Kinsley

His belly was still swollen and painful, but the agony had receded. It felt like creepy things crawled on him—invisible spiders on his skin. The heat from the fire was palpable; it filled the room with rainbow-like, glowing concentric bands of light—orange and pale red and yellow.

The cabin breathed, expanding and contracting. He realized he floated several inches above the fragment of carpeting. Life was everywhere…insects in the walls, moss growing on the roof, mice under the floorboards, and outside, something watched. An opossum, Robert realized, with beady red eyes and stupid thoughts flowing like cold syrup.

Farther way, there were more open eyes. People, their domestic animals and deer, a fox family snuggled nose-to-tail in a warm den, a bobcat smelling the air and a cougar, angry and stalking. The world was filled with eyes and hearts and souls, rising from the land like waves of heat from sun-drenched desert pavement. There were pockets of joy, but mostly there was pain. Cruelty was the way of nature.

From the south and west, with slow precision, power approached. The federal agents and the police, seeping across the border and seeking them.

Also, a man—the father of one of the children a freed tiger had killed—filled with guilty visions of neglecting his laughing daughter and a white-hot rage—was coming. If he found them, he planned to kill them slowly and bury them deep, but he was alone and looking the wrong way.

To murder was a Godly power to be grasped only by the bold. Robert realized he liked the pure, cleansing intoxication of it.

Nature's way is to murder and move on.

He became aware of something in the hills, a pocket of alien intelligence. Something ancient and strange. Irritatingly, the whispers of old voices were swept away when Raven spoke.

"Love," she said. "It fills the cracks of the world and softens the sharp edges. Pure love is a light that warms and illuminates. Love is God's gift."

Love is fool's gold, Robert thought. *Love is a cheap trinket, a sparkly plastic bead gleaming out of a mountain of shit.*

He clenched his fists and admired the ripple of sinew and muscle in his arms. He was strong of body and strong of will and did not have the stupid softness of others. His legs were strong and his mind was strong. His prick was strong—swollen and erect. He opened his eyes and looked at Raven. She was curled up in a fetal position on her dingy scrap of carpet. He could smell her feminine essence and it called to him for violation and dominance.

Roughly, he rolled her onto her back and forced open her thighs. Hovering and ready, he waited long moments before the plunge. She whimpered and tried to push him off, but this only inflamed his desire more. Like a jack hammer, he pounded her until blood raged in his head, and then he poured endless waves of primal fluid into her loins.

When he was done, he rolled off and she curled up again, muttering and weeping.

"True love is real magic," he heard her say.

"I wish you'd shut the fuck up and let me sleep," he said.

CHAPTER SEVENTEEN

Maria

THERE WAS COMMOTION from outside the cave. Her headache crept back as if probing little fingers poked at very sore spots.

She rubbed the back of her neck.

"You brought something with you…they know, I'm sorry, but you'll have to give it up."

"I don't know what you mean."

"A bone, am I right? You have a skull that is theirs?"

Maria stood and pulled the cloth-wrapped bundle from her jeans pocket; she unwrapped the little skull.

"This?"

"Yes, they will take it. It's better that you offer it up. Just stand in the open and they will come."

Her headache intensified and she heard faint voices, perhaps imagined.

She left the nook. A group assembled—five of the creatures, large and dirty. Waiting. She offered the skull and one of the creatures snatched it from her hand. She got no sense of gratitude, only hostility. Elmer stood by her side.

"Oh, no, I knew this was coming. You will not want to watch."

He tugged her arm to pull her back inside, but she shrugged him off.

"Whatever it is, I want to see."

"I already told you."

As they watched, a mass of creatures gathered in the center of the cavern. The injured boy was placed on a flat stone and one of the females smashed his head with a large rock. They converged on him and ripped him to pieces—hacking with crude rock hatchets. Gore dripped down the rock. Bloody chunks were hauled to corners.

"That was brutal," Maria whispered. "Inhuman."

"That's right, they are not human. Please, it's over, we should go back inside. Your head hurts? I will beat the drum, which will help."

She went inside and plugged her ears, which only made the voices in her head more vivid. The effect was uncanny. With her ears stopped up, the noisy drum did not bother her this time. When he stopped and came back in, her headache receded.

"Thank you, that works."

"Yes, they are persistent; they will come back, but let me know, I'll do it again."

"They punish the injured child with murder and cannibalism? They will eat the child?"

Elmer squirmed as if uncomfortable. "That's not exactly right. You've seen all the children, there are lots of them, but they kill most, like I said, around the age of six. I don't know how they select them; it doesn't always appear that they select the strongest. And the injured? You saw it. They are killed to make way for a new adult. Nothing goes wasted. When I die, they'll eat me too. I don't care. If I leave here and get a Pepsi, then they'll probably track me down. I don't know. You have something else. There is a diamond…they want the stone too. You were supposed to bring it."

"What is the deal with the rock?"

"The diamond? They trade with the humans sometimes, gold and diamonds for some of the things they want, but I think they are afraid. Is it the DeBeers? Are they still in control of the diamond market? It's silly really, just carbon. Common. Amazing what people will buy, all sparkle, no intrinsic value, diamonds are forever, a girl's best friend, all that rot. This does not answer your question, I'm sorry. I think they are worried; there are lots of diamonds in the caves. If the diamond cartels come in that will be the end of the people. They're not going to live in a zoo or on a reservation with humans meddling; they'll fight and hide deep in the caves. It will be open warfare."

"Limiting their population so strictly seems cruel..."

"It is, but they despise us for our unrestrained growth and reliance on technology. When the next ice age comes and the oil runs out, there won't be much area to live in—a swath around the equator, how many will that support? One-hundred million? More or less? I don't know. Many billions will die. How will *they* be selected? The rich will buy the land and build secure—gated—communities. They'll live in comfort while billions die in drought, pestilence and disease. Which method is crueler? Do we decide by comparing body counts? By comparing the numbers of the survivors? I wish things were simple, but here I am, living with the people. We live in a golden age of warm temperatures and we act stupid—we don't realize the friendly climate will someday come to an end."

"Perhaps technology will avert the disaster."

"Yes, technology, that is our religion and our hope, I know it and so do they. It's possible, certainly possible, but likely? I don't know. They just need to hide for a couple of thousands of years and we'll find out. Not us, of course, we'll all be dead, but our descendants."

"I'm embarrassed to ask...this may be a very dumb question. Are these creatures telepathic? I feel them scratching at my mind."

"Yes, of course, you noticed the bulge over their forehead. I've studied the effect, the blood, under high pressure, flows quickly in circles, sort of an inductive loop; the iron in the blood is magnetized? I don't know the details, but yes, they communicate to an extent, non-verbally, simple concepts, nothing complex. In engineering terms, low bandwidth, low data rate, do you follow?"

"Why did they allow me to come here?"

"That's right, you don't know. In your family, there was probably an Indian? I can see it in your face—in your cheekbones and in the color of your skin. Four, maybe five generations back? You have the blood of the people in you. You are a relation, in small part, yes, that's true. Sometimes the people mate with humans. Not often, but sometimes, yes."

Willie

It grew cold on the deck; Willie wriggled in his chair to loosen his stiff joints. He'd been immersed in his book. The plot twists unfolded and it amused him how, when things were going well, the book seemed to write itself, like he was a conduit between something mysterious and the page. He wondered how long Maria had been gone.

A few hours?

The sun was low on the western horizon and the temperature dropped as the evening wind kicked up. He gathered his papers and went inside.

She'd come back after dark before, but still, Willie worried. She could have fallen—broken a leg or been mauled by a bear—there were many hazards.

What would I do without her warmth and light?

Fumbling around, he managed to light a lantern and get the propane stove going. As night fell, he sat with the forgotten manuscript on his lap and fitfully dozed.

He remembered being balanced between his dead wife and his savior, Maria. Victoria gave him permission to be happy again after she was gone. 'Not too soon,' she'd said, with a glint of humor in her eye. He had felt guilty, as if he was betraying Victoria's memory, but Maria was so beautiful and so good for him. He could not let her slip away.

Thank you, Lord, for loaning me your two angels. And Lord, while you're at it, please protect Maria—wherever she is out in the cold woods. Is that asking too much?

When his manuscript fell to the floor, he woke up. Straining his ears, he hoped to hear the sounds of Maria coming back, but all he heard was the wind and the hiss of the propane flame radiating heat in the lonely darkness.

Clayton Powell and Graham Wallace

They pulled the kayaks onto the rocks. Graham knew the routine, but after scanning the area, he did not see the camp bundles hoisted in the trees. Clayton shouldered his pack.

"How far?" Graham asked.

"Half a mile, no more. This is one of my favorite parts of the trip. This will blow your mind."

"Alright, let's get it done."

They were immediately immersed in a thick forest, one of the few parts of their trek where the trees seemed completely healthy. The evergreens were tall, stately and green. The trail followed a stream for a few hundred meters, and then they climbed a steep bank.

"You didn't tell me the half mile was vertical," Graham complained.

"Stop crying like a baby. We're almost there."

"Asshole," Graham muttered.

"Whiner," Clayton replied.

On the hillside, the tree trunks were massive, some ten or more feet in diameter. Graham looked around suspiciously.

"We're here," Clayton announced.

"Where?"

"The internationally famous Clayton Powell's Doug Fir Hotel," he said proudly while pointing upward. A rope ladder was tied against the base of one of the firs. Graham stood back to look up the tree. The ladder disappeared into foliage.

"Where are we going?"

"Up," Clayton replied, while untying the ladder.

Soon, he had clambered up. Graham watched him while holding the bottom of the ladder steady.

"What the fuck is this?" he muttered.

Afraid to look down, Graham climbed and climbed. The last section of ladder ended in the floor of a large structure. The tree swayed and Graham fought against the feeling that he was falling. Inside, Clayton reclined on a leather couch.

Offering a bottle of beer, Clayton said, "I'll bet you've never seen anything like this."

Graham, taking the beer and drinking deeply, walked to a picture window. Outside, the terrain fell away. He could see for miles, even as far as the falls, which seemed closer than they should be. The vista was incredible and he was speechless.

Waving his hands to show off the features of the treehouse, Clayton said, "We have bunk beds, a shitter, a DVD player, everything. Our refrigerator is filled with beer and steaks. We have a gas stove. Outside, there is a little Honda generator for the lights and electronics."

"I have to say, I'm impressed. How much did all this cost?"

"Hell, my man, you know it cost a bundle of cash, but I damned well don't care. Besides, my accountants will write it all off as a business expense."

"Is it safe?"

"After all you've been through, that's a hell of a question. Compared to a death-defying jump over a waterfall into a flimsy net, you're damned right it's safe. Barring a thunderstorm, we'll be fine. I have a satellite phone. My people will call if the weather gets rough, but the forecast is good. Sit back, kick off your boots, and have a cigar. You can tell your grandkids about spending a night in the world's coolest tree house with your pal, Clayton Powell."

"A pal wouldn't keep trying to kill me," Graham complained.

"You're a real pain in the ass, you know that? If I wanted you killed, I'd make a phone call, spend a few bucks and before you know what hit you, you'd be cooling on an autopsy table with your guts chopped out and on their way—via courier service—to be implanted in rich brats dying in Massachusetts and Texas. No harm, no foul, am I right? Quit belly-aching and take a load off. If there is a place closer to heaven itself, then I don't know it. You earned a break—it's time to relax and enjoy."

Pacing, Graham explored the room. Behind a pocket door, the shitter was a toilet seat hanging over empty space. Looking through the hole with his stomach in his mouth, he noticed how the drop zone was well away from the climbing area. A good design touch, he had to admit.

Uninvited, a grin spread across Graham's face. There was no arguing the point, the place was breathtaking. He could do with less sway, but perhaps he'd get used to it. He shrugged off his pack, unlaced his boots, and then slowly eased his tortured body gently onto an overstuffed leather chair.

Gesturing at the bottle of Glenlivet single malt scotch from which Clayton sipped, Graham said, "Okay, I confess, I'm very impressed. Now, don't be a manipulative, self-centered, ass-biting booze hog. Pass the bottle."

Robert Kinsley

Awake and staring at the ceiling, Robert listened to Raven snore. He pushed her to make her move, which helped for a while, but soon enough, she'd saw away again.

Irritating.

His stomach ached and his drug-fueled mind raced—filled with fragments of images and glimpses of the horrible power of cruelty in the world. He was just a college dropout, stuck in the woods with no money and no hope; still, he felt destiny calling. He belonged in the pantheon of greats: Napoleon, Adolf Schicklgruber Hitler, Pol Pot, Stalin, Mao, Castro, Charles Manson, Jim Jones, Ron Hubbard, Mumia and dare he dream of it?

Robert Kinsley.

One day, his face would be silk-screened onto millions of t-shirts worn by enlightened college students.

The worldwide animal, environmental and hemp rights movement, spearheaded by their handsome, young, international hero, Robert Kinsley.

He craved this respect and power with his whole essence. He dug an elbow deep into Raven's ribs. She groaned and shifted on her side and was quiet. In this quiet, he heard it.

Something creeping up the driveway.

A car or two, perhaps three. Headlights off, they approached slowly. Robert laughed. Clearly they thought he and Raven were armed and dangerous. His mind was altered; he heard strange voices and saw bright flashes of light sweeping through his mind like sheet lightning. He pulled on his jeans and shoes and climbed down the loft ladder and tip-toed into the kitchen. At random, he threw items into plastic bags.

From behind, Raven startled him.

"What are you doing?" she said.

"Keep your voice down—they're coming up the driveway."

"Oh, no, are you sure? I thought we'd have more time." She peeked out the window. "Oh, God, you're right, I see them. Why are you dressed? We should both be bare, skin to skin. We have to do it now, or it will be too late, my darling." She slipped an end of the hemp rope over his neck and kissed him on the back of his neck. "Take off your pants and we'll be united on the other side."

Turning to face her, he took a last feel of her spongy left breast. She pulled the rickety kitchen chairs under the beam and stood on it with her knees shaking and the chair legs vibrating.

She slipped the other knot over her head. Loosening his knot, he slipped off the rope.

She had time to say, "What?" before he hauled back and kicked her chair away.

He hooked the loose end on the woodstove and watched as she struggled and wriggled, scratching at the rope with her fingernails. Looking around the room, he noticed the prayer rug, which he rolled up and tucked it under his arm. Weighed down by the plastic bags, he took one last look around. Her face turned purple and her eyes bulged.

Very attractive. Like I'd enjoy mating with that as I die.

"I hope you enjoy your trip, you dumb bitch," he muttered, before slipping out the back door.

He knew the pathway to his pissing tree very well and traversed it silently in the darkness. Beyond the outhouse, there was a deer trail—rough, but better than going cross country.

Through the silent woods, he heard shouting and banging as they charged the cabin. He hustled and was soon a mile away.

Free and clear.

CHAPTER EIGHTEEN

Maria

THINKING, MARIA SAT in the cave and sipped from a bottle of water. She pulled out granola bars stuffed away in her pack, but Elmer waved them away.

"I'm used to the people's food. Yes, it's rank and rotten, but my system is adapted to it—your chemical food would just make me sick. Is people food addictive? I think so, it has mold, it makes me feel good, I get sick without it. I wish it weren't so, but it's too late. Will I ever get my Pepsi? I dream of it. The people have bad food, yes, but it's completely organic and natural. No technology, that's the way here."

"They'll let me leave?"

"Oh, that's no problem, you can come and go, go and come, just don't eat the people food, or you'll be an addict too, here in the cave with the people—craving a cold sugar-drink. Not so bad, I would share my dwelling. We could mate and rut. I'm a gentle man, I know how I must look, but soon you'd be like this too, smelly and filthy-dirty, but happy, in our way, waiting for the great change—for the sun to dim and the ice sheets to grow."

"Thank you, but, no, I will return to the world. Come with me?"

Elmer wept. "I would have to leave and not come back, except for my bones. They would find my body and take those, but never alive, me, no, I couldn't come back. Only my bones—which they'll pound into paste and eat."

"My husband will be worried. I should go."

"I must warn you. Time flexes around the people. I don't know how it works, is it biological? I don't know."

"I'm not sure what you're warning me about."

"Nothing really, but it will be later than you think when you leave. Time ebbs and flows here. It passes differently among the people."

Standing, Maria gathered her pack. "I don't think I'll come back. My head hurts and these *people?* Well, they're bad."

"No, not bad. Different, yes, very different, but I understand. Go with the organic spirit, thank you for your company, you've given me much to think and dream about, come back if you wish, stay away if you must, that's the way things work. Go ahead, I will beat the drum and they will not molest you. Goodbye, farewell, we're friends, am I right?"

Unsure what to do, Maria held out her hand for a handshake. Elmer looked at it with a moment of confusion then smiled. He gripped her hand and shook it enthusiastically.

"I remember, shaking hands, yes, that's good. Goodbye."

She walked out slowly, scanning the creatures who watched her leave as Elmer beat on his drum. Outside, it was fully dark. Elmer was right; she expected it to still be afternoon. A sliver of moon cast cold light and, though it was slow-going, she was able to pick her way back; up the cliff and through the woods—finally to her favored perch over the lake.

Sweating profusely and with her mind a jumble, she rested. From the woods, eyes watched, but she ignored them. When she was ready, she hiked down the hillside toward the cabin.

Willie and Maria

Willie could not sit still. He wandered from the kitchen area to the back door—peering through the dusty windows into the darkness. Sometimes he would hear something and call out her name.

"Maria?"

But there was never a response. It was after midnight before he finally heard her coming down the trail. He threw open the door and gathered her into his arms.

The smell was overwhelming. He didn't want to, but he was forced to push her away.

"My Lord, Maria, have you been wrestling with skunks? My eyes are burning. Don't come in, where have you been? I've been worried sick about you, but by the spirit of Ayn Rand, you reek to high heaven. Take off your clothes. We'll have to burn them. Throw your pack downwind. I can't stand it."

Maria laughed. "That has to be the lamest come-on I've heard. *Take off your clothes, you stink.* Very smooth, Professor."

Coughing, he pushed her back to show he was serious. Standing on the back landing she pulled off her clothing and stood outside shivering.

"Don't bring them in, we'll burn them tomorrow."

"Dammit, Willie, I'm freezing. Bring me my bathrobe."

"I'm sorry, Maria, but you'll have to scrub first."

"The lake is forty degrees, for God's sake."

"And wash your hair." He threw out a bar of soap and slammed the door.

"Some damned home-coming," she muttered.

Emptying her head, she ran to the end of the dock and dived in. The frigid water was as much of a shock as she knew it would be, but it didn't help to agonize over it or try to climb in little-by-little.

Better to just dive in.

She hurriedly scrubbed and rinsed, then ran back up to the cabin. Willie had turned up the propane heater and stood waiting with her fluffy bathrobe.

"You still smell, but that's much better," Willie said.

"Thanks so much for your approval. I'm exhausted. I'm going to bed."

"No, wait, you have to tell me where you've been. It's after midnight. I've had many horrible thoughts; you could have been injured or lost. I was losing my mind."

She stood with her arms crossed across her chest.

"You tell me I stink and make me jump in ice water, Professor William Jefferson Washington Walters. I'm cold and I'm angry. I'm going to bed. You can wait for my story tomorrow, and you'd better not complain about making me coffee in the morning, mister."

She turned and dived into the bed and pulled the covers over her head.

"Well, you really did stink. Cripes, woman...you're intolerable."

From the main room, he sat and watched her burrow into the bedding. Lighting his pipe to cover the remnants of her stench, he extended thanks to the powers in heaven for bringing her home to him.

Clayton Powell and Graham Wallace

Graham, wrapped up warmly in his soft down comforter and fighting a headache from the Scotch, did not want to wake up. However, Clayton banged around the galley and cooked something in a frying pan. The treehouse filled with the scent of sizzling bacon mixed with the aroma of percolating coffee.

The room swayed gently, but Graham, in the night, decided he liked it. It was soothing, like floating on an inner tube on a placid river.

The events of the last few days flashed through his mind—it seemed as if a year had passed since Clayton extended his invitation and J-C and Lili had cruelly driven him in preparation.

Was it really just two weeks, nearly?

Stretching, he decided to get up.

Scratching his head, he pissed a yellow stream into space. Back in the main room, Clayton dropped plates on the table and distributed flatware, and then filled mugs with steaming black coffee. The crisp bacon was accompanied by fried potatoes and scrambled eggs. They both reached for the Tabasco sauce at the same time and tussled for it briefly.

"I cooked."

"I'm your guest," Graham said, winning the battle.

"After all this," Clayton said, waving his hand around the house, "you're ungrateful?"

"No, this is one of the greatest and coolest things in my whole life, almost as good as my first orgasm with a woman involved, but you're not going to soften me up. I'm onto your bullshit, Powell."

"That's fine, but if you're done with the hot sauce—please pass it over."

Graham shook out one more sprinkle, then politely handed it across the table.

"No problem, here you go," he said formally.

They ate while listening to air currents ruffle fir needles. Occasionally a pine cone would hit the roof and tumble off. A squirrel peeked in the window and chattered at them.

"You cook pretty good for a rich fucker," Graham commented after tossing a last bit of scrambled egg into his mouth.

"Yeah, but sometimes my admin reminds me what it costs. I make something like four thousand dollars an hour. It doesn't even pay for me to bend over and pick up a dollar bill if it floats by. I need to do productive things with my time—not things I can pay other people to do. Believe it," he said, sighing, "money and fame can be like a prison sentence. I can't go to the grocery store without some jerkoff trying to hand me a business card or a hit me up for angel money for some damned hopeless scheme. I remember when I was nobody—like you—and I miss those carefree days."

"Nobody?"

"That didn't come out right. No offense intended. You can go to a baseball game without people staring or coming up and saying stupid things, like their damned software is crashing or something. Like it's my damned fault they're too cheap to upgrade their servers or buy sufficient storage space or whatever. See what I mean? Being one of the richest men in the world and the most powerful man in the industry is not all awards and stock option redemption, it can be hard work."

"And I'm the cry-baby whiner."

"That's why these trips are so important. They allow me to stay centered and in touch with the primal side of my nature. I can decompress and clear my mind of all the bullshit. Secondarily, I can measure a man before going into business with him."

"You can rediscover your inner dickhead."

"You know, Graham, I'm actually starting to enjoy your spirit. To a point, of course, I wouldn't want you to forget who's the boss and who's the service-provider."

"Well, you like me so much, maybe you'll stop trying to kill me, huh?"

"You've made it, or nearly. There's one more real challenge."

"Great, quit jerking me off and tell me all about it."

"It should be no surprise. I already told you we're going bear hunting."

"I'm not shooting a damned bear."

"We'll see about that," Clayton said with a thin-lipped smile.

Robert Kinsley

It was cold. Robert kept warm by staying on the move, up and down hills, pushing through brush thickets and listening for any sign of anyone following. It seemed like he'd gotten away clean—maybe they wouldn't even know he had been there.

He tried to think of any evidence he'd left behind. It was hopeless, there was too much, like the dirty dishes and his clothes. They'd know. Dawn was imminent when he came out onto the highway. Trying to evaluate the options, he decided to head north. That way, at least he wouldn't have to pass by the cabin.

No telling what was going on there.

Almost instantly, he flagged down a ride with a young man in a piece of crap Datsun; it seemed to be held together with hanger wire and duct tape.

The kid turned down the death metal music slightly. It appeared he had a thousand dollar stereo blasting away in his two hundred dollar car.

"What the heck are you doing out here?" the kid said.

"I'm headed up north to see some friends," Robert improvised.

"Ah, Prince George?"

"Yeah," Robert said.

Where the hell is Prince George?

Two miles? Two thousand miles? Goddamned Canada.

"Well, I can't help you. I'm only going to Lytton—a hundred kilometers or so."

How far is that? 60 miles? 160 miles?

Will this shitty car make it that far?

"Thanks, every little bit helps," he said.

"You like Toxic Shock Syndrome? This is their latest," the kid said, banging out the beat on the dashboard. "If I could afford a set of drums, I'd play this music."

It sounds like a chainsaw ripping flesh. This is going to be a long trip.

"No, I'm not familiar with their work."

The highway, blasted thorough solid rock along the river, weaved through several tunnels. The kid pounded on the horn as they passed through each one.

"Tradition," he said.

It occurred to Robert that he could be in the middle of a drug-induced hallucination.

Am I back in bed with Raven and imagining this whole thing? Her hanging? The race through the woods? The horrible hammering mix of the music and the over-strained sewing machine engine laboring under the hood of the Datsun?

Will I wake up soon and give Raven another vigorous bang with my sore cock?

The kid interrupted the reverie.

"Okay, end of the line, mi amigo."

"Look, you wouldn't happen to have dope you could spare?" Robert asked.

"Oh, no, you really have the wrong idea. I'm a Jehovah's Witness. We're hip these days, I wear a mullet and piercings, but I'm one with God's spirit. I use no chemicals to alter the balance of the vessel."

Robert unfolded himself from the tiny car and gathered his plastic bags and the prayer rug.

No, this is too bizarre to be anything but real.

Looking around the little town, he could see agitated water mixing from two rivers. The road split too. On the east fork, up Highway 1, an RCMP car idled in the parking lot of a café. Robert began walking north on Highway 12.

"Stay on Highway 1 if you want to get to Prince George," the kid yelled.

Plastering on a goofy grin, Robert waved and picked up his pace.

People in remote British Columbia are friendly. Robert got another ride immediately with an older couple driving in a spotless old Buick.

The hunched woman, peering through the steering wheel, drove. The old man looked over his shoulder stiffly at Robert in the spacious back seat.

"Where you headed, son?"

He'd seen a sign, so "Lillooet," is what he said.

"You're in luck, 'cause that's where we're headed too," the old man said cheerfully.

Duh, like this road goes anywhere else.

After a few miles, Robert spotted a bridge over the river.

"Hey, let me out here," he said.

The man looked skeptical. "Are you sure?"

"Don't argue with the boy," the woman said. "I didn't want to pick up a hitchhiker anyway. If he wants out, then we'll let him out. No offense, it's just that you never know. You could be a mass-murderer or something, though you seem nice enough."

"I picked up hitchers all the time when I was driving," the husband said.

"Well, you're not driving no more—not after you wrecked the RV."

"Are you going to keep bringing that up forever?"

By this time, the car was stopped. Robert got out and left them to their bickering.

He spent a few minutes on the bridge watching the water rush by below. Traffic flowed on the highway, but the bridge appeared to be little-used. It was stupid to stand around in plain sight, but Robert was mesmerized by the river. After a few long minutes, he was ready to walk. The road climbed a rocky rise and disappeared. Robert arranged his plastic bags as best he could and began walking west—into the wild country.

CHAPTER NINETEEN

Willie and Maria

ONCE THE COFFEE was hot, he stirred in creamer and sugar the way she took it. The sun was high in the mid-morning sky; he waited as long as he could stand it before risking disturbing her. She sat up in bed. Her bathrobe fell open to expose a brown breast.

"I've been going mad with speculation, dear," he said. "What happened up in the hills?"

She folded her arms and pushed up her breasts.

"You're going to make love with me and make me breakfast, then *maybe* I'll tell you."

"I'm an old man. You can't expect me to perform on command."

"Shut up and get busy."

After, she dozed while he banged pots and pans together in the kitchen.

"I made you French toast," he said proudly.

"What a surprise," she said. That was all he knew how to cook. Spaghetti for dinner, French toast for breakfast. Sure, he could heat up meat and leftovers, but that was the full extent of his kitchen skills. "Bring me my coffee," she commanded.

"It's on the table. If you want it, you get up and get it."

"You're an inhuman monster," she said, while rotating in the bed and using her feet to search for her slippers. She'd been trying to figure out what to tell him. She could tell the whole story, but he'd either decide she was whacked out of her mind or decide he needed to see for himself. Probably both. She couldn't visualize her elderly husband making the trip.

What would the creatures do? Would they let him come and go? Would they smash in his head and make soup of his bones?

She didn't know.

He mixed orange drink from a powder; she made a sour face when drinking it. Otherwise, the breakfast was fine. She was much hungrier than she realized. When she couldn't take another bite, she pushed the plate away. He immediately put another slice of toast on it.

"No, I'm going to explode. No more," she said.

"Fine, breakfast done, time to talk. No more making me wait. Spill it."

She took Willie's hands. "I was hiking along the ridge north of here. I was enjoying the woods and I lost track of time. I took a shortcut coming back and I tripped into a skunk den. Naturally, they sprayed me. I rolled around in the dirt and tried to kill the smell the best I could, but by then it was getting dark. I had to wait until the moon rose because I didn't have a flashlight, and I couldn't walk very fast, but I knew you'd be worried, so I came home as quickly as I could."

Willie looked very skeptical. "That's it?"

"Yes."

"I know what skunk musk smells like."

"Maybe they are a different species. There are lots of different kinds of skunks."

"I don't think this adds up. What aren't you telling me?"

"Baby, I'm hurt." She batted her eyes and tried to look innocent. "You know I would never, ever lie to you unless it was absolutely necessary. I love you."

"I love you too," he said absently.

"Okay then, I'd better get outside and get those clothes burned; I can smell them from here. They reek—gotta be driving you crazy. Light up your pipe, I'm sure that helps, I'll be right back." She kissed him on the forehead, but his mind was miles away.

With a stick, she threw the clothes farther from the cabin and into a heap. Pouring on kerosene, she set the bundle on fire with a wooden match. From outside, as she stirred the fire, she watched Willie; he was in one of his trances.

Probably disassembling her implausible story with his unassailable logic.

After an hour, the clothes were fully consumed and there was no excuse left for tending the fire. It smoked a little, but it was over. She went in the cabin quietly and set herself to cleaning the breakfast dishes.

Nope," he said, startling her. "Fell into a den of skunks? I don't think so. However, I believe you wouldn't lie unless there was a very good reason. How about a hint to ease my mind a little?"

"How is your book coming along?" she asked sweetly, while wiping a coffee cup with a kitchen towel.

"So, that's how it's going to be?" he asked. "Very well, my dear, a challenge for my intellect. I'm very bright and I write mystery stories, as you well know. Given time, my mind will decode your deception. Of that, I am sure."

"Need a refill?" she asked, holding up the coffee pot. He didn't say anything, so she smiled and topped off his cup.

Clayton Powell and Graham Wallace

The climb back down the tree took a long time, but they made it to the ground. Resting, they looked upward.

"I admit it. You impressed me with this one," Graham said.

"You're welcome," Clayton said.

"Ever think about throwing the whole thing over? Cashing out and living in a treehouse for the rest of your life?"

"Every damned day," was the reply.

"What's next?"

"Easy, we hike cross country for a while. A few rope bridges and a scoot across Highway 99 dodging logging trucks. That will be the only real excitement. We'll be tired by the time we make camp, what with all the climbing. It's bumpy country out there, but nothing that will piss you off, I promise. There's a lot of miles between here and there, shall we get after it?"

"After you, boss man," Graham said.

From the top of a ridge, they could see the treehouse about two-thirds of the way up a massive Douglas Fir tree. It was lashed with cables and supported by struts. It looked sturdy enough.

"How'd you ever get a permit to build that thing?" Graham asked.

"Permit?" Clayton snorted. "I don't need no stinking permit."

"I recognize that line—it's from a John Belushi movie."

"No, I made it up myself," Clayton said in an offended tone.

They continued on a faint trail and soon the treehouse was out of their sight.

They made good time, but Clayton was right—the endless climbing wore Graham out. His foot, well bandaged, held up okay; it was his biggest worry. The swelling in his knee subsided. They scrambled down a gravel bank and soon found themselves at the river's edge. A pair of ropes stretched across—one low and the other at chest height above the other.

"High Bar is that way," Clayton said, while pointing downriver.

Refusing to be distracted, Graham skeptically studied the ropes. At the center, they were about three yards above the boiling river.

"How do we do this?"

"Easy. Feet on the bottom rope, hands on the top rope, shuffle along. Don't let go and you'll be fine." He hopped up and started across. "See, it's simple."

Graham uncoiled a short line from his pack. By the time he'd fashioned a safety strap, Clayton was halfway across and calling out to him.

"No dawdling, chickenshit."

"Screw you, Powell," Graham yelled back.

He climbed on and started over. The ropes flailed and Graham had a distinct vision of dropping into the river. With the pack on his back, there was no way he'd be able to swim out. Near the center, he almost lost his footing, but, holding on with his eyes clamped shut—skating on the edge of total panic—he waited for the ropes to settle and was okay. He continued without incident, but was very happy to put both feet back on solid ground.

"Real men don't need safety equipment," Clayton said, rested and squatting on his haunches.

"I think I shit myself," Graham replied.

They hiked and the sun was low on the sky when they found the next rope bridge. This one was a lot shorter and the stream was shallow. Clayton was across and waiting by the time Graham patiently rigged his safety rope and edged across.

"This is going to take forever if you keep playing it safe."

"Bite my nut bag," Graham said.

As darkness fell, they found themselves on the edge of a small lake. After looking at GPS coordinates, and after a few minutes of searching, they found kayaks hanging in the trees.

"Seton Lake," Clayton said.

"I really don't care," Graham replied. "Where's camp?"

"Across. Not far. No time to rest, we gotta get on it," Clayton said.

They paddled across the lake and dragged the kayaks into the brush. Clayton brought out a flashlight and Graham put a headlight on over the headband of his Tam o'Shanter.

"You look like a real bozo," commented Clayton.

"Are we going to stand around gabbing about it?"

In full darkness and stumbling along, they finally found the campsite. Graham inflated his air mattress and unfolded his sleeping bag and mosquito net. Within a minute, he floated on the edge of sleep. Clayton opened an MRE and a bottle of wine and leaned back—staring into the gloom.

"We covered a lot of miles today. Feels good, doesn't it? Graham?"

"Leave me alone," was Graham's muffled reply.

"I like a glass of wine and a nice conversation after a long day."

Far away, an owl sounded like a faint freight train whistle. That was the only response to his comment.

In the morning, Graham, famished, ate two MREs and a large Baby Ruth candy bar.

"What's the game plan for the day?" he asked.

"Sure, now you want to talk. Prick," Clayton said.

Hiking on after breaking camp, the terrain turned more rocky and rugged.

Arid country, Graham thought while resting and looking out over a valley.

Highway 99 *was* scary; they came across it at a sweeping bend etched in rock. Trucks roared by with air brakes howling. Picking a quiet moment, they darted across, but were still buffeted by truck turbulence on the other side as they searched for their trailhead.

"That was frightening," Graham commented.

"But I warned you ahead of time, so we're okay, right?"

"Yes, no problem. Let's get out of here."

"Good, I know how touchy you can be." There was a flash of orange painted on the roadway. "This is it," Clayton said.

They scrambled down a gravel bank and found the trail, again marked with a slash of orange.

"I think I'm onto your system. Orange paint marks the trail," Graham said.

"I'm in awe of your great genius," Clayton replied.

"Where's the next camp?"

"Between Skihist and Stein mountains."

"How far?"

"Thirty klicks, give or take."

"How long?"

"All day, depending on how many stupid questions you ask."

"No, I asked about the next camp. We can't walk thirty kilometers today."

"You'll see," Clayton said mysteriously.

After a mile or so, they came upon a fiberglass shed. It was locked with a digital padlock. Clayton punched in numbers and the clasp sprang open. Inside, there were ATVs—big Japanese ones with huge knobby tires.

"Ever ridden one of these before?" Clayton asked.

"No, but how hard can it be?"

"Not hard, just try to keep the rubber-side down, okay? Key, ignition, gear shift, throttle, brake," Clayton said, speaking quickly and gesturing around the vehicle.

"Helmet?"

"I didn't ask for any, but you can look."

Graham poked around the dark interior of the shed and found helmets and thick gloves. He offered the equipment to Clayton, but Clayton waved it away. While Graham adjusted the strap on his helmet and worked the gloves on, Clayton started his engine and roared away. Graham started his engine and played around, driving in circles in the clearing to make sure he could work the gears, the throttle and the brakes. When he was satisfied, he followed Clayton's trail.

Following fresh tracks on gravel roads, Graham didn't see anyone else along the way. It took almost an hour, but he finally found Clayton sitting on a rock drinking a soda.

"It's about damned time you decided to join me," he said. "Trail's there."

Graham saw the flash of orange paint, though he might have missed it driving down the road at speed. Choking on Clayton's exhaust, he followed into a stand of dead trees.

As dusk fell, Graham's butt felt dead and his back was stiff. Clayton swept his ATV in a wide circle, scattering pine needles and gravel. He pointed left and right at rugged peaks.

"Stein. Skihist. Told you'd make we'd it."

Killing his engine, Graham climbed off, pulled off his helmet and stretched out his back. "That was fun for the first few hours," he said.

"If you want to walk, you can walk. We have another thirty klicks to cover tomorrow. You could do it, though it might take a few days."

"I'm sure my ass will be recovered by tomorrow," Graham said, rubbing his cheeks under his kilt. "At least, I hope so." He looked around. "Where's the camp stash?"

"Everything is on the ATVs."

They unpacked and started a fire. Graham realized something.

"I don't think I've swatted a single mosquito."

"Dryer out here—fewer mosquitoes." Graham felt a pain on the back of his arm and swatted at a large fly. "Gotta watch for the deer flies though," Clayton said, laughing, "they'll take a chunk out of you."

"Thanks for the warning," Graham said, while rubbing at a bloody spot on his arm.

After a few beers, they watched the sunset and Clayton's mood mellowed. The scenery was harsh after the lush woods farther north. Mountains followed mountains—some had trees while some were nearly barren—bearing fan-like cascades of metallic colors; rusty red for iron, bright yellow for sulfur, a vivid green for copper.

Clayton offered a toast, "Hard country for hard men."

"Hard men on their trusty Japanese automatic transmission four-wheel-drive all terrain vehicles," Graham said, grinning.

"A couple more days and we'll be at the spa getting deep muscle massages and teasing the girls about happy endings."

"I'm sorry?"

"A good massage finishes when they roll you on your back and give you a happy ending. You figure it out."

"Oh," Graham said. "I didn't know about that. No wonder massages are so popular."

"Well, you have to be careful, not all the girls will do it…"

"Right. I suppose you made special arrangements for when we get to Harrison."

Clayton acted offended. "After all we've been through, I'd forget a detail like that?"

"Of course. I'm not doubting you. Take it easy."

"If you make me angry, I'll make sure you get an ugly masseuse, or a man, how would you like that?"

"Up yours."

"That's what I'm talking about, is that the way you like it?"

"I'm not gay, asshole."

"Just checking. I want to know who I'm partnering up with."

"A detail like that you'd know a long time ago. Don't blow smoke up my ass."

"Let's get serious for a minute." Clayton leaned up on an elbow. "You impress me. Everything that came up on this trip, you made it through. I'm even a little worried about losing our wager...giving up my Hummer and letting you keep your pretty little Porsche. I'd be bummed."

"Bullshit, buy another one. Buy a fleet. Buy a whole dealership of them. You can swing it—write a check."

"Well, I'm attached to the one I have, but that's neither here nor there. Now is the time to speak of the final challenge. You see, we're not leaving these hills until I bag a bear."

"I afraid to even ask. We've seen some little ones, black bears, am I right? But that's not what you're talking about, is it?"

"You nailed it. We're taking down a grizzly."

"I suppose it would be too easy to use a big-ass large-bore high-powered big game rifle..."

"You know me too well. We're using our long bows."

Graham glanced over at his, he'd been carrying it so long, he'd forgotten about it.

"Does your life insurance company know about your deathwish?"

"I *own* the insurance company, dickweed."

"Well, I already told you. I'm not shooting a bear."

"That's fine. Assist me."

Graham mulled the idea over. "What the hell. Yes, I'll assist you kill a noble, innocent bear who probably hasn't ever hurt a fly."

"I don't think *innocent* is a proper way to describe a grizzly, but that's beside the point. What I'm saying is, you'll help me with the bear. You won't turn tail and run away like a little girl?"

The silence extended. Graham stared off into the distance.

"It was a serious question, Graham. You'll stand your ground and help me kill this bear."

It took a while, but Graham finally responded.

"Yes," he said.

Robert Kinsley

It was nearly dark when Robert began to realize how much trouble he was in. It wasn't raining—that was a plus—but he was not at all prepared for roughing it in the outdoors. Wearing flimsy tennis shoes, he had almost no food, just random things from the kitchen. Among the items were a loaf of bread, a box of instant oatmeal, a big box of wooden matches, a bottle of water and a can of Pepsi.

In the bottom of one of the bags, as he was doing partial inventory, he found a bag of tampons which he threw away in disgust, but then he picked them up again.

Might be some use for them.

Can't afford to waste anything.

He was a few miles in the woods, generally following the declining sun. His isolation seemed complete.

Let them try to find me out here.

He'd had the presence of mind to bring the remaining swallow of mescal and the pot from the cabin.

He was not completely sober or off the mushroom high—sometimes he saw things at the periphery of his vision—odd things that could not be real. Spiders with wings like butterflies. He was sure they didn't exist, not even in Hawaii or Galapagos, where other weird things lived.

Had to be the drugs.

He worried that there might be something permanent done to him—a rewiring of the connections in his brain. Things like that can happen.

Bad trip. One way.

At one point, while stumbling through the woods, it struck him—what he'd done to Raven.

Cold-blooded murder.

He fell to his knees and cried for her and made up his mind to kill himself and complete the pact. At the first cliff tall enough to make the job certain, he'd jump and die with Raven's name on his lips.

As he walked, he realized she had wanted to die and it wasn't his fault he had decided to live. For her part of things, he was simply following her instructions.

That's not murder, it is assisted suicide, and it's legal in a few states, perhaps even Canada.

How angry can God get if it's legal? What am I thinking? Killing myself because I obeyed the wishes of a dumb broad.

Stupid.

She got what she wanted. To hell with her.

As night fell, the stars popped out. Abruptly. One instant he was tripping over half-seen things in the dark—the next, he looked up and there they were, gleaming and cold. He stood and stared. The constellations were wrong, bizarre. A headless man with a bloody sword, a fish with huge teeth—and a dragon, with mouth opened wide to burn him with unholy flame.

He shook his head and the familiar constellations appeared. Orion, Cassiopeia, and the Big Dipper with its pair of stars pointing the way to the North Star. He needed to be careful; his mind played evil tricks. To survive, he needed to be sharp.

By starlight and slivers of moonlight that pierced the trees, he found a place to sleep—tucked between two fallen logs. He gathered pine branches and made a hiding place where he could look out and see anything approaching.

It was cold, but not freezing. He toyed with the idea of making a fire but decided against it. It would be seen from far away and he couldn't take the risk. He needed a plan. Perhaps he would find a cabin or house, which would be perfect. Someplace where he could hide out for a while—until the law forgot about him and he could be free.

The bugs drove him crazy. They weren't so bad when he was moving, but when he was nestled in his lair, they found him and bit his face and arms—even through his shirt and pants.

Was it too much to expect a stupid girl to buy bug repellent?

How he hated her. She'd made him a murderer.

Grumbling, he covered himself with the plastic bags as much as he could, but the bugs found the bare spots. He couldn't remember ever being so miserable. He fed a whole forest of insects—buzzing and biting. He wanted to jump out of his skin. His thoughts were fractured and out of control. Through branches, the stars looked down; they were bright pinholes, like the holes being drilled into his skin—punctures in the skin of the universe.

His mind drifted. He was in big trouble, that was sure, but what if he could make up for it? Do something big that would make him a hero for the cause. Fund-raising, that was the ticket. The law couldn't touch people with money, everyone knew that.

Perhaps redemption is unlikely, but it is possible.

He could cling to hope. Tormented, he finally slept and made it through to the next morning.

CHAPTER TWENTY

Willie and Maria

SHE KEPT BUSY around the cabin by sweeping the main room, washing the windows and peeling potatoes for a pot of home-made soup. She found herself sweeping again and threw down the broom. It could have been her imagination, but it appeared that Willie, watching, smirked at her.

She wondered what theory he'd come up with for her mysterious absence. He was scary, sometimes, with his non-linear analysis and uncanny perception. She couldn't stand it, so she took him a cold glass of lemonade.

"What's the best theory you have so far?" she asked.

"Curious, are you? I don't blame you, dear. Some of my speculation leads me down fascinating paths. One theory I discarded because of a poor match to the available facts is that you were with a lover and, in the intoxicating depths of illicit passion, lost track of time. Knowing the extreme potential of my rage, you threw yourself into a den of skunks to cover the scent of your betrayal. However, this theory does not hold up, as, once a woman has been with me, there is no one else who would tempt her. Theory discarded."

"At least you are honest with yourself and can admit to a wrong turn in your thinking. Tell me again, what is the total extent of your intimate experience with women? Precisely two? Not a very large dataset for drawing broad conclusions, would you agree?"

"You can try to obscure the main issue, but that will not work."

"Give me a theory you have not discarded."

Willie turned serious and wore a troubled expression.

"I changed my tactic. I tried, as you suggested and satisfy myself that there is some important reason you can't tell me the whole unvarnished truth. But, I can't. I simply must know for my own peace of mind. I can't work while this matter is unresolved. So, I must, on my own, go out into the woods to see if I can trace your path, and see for myself what you were up to."

"Willie, I love you and you get around great for your age, but you should not be roaming the woods. Break a hip out there and it would be very serious. Please trust my judgment on this."

"I'm sorry, Maria. I tried to let it go, but I can't."

"Okay, can I have some time to work through this in my mind? A week? Please, my darling?"

"Twenty-four hours, starting now—that's what I'll grant you."

"Forty-eight hours."

Willie studied her. "Okay, I agree, you have forty-eight hours. At that time, if you don't confide in full, then I will go out," he said, gesturing toward the woods, "and explore for myself. I will uncover this deep dark secret that cannot be disclosed between man and wife, whatever it might be. Until then, however, my mind will be working and perhaps I will unravel the mystery without a dangerous adventure in the woods."

"Okay." She held out her hand for a formal handshake. He took her hand and kissed it.

"Are you ready for another theory?"

"Sure," she replied.

"I think this has something to do with Sasquatch," he said calmly.

She made every effort not to respond…she kept her eyes steady and, in spite of the instinct to jerk her hand away, she left it resting in his. As far as she could tell, she didn't twitch or react in any way, but still, he seemed to read something in her. Was there a sign? Did her eyes dilate? Did her skin flush slightly?

His mind could be scary-quick sometimes.

"Okay, Mastermind, let's hear the backup for this incredible theory."

"Okay, to start, could I take another look at the skull I brought home yesterday?"

"Um," she stammered, thinking.

"Don't bother; I know you don't have it. You took it with you yesterday and you did not return with it. An interesting circumstance. Perhaps it was lost in the skunk den. Here's another question, might I see the sketches and drawings you spent a whole day working on?"

"Well..."

"Again, don't bother to answer. You think I don't notice things, but I do. When you burned your rancid clothing, you burned the sketches too. I watched you delete the photographs from your digital camera's memory card. A curious thing to do, don't you think? Perhaps you've thought of a reasonable explanation by now—you're a bright lady, you may have something. Why do you not have the skull and why did you burn your sketches?"

"I can't answer."

"Right, I understand. You'd like to stall for two days and hope I'll lose interest or something, but that's doubtful, am I right? As a last data point, most of the eye-witness accounts of Bigfoot sightings talk about their rank odor. I know what skunk musk smells like, all the varieties smell much the same and none of them bears any resemblance to the way your hair smells even now. In spite of my olfactory senses being distorted by the pipe tobacco, I can smell it on you and it's not skunk. I put all this together and, as unlikely as it appears, Sasquatch is the answer that fits the best. Any comment?"

"I cannot."

"Yes, I know. Now I will apply myself to this dilemma. Why can't I be told? Obviously, there is danger, but what? Sasquatch does not like highly intelligent black men? Possible, but likely? I don't know. To this, I will apply my power of reason for the next forty-seven hours and then hold you to your promise to tell me everything at that time."

"Anything else, Monsieur Hercule Poirot?"

"Yes, actually, there is. Chief Sam Joe is stopping by later and I suspect your conversation with him will be revealing. He too, is someone who knows more than he's saying, I suspect. Otherwise, I think I'm done now, but I will be thinking and watching. If you change your mind and want to talk, you know where to find me."

"I'll go in the cabin and sweep up now."

With a wry and self-satisfied smile, the Professor tamped tobacco into his pipe, lit it, and stared out over the water.

She served potato soup to Willie on the deck. Giving up on work, she curled up on the couch and reread, over and over, the same page of her William Gibson book. She couldn't focus on the words and was relieved to hear the motor of Chief Sam Joe's boat. She walked out on the deck and waved as he tied the boat to the dock. When he walked up to her, she kissed his cheek and handed him a bowl of soup. He buried his nose in her hair and sniffed.

"Oh, my," he said.

Sitting on the deck without speaking they watched the Chief slurp his soup. Finally, he was done and he set the bowl down on the deck.

"Well, where are we? You saw Elmer? I can smell it on you."

Maria nodded.

"We're speaking of Sasquatches and other mythological creatures," the Professor said.

"She knows and you don't. Am I reading things correctly?"

The Professor nodded. "You got it. She won't tell me anything and she doesn't want me exploring the woods on my own to find out. It's a mysterious bundle of confusion. I think she found them or they found her, but for some reason, she won't talk about it. She wants to protect them? She wants to protect me from them because they are a danger to me?"

"Complicated," the Chief said cryptically.

"Clearly," the Professor replied.

"A lot of us up here don't like what they've seen, but think the *people* have a right to be left alone. One day, someone will come around—one of the Bigfoot hunters perhaps, and that will be that. The world's attention will focus here and it will make the gold rush look like nothing. The world has endless supplies of cameras, tourists and meddlers. That wouldn't be right."

"I'm not that kind of person," the Professor said mildly. "I can keep a secret."

"It's not that," the Chief said. "Maria is right, these things are a hazard. They might kill and eat you, every last bit of you, right down to your bones."

"They didn't kill Maria."

"Ah, that's true. Go ahead, tell him, Maria."

"Okay. They can mate with humans." She rubbed the slight ridge of bone over her eyes. "I have some of their blood in me. It's no guarantee, but it got me out of there. They're not human, Willie. They are vicious, nightmarish, horrible creatures. You're better off staying away from them. You would not be safe among them."

"I'm sorry, but I need to see for myself."

"Maria, there's something going on out there, can you feel it?"

"No, I've been so focused on Willie…oh, you're right, what is it?"

"I don't know, but I think we'd better go. We might as well take the Professor along. I think that's the only way to shut him up. And Maria?"

"Yes, Chief Joe?"

"Better bring along your medical supplies, I have a feeling we'll need them."

Clayton Powell and Graham Wallace

Clayton played with his GPS and spread out a large map and detailed satellite photograph. He pointed out areas of interest.

"The bear is currently here and we are currently here."

"How do you know where the bear is?"

"He has a transmitter on him," Clayton explained with exaggerated patience, as if he was talking to a slow child. "Now shut up and listen. He's being driven. We're taking him down here at about three this afternoon," he said, pointing at a spot on the map.

"Excuse me for butting in, but if there is one thing I learned on this trip, it is to pay attention to the details. Why there at a specific time?"

"The area is clear of trees and the whole thing will be photographed by a satellite flying over. We'll get great action shots."

"So, you have crew and they can act as our backup."

"They are under strict orders. Once we engage, they pull out. It's you, me and the bear, that's it."

"What if we need medical attention?"

"Then we're fucked. We can't do this with backup; otherwise we might as well just shoot a bear in a zoo. You and I will risk our asses to take down this bear. If you want to chicken out, then I'll call in the chopper right now and haul you out along with your stupid kilt. No contract and you can kiss your cute little Porsche goodbye. Along with any claim to manhood."

"You're one twisted fuck."

"You in or out?"

"I already said I'm in."

"Okay, so, shall we get this done?"

"Fine by me," Graham replied.

They parked the ATVs and Clayton arranged his equipment. The terrain was barren and rocky and they could see for miles—the mountains marched in hazy formation to the horizon. Clayton showed off the arrows stowed on the ATV. Graham reached out to touch.

"Careful. The edges are molecular. They'll take off a finger like it's nothing."

"Thanks for the warning," Graham said, yanking his finger back.

"What are friends for?" Clayton replied. "I think we're ready."

Graham slung his bow over his shoulder like Clayton, but looked through the ATV storage compartments and his pack for other weapons. He came away with a Gerber hatchet from the camp supplies and his large clasp knife, selected for him by J-C.

Clayton laughed at the sight of Graham wearing his kilt and holding his selected weapons.

"You look like a damned fool. Wave to the cameras, I want to make sure we get good photographs."

With a middle finger, Graham gestured to the sky.

"Fuck you, let's get on with it."

"Okay, partner, the bear should be right over the ridge. Let's see if we can find him."

As they walked along, Clayton had an arrow notched and ready. He saw the animal first, standing on his back legs and sniffing curiously at the air. It was monstrous, at least ten feet tall.

"Shit, Clayton, that thing is huge."

"You didn't think we'd come all this way for a little one?"

They stalked. The bear was on all fours—tearing at something bloody.

"You baited the bear?"

"Shut up."

Clayton took his time and found a clear spot about forty yards away. With his boot, he cleared twigs and loose rocks and took a stance.

"First arrow away," he said.

His aim was true. The arrow slammed the bear behind the front leg and rammed in deep. At first the bear looked around without reacting, but then seemed to recognize the injury. He roared and looked for the offender. Clayton loosed another arrow and it sank in near the first. The bear saw them and loped their way…head on. Clayton loosed another arrow and it went in under the neck.

The sharp points had to be cutting the bear's insides to shreds, Graham thought with sympathy for the poor beast.

Faster than seemed possible, the bear ran at them. Graham's estimate of its size increased.

The damned thing is enormous.

"Are we going to run or what?" Graham said, fighting panic.

"Can't outrun them," Clayton muttered. "All you can do is kill them."

He loosed another arrow. The bear was on them, howling and furious, all claws and huge teeth. They jumped left and right and the bear, like a bull in a bullfight, ran between them before clawing to a shambling stop. Clayton loosed another arrow into his chest.

"Okay, he should fall down now," Graham heard Clayton say just before the bear grabbed his head with his jaws, lifted him off his feet and batted him ten feet with a massive paw.

With the top of his head streaming blood, Clayton crumpled by a stump, screaming.

Graham lost his mind. As the bear approached Clayton to finish the kill, Graham bellowed and attacked with the hatchet and knife. He was able to jam the knife in the bear's right eye socket, and then he raised the hatchet, two-handed, and embedded it in the bear's skull—directly between its eyes—with a satisfying crunch. He jumped to the bear's blind side and avoided, by inches, a deadly sweeping paw. The bear, now beaten, mewed and tried to pry the hatchet out of its head. Giving up, it slowly walked in tight little circles, and finally fell when its legs collapsed.

Gasping for air, Graham watched it for a moment. Suspiciously. Though twitching, it certainly appeared to be very dead. Graham walked over to check on Clayton—sure he was dead too. White bone was visible on Clayton's skull—a large flap of hair and skin was torn and hanging.

He moaned. Clayton was alive. Gritting his teeth and feeling faint, Graham pulled the flap back over Clayton's skull, where it sat like a cheap toupee.

"Time to call in the cavalry."

"I told you, we're on our own. Are you hurt?"

Graham took a quick inventory. "No. I'm nearly scared to death, but I'm fine."

"I have a broken arm and my head. My head. Is there any sign of brain matter?"

"From you? None."

"Very funny, asshole. Is my skull fractured? Are my brains dripping out?"

"How the hell would I know? I'm an engineer, not a doctor. I don't see anything but blood."

"All right, help me up. We're not far from the Hot Springs. We'll get help there."

Clayton looked like a dead man with streamers of blood pouring down his face, but with Graham's help he was able to walk to the ATV. Graham ripped up a shirt and wrapped up Clayton's arm as tightly as he could, then got him on the ATV.

"Are we carrying a first aid kit?" Clayton started to speak, but Graham interrupted. "I know. Safety equipment is for pussies. Jerk. Which way?" he asked.

Clayton pointed toward the southeast. With the sun hovering on the western horizon, they started out. After a couple of hours, it was clear they were not going to make it before dark. Graham started looking for shelter.

In a dark section of trees, he saw the opening of a cave. There was something odd about it, but they were picking their way slowly by the ATV headlight. Darkness. It was time to stop.

"Christ, did you cut one? What's that horrible smell?" Clayton said.

"Shut up," Graham replied.

Robert Kinsley

On waking, his eyes were nearly swollen shut. Feverish, his mind was foggy—he wasn't sure where he was or why he was there. He couldn't hold a coherent thought—his mind was filled with broken fragments and disturbing, disjointed images.

He was freezing. The cold, pale, unhelpful moon illuminated the cloud of mosquitoes taking turns draining his blood. As much as he wanted to rest, his situation was hopeless—he needed to keep moving.

He heard an engine.

Without other options, he headed in the direction of the sound—which he hoped was no hallucination.

CHAPTER TWENTY-ONE

Clayton Powell and Graham Wallace

HELPING CLAYTON WALK, Graham entered the cave and stood in the large cavern examining the corners with their flashlights. A ragged, dirty man stood quietly against the cave wall—he surprised them when their lights found him. He covered his eyes.

"Hey, lights are not good here. Turn them off, they hurt."

"Sorry," Graham said, killing his headlamp. "We need help, my companion is injured."

"No, sorry, no help around here," the man said.

"Who are you? What is this place? What is that smell?"

"You must leave right away. They retreated into the deeper caves, but they will come back soon and it will not be safe for you. Go now."

"Outside, we're stumbling around in the dark. We'll go in the morning."

"I told you. What more can I do? Protect men from their own ignorance? That never works. Good luck to you."

The man walked to an enclosure and lifted a flap of fur. He disappeared.

"Well, that's fucking helpful," Clayton commented.

"You and your damned bear got us into this. Now we really could use a helicopter and you can't get one. I'll bet you were sure it would be *me* mauled by the bear. What did you do? Rub a dead fish on my pack?"

"It was fifty-fifty the bear got one of us while the other escaped. I took my chances and lost," Clayton said with a crooked grin. He looked ghoulish with the dried blood on his face and the crooked way his scalp rested on the top of his head. "Dead fish, that's a good one, I didn't think of it."

"What about the bear? Just going to leave it out there?"

"It'll be stuffed and in my study by the time I get home."

"Choppered out?"

"Sure. But not us. I didn't get to where I am today by choppering out when I'm this close to finishing a journey."

"Damn you, Powell, that doesn't make sense. You could be dead tomorrow—let's get out any way we can. I thought I'd seen the pinnacle of your lunacy and you keep amazing me."

"Would you two please shut up so I can meditate," Elmer said.

"Fuck off," Graham and Clayton said in unison.

They noticed movement in from deep in the cave.

"What's that?" Clayton said, pointing. "We should not have come in here without arms. Did you bring my bow?"

"It's with the bear. All I could think of was getting out of there."

"Maybe we should be thinking about getting out of *here*."

Agreeing, Graham got up. Three large not-human creatures blocked their way back.

"What the hell?" Clayton said, stunned.

"Here comes the bloodshed," Elmer muttered in his enclosure.

Surrounded, Graham and Clayton retreated to the center of the cavern. There, they noticed a flat rock with disturbing dark stains showing faintly in the dim light.

"Bigfoot," Clayton said, redundantly.

"I can see that," Graham said through clenched teeth, with his hatchet and knife held ready.

"I heard the stories, but I thought they were all bullshit."

"They don't seem very friendly," Graham said.

"I can see that too."

"They're ugly and they stink."

"Shut up."

Willie and Maria

It was slow going as they hiked, scrambled and climbed. Willie needed many breaks to catch his breath. Finally, they stood in front at the cave entrance.

"That's a familiar odor," Willie commented. "Are we going inside or stand around all night?"

Maria and Chief Joe exchanged glances, and then led the way. The scene inside was quiet. Two figures sat on the edge of the killing stone surrounded by dark figures.

"Wow, they really do have big feet," Willie said with wonder.

Clayton Powell, Graham Wallace, Willie and Maria

Maria, with her medical bag, pushed through the assembled creatures. She glanced briefly at Graham, but focused her attention on Clayton.

"Did the people do this?" she asked.

"Bigfoot? No. Bear," Graham said. "You're a doctor?"

"I graduated from medical school."

"Close enough," Clayton said.

"You're a mess," Maria commented. "I'm surprised you're conscious. Beyond the obvious, how are you doing?"

"Other than a massive headache and a broken arm, I couldn't be better."

"I'm going to press on your skull and see if there is a fracture. There will be pain."

"What else is new? Be careful with me—I'm one of the richest men in the world."

"I already know you're one of the mouthiest."

She finished her inspection.

"The bandage on your arm will hold and there's a good chance you'll keep your scalp if I sew it up now. Then, if the creatures let us go, we could be in Harrison in a couple of hours, but I don't think we should wait that long. I have suture thread, can you stand it?"

"Do your worst."

"I'm going to consider that a medical release. Will you witness?" she asked Graham.

"Sure," he said.

"Okay, here we go."

The procedure took an hour and when she was done, Clayton looked like one of Dr. Frankenstein's unsuccessful prototypes.

"I think that's going to be fine. When your hair grows out it will cover the worst of the damage. I'll splint your arm better and then we'll be ready to roll."

Robert Kinsley

The mouth of the cave glowed dimly and he heard voices both acoustically through the air and directly embedded in his head. Through the trees, he saw a shooting star, which he took as an omen. Then he saw more and realized they were imaginary streaks of white light in his head.

The air was foul…the thick scent made him gag. He wanted to enter the cave, but did not have the courage.

What to do?

Smoke a joint.

Sitting on a rock between massive tree trunks, watching, he took the last doobie from his stash and lit up. The smoke filled—and tickled and teased—every living cell of his lungs.

Between tokes, he swigged the dregs of the Mescal and dribbled the last caustic drops onto his tongue. His consciousness expanded. He was one with the forest and its creatures.

Owl, mouse, bobcat and opossum.

Dead bear.

Sleeping chipmunk, fox and coyote…whimpering at the moon.

The spirit of the trees. Whispering.

And, inside the cave, old, ugly creatures with gnarled souls.

Cruel souls.

The puzzle was missing an important piece.

Him.

Finally, he was ready to move into the scene that awaited.

His destiny.

He gathered his things, worked down the rough trail and entered the cave.

The humans in the center of the circle appeared to be under siege. The creatures, settled on their haunches, surrounded them. They were foreign. The scene, lit by dim light from the cavern walls, rushed through his mind like a wave.

Sasquatch!

He would be their savior and they would be his salvation.

There were thousands of acres of forest protected for Spotted Owls—imagine the forest preserve for the alien humanoid creatures discovered by Robert Kinsley.

Imagine an international environmental group founded and headed by the legendary Robert Kinsley. The Robert Kinsley Wildlife Federation. Accolades and awards. Grants and donations. The Nobel Prize.

What law could touch such a man?

He stumbled into the cavern feeling larger than life.

Happy.

Saved.

His new life unfolded before his drug-addled eyes. Private jets. A reception at the White House with the President. Movie stars. A prize-winning documentary. An Oscar. His impassioned and heartfelt speech. A pretty starlet hanging on his arm. Malibu. Kinky sex with two girls in a marble hot tub.

"I love you all," he shouted, "and I know exactly what to do. You will save me and I will save you."

He saw a shadow move. Something large arced through the air. With his head filled with light, the back of his skull was crushed by a rock.

And the light slowly faded in his eyes.

Clayton Powell, Graham Wallace, Willie and Maria

The group watched in horror as the young man was smashed in the head. There was no hesitation—in less than a minute Robert was butchered. His pieces were dispersed while his belongings were left scattered on the cave floor.

"Oh, I see," Willie said in a shaky voice.

In torn plastic packages, the scattered tampons soaked up blood and the can of Pepsi peeked from under a scrap of Robert's shirt.

From the mass of creatures, two came forward. One took Willie's arm and the other took Clayton's. They began pulling them away.

"No," Maria shrieked.

Graham brandished his hatchet and pulled Clayton's other arm. The noise in the room increased. The creatures were angry. Even Willie felt a tickle in his brain. Maria's headache became blinding. The creatures converged and more hands grasped at Willie and Clayton.

Willie pulled out the diamond and held it up. The grasping hands fell away. The diamond seemed to suck up the faint cave light. It glowed. The people took a step back.

He turned and placed the diamond on the bloody altar.

"That's all I have," Willie said. He said to Graham, "If they approach, smash it with the hatchet."

Graham nodded.

"This would be a great time to start beating that goddamned drum, Elmer," Maria shouted.

Elmer appeared in the doorway of his enclosure.

"I don't think I shall," he said petulantly.

Reaching down, she grabbed the Pepsi can and held it up. The creatures stepped forward and restarted their tug-of-war—pulling at Willie and Clayton. Graham raised the hatchet.

"Hey, Elmer, want a Pepsi?" she said loudly.

"Oh," Elmer said. "I never..."

The scene was frozen.

After a moment, Elmer pounded his drum—the deafening sound reflected off the cave walls. Leading, Maria pushed through the circle that enclosed them. The creatures hissed and howled, but allowed them to pass. At the mouth of the cave, Maria tossed the soda can to Elmer; he dropped his drum and caught it neatly. They streamed out into the cool, refreshing air.

Picking their way back—eventually they were at the cabin. No one spoke. Piling into Chief Sam Joe's boat, he pointed the bow south and they headed toward Harrison guided by the light of the moon—partially obscured by clouds.

CHAPTER TWENTY-TWO

Clayton Powell and Graham Wallace

A MEDIC EVACUATION helicopter from Vancouver lifted off from the Harrison Hot Springs parking lot. From a window, Clayton waved at the group as the chopper ascended.

"Wait for me, I shall return," he shouted.

Though it was late, a crowd had gathered to watch. Wearing a bathrobe, a red teddy and a sleepy expression, Lili came out to see what was going on. She spotted Graham and ran—with her bathrobe streaming behind like wings. It was at that instant that Graham, impulsively, decided to ask if she'd marry him. She hugged him and kissed him on the cheek.

"Are you in one piece?" she said.

"Barely," he replied. "I have a question. Are you a lesbian?"

"I played around in college. Who didn't? But, no, I'm not a lesbian."

"In that case, will you marry me?"

"Sure. It's about damned time you asked—my patience had nearly expired. I thought I'd have to ask you myself."

Their kiss went on until Maria tapped Graham on the shoulder.

"Sorry to disturb you," she said, "but we're headed back to our cabin. Goodbye."

"Clayton won't say it," Graham said, "but thanks for everything. It was an adventure, wasn't it?"

"Oh boy," she said.

He shook hands with Willie and Chief Joe and they took their leave.

"We have to get you out of these clothes," Lili said, wrinkling her nose. "I hate to mention it, but you're stinking up the place."

"Whatsoever you say, that I shall do, Lili," Graham said.

"I like the sound of that," she said.

Willie and Maria

Back at the cabin, Willie took care of burning their clothes this time. He spent a long time tending the fire and thinking. Maria came up behind him and threw her arms over his shoulders.

"Unless I'm seeing things, you seem to be burning the manuscript for your Great North American Sasquatch Novel."

"Yes. I completely lost my taste for it. I think I have a lot of it figured out, but I'd like to compare notes with you. No more need for secrecy, right?"

"Right, but no hurry?"

"I agree, no hurry. I'm thinking of another book."

"Let me guess, evil government agents rob life and liberty from hard-working taxpayers?"

"Sure, mock. No, this one is a bit different. I'm thinking of a day, not so very far in the future, when real estate around the equator gets really, really valuable. What do we really know about the climate cycles of ice and fire? I'm considering a working title. How about *The Gated Equator*?

She considered it with a sour expression.

"Clumsy. How about *The Golden Age*?"

He turned and swept her up in his arms.

"I like it," he said.

Graham and Lili

A priest, leading a group of singers, was staying at the hotel. He agreed to perform a simple ceremony for them. Lili wore a white sheath dress and tied flowers in her hair. Graham wore his Utilikilt.

After, they loafed around the hotel for a few days. Graham caught up on his e-mail while they waited for Clayton to return and consummate their deal. The time allowed Graham to think and make a few executive decisions. Finally, the day came and Clayton was deposited back in the parking lot by a chartered helicopter. They met in the hotel bar. He looked much better—a large floppy hat covered his bandaged head. His arm was nestled in a light-weight high-tech splint.

"I heard you got married. Congratulations."

"Thanks. You look like shit."

"I might be ugly, but you should see the other guy. The bear is installed in my house already, front and center. Our satellite video is all over the Internet—you really did a number on the creature with your knife and hatchet. Hollywood will probably call. Of course, I slowed him down with fine archery, but that's beside the point for now. This is your big day, mi amigo." He pulled the envelope out of his pocket, slipped out the contract, signed it with a flourish and pushed it across the table. "Voilà, you earned it and you deserve it."

With an inscrutable expression, Graham took the contract and slowly and with great care, tore it into tiny pieces.

"Hmmm, that's interesting," Clayton said. "Are you thinking of a different price?"

"No, I'm thinking of a completely different deal."

"I'm listening," Clayton said. And he did, for a couple of hours and several rounds of single malt Scotch whisky.

At the end, they shook hands.

Graham had his deal.

Feeling no pain, he stumbled away from the bar, and then turned back to Clayton.

"I almost forgot…there are two more things," he said.

"We already shook on our deal," Clayton complained.

"The Hummer. Have it delivered up here. I want to drive Lili home in it."

"Oh man, I love that car. I'll buy you a brand new one, how about that?"

"No."

"Crap—it has a sound system with sixteen speakers. You're such a jerk. Alright, what is the very last, absolutely final thing?"

"No big deal. GPS coordinates and a chopper ride for my wedding present. That's all."

Graham and the Strategic Services, LLC Executive Committee

The Harrison Hot Springs conference center was on the first floor. It was the usual set up—the staff brought in a portable white board and coffee and sweet roll service. The whole team was assembled. Anderssen wore a colorful Flower Kings t-shirt that covered his large belly like a tent in desperate need of staking.

"Okay, it's time to get started," Graham announced. "I have news and we have decisions to make. News even Lili does not know."

"And I'm his wife," she said pouting. "I have half a mind to get fat if he's going to treat me this way," she added, speaking around the remnants of an apricot Danish.

"Please sit down," Graham urged. "As you know, the last couple of weeks, I've had time to get out of myself and look at things from an objective distance. Strategic Services is aptly named, we're a services company. You'll never control your own destiny if you're just supplying services. That's why I made an offer to Clayton Powell and he accepted. I'm selling the company to him for twenty-four million."

Lili sputtered and Anderssen was angry. "Dude, its worth twice that much."

"Hold on," Graham said. "The devil is in the details, right? When you're done spouting off, I'll give you those details. Alright? Everyone calm? First of all, everyone in this room is a millionaire, okay? You get cash when the sale closes and you can work for Powell if you want to, no problem. However, part of the deal is I'm allowed to make certain key officers," he said, waving around the room, "offers of employment. There is no waiting period or other legal barrier. I'm starting a new company, a hardware company. If you want more independence, you gotta sell hardware. The company will be based on a product idea I had while on my trip."

"We don't know anything about hardware."

"We'll do the market research and write the specifications. The detailed electrical design will be done in Taiwan or China. That's the way things are done these days. We can do it."

"What's the product?" Lili said.

"You know how there are all these pods? Audio i-Pods, v-pods, game-pods? I have a concept called life-pod and it's really cool. It's both hardware and a subscription service. To learn more, you have to sign up for the new company. Who's in?"

Everyone raised their hand except for Wilkins, who was text messaging.

"Wilkins?"

"Oh, sorry, I was placing an order for a Maserati MC12. Sure, I'm in, absolutely."

"Okay. The idea of the life-pod is we document and sell a subscription to real time access to famous people's lives. Anytime, anywhere, you can log in and see and hear what George Clooney or Angeline Jolie are doing."

"What if George is taking a crap?"

"If you haven't bought a premium all-access subscription, we cut to a commercial. Any other stupid questions?"

"Is Clayton putting in seed money?"

"We're working on it. He wants twenty-two percent ownership for his money and he's not getting any more than eight. The point is to own our destiny, and not sell our souls so quickly this time. He'll come around, I'm sure."

After the meeting dissolved, Graham and Lili sat alone in the big room.

"We need to buy something for J-C," Graham said. "He saved my ass out there."

"Can we afford to buy him new knees?"

"Yes. Now go pack a bag. I have a surprise for you. We're going away for a couple of days."

"I like it right here, so this better be good."

"It is, now scoot," he said, slapping her on the butt. "Meet you in the parking lot in ten minutes."

Graham asked at the desk and tracked down Clayton. He was in the sauna getting a massage from a thin blonde wearing tight shorts and a halter top. She kneaded his back with strong fingers.

Clayton's hacked-up hair was slicked back; his wounds were on grotesque display.

"You're one ugly son of a bitch," Graham commented.

"Great to see you too, partner." Gesturing at his head, Clayton said, "I'll bet you a house—by this time next year, head scars like this will be the latest fashion statement...the hottest cosmetic surgery around."

Graham considered it.

"I think I'll pass."

"Good call. People Magazine will pay a bundle for the right to the first photographs of my ugly head. Then, I'll fund the first business plan presented by someone hacked up like this." With an evil grin, he said, "The second can pound sand. Believe me, this look will be hot."

"Well, you asked to see me—the chopper leaves shortly. What is it?"

"About next summer, I'm taking Steve Ballmer salmon fishing in Alaska. He doesn't know shit about the backwoods. You in?"

Graham pondered the question.

"You scared me—I thought you'd say something about..."

“Those god-forsaken, ugly things in the woods? Those stinking things can rot in their holes. Screw them. Well, I wouldn’t mind having one stuffed for my collection, but that can wait.”

Thinking, Graham considered everything he’d been through.

A big grin spread across his face.

“Sure, I’m in,” he said.

“Excellent, now beat it.” Clayton said. He winked. “Because I’m about to get flipped over.”

AFTERWORD

Graham and Lili Wallace

GRAHAM'S INTUITION WAS correct…Lili liked the treehouse. She squealed with joy and jumped up and down when she saw the interior. Once Graham figured out how to turn on the circuit breaker and use the solar panel mounted on the roof to charge a battery pack, they watched DVDs and listened to music.

Their first child was conceived on the third day of their stay.

"You lost weight," she said on that day. "You look reasonably healthy for such a large guy."

"Shut up. Let's watch the Terminator again."

"No," she said.

"Don't make me watch another movie with Sandra Bullock in it."

"Okay, how about one with Drew Barrymore?"

"No. Same thing."

He watched her sort through the collection of DVDs. She wore a pair of Hello Kitty panties and one of his shirts unbuttoned to the waist.

"Often, life sucks," he said. "It's filled with flu and runny noses and hemorrhoids. Earthquakes and train wrecks and bad fish."

She turned.

"What are you talking about?" she said.

"But, sometimes, just for an instant, a door opens and we get a brief little glimpse of heaven. The stars align. A perfect moment appears before our eyes and the gods dare us to grab it…to capture it and try to hold onto it."

"You're an idiot," she said. "I found it. I knew it would be here somewhere. Behind the Oxford dictionary…his collection of porn."

"I'm serious. We have to pay attention or we'll miss God's little gifts…the tiny, leftover bits of ecstasy that fall off his table and make all of life's crap worthwhile."

"I'm serious too." She held out two DVDs. "Which do you prefer? *Pippi Grows Up* or *The Naughty Cheerleaders?*"

He tugged the tails of her shirt and pulled her close.

"Let's forget about the DVDs for a few minutes, shall we?"

She laughed.

"Okay, but when we're done, we're watching the cheerleaders. Any movie with a lead actor named Lance Shaft has to be really frickin' good, don't you think?"

"Whatever you say, dear," he said.

Outside, the wind gently massaged the trees.